The Hired Man on Horseback

BOOKS BY EUGENE MANLOVE RHODES

The Proud Sheriff
Beyond the Desert
The Trusty Knaves
Once in the Saddle
Copper Streak Trail
Stepsons of Light
West is West
The Desire of the Moth
Bransford in Arcadia
Good Men and True

EUGENE MANLOVE RHODES

THE
Hired Man
ON HORSEBACK

My story of Eugene Manlove Rhodes

BY

MAY DAVISON RHODES

ILLUSTRATED

HOUGHTON MIFFLIN COMPANY · BOSTON
The Riverside Press Cambridge
1938

The Riverside Press
CAMBRIDGE · MASSACHUSETTS
PRINTED IN THE U.S.A.

TO

MY FRIENDS

TURBESÈ LUMMIS

AND

HENRY HERBERT KNIBBS

AT WHOSE GENTLE INSISTENCE THIS RECORD WAS WRITTEN

My earnest thanks are tendered Henry Herbert Knibbs, Turbesè Lummis, William MacLeod Raine, Eugene Cunningham, Edward H. Crussell, and to all the Rhodes Fans who so generously sent their letters for me to copy.

MAY DAVISON RHODES

The Hired Man on Horseback

(With apologies to G. K. Chesterton and Don Juan of Austria.)

The typical cowboy is . . . simply a riding farmhand. —James Stephens; *International Book Review.*

The cowboy, after all, was never anything more than a hired man on horseback. — Editorial Page; *Minneapolis Tribune, San Francisco Chronicle.*

Harp and flute and violin, throbbing through the night,
Merry eyes and tender eyes, dark head and bright;
Moon shadow on the sundial to mark the moments fleet,
The magic and enchanted hours where moonlight lovers meet;
And the harp notes come all brokenly by night winds
stirred —
But the hired man on horseback is singing to the herd!

(Whoopie-ti-yo-o-o! Hi yo-o, my little dogies!)

Doggerel upon his lips and valor in his heart,
Not to flinch and not to fail, not to shirk his part;
Wearily and wearily he sees the stars wheel by,
And he knows his guard is nearly done by the great clock
in the sky.
He hears the Last Guard coming and he hears their song
begun,
A foolish song he will forget when he forgets the sun.

The Hired Man on Horseback

(*Whoopie-ti-yo-o-o! Hi yo-o, my little dogies!*)

'We got 'em now, you sleepy men, so pull your freight to bed
And pound your ear an hour or two before the east is red.'
If to his dreams a face may come? Ah, turn your eyes away,
Nor guess what face may come by dream that never comes by day.
Red dawn breaking through the desert murk;
The hired man on horseback goes laughing to his work.

The broker's in his office before the stroke of ten,
He buys and smiles and he sells and smiles at the word of other men;
But he gets his little commission flat, whether they buy or sell,
So be it drouth or storm or flood, the broker's crops do well.
They are short of Katy Common, they are long on Zinc Preferred —
But the hired man on horseback is swimming with the herd!

White horns gleaming where the flood rolls brown,
Lefty fighting the lower point as the current sweeps them down.
Lefty fighting the stubborn steers that will not turn or slow,
They press beside him, they swim below him — 'Come out, and let them go!'

But Lefty does not leave them and Lefty tries once more,
He is swinging the wild leaders in toward the northern shore;
'He'll do to ride the river with!' (Bridging the years between,
Men shall use those words again — and wonder what they mean.)
He is back to turn the stragglers in to follow the leaders through
When a cottonwood snag comes twisting down with long arms lashing hate,
On wearied horse and wearied man — and they see it come, too late!
— A brown hand lifted in the splashing spray;
Sun upon a golden head that never will be gray;
A low mound bare until new grass is grown —
But the Palo Pinto trail herd has crossed the Cimarron!

A little midnight supper when the play is done,
Glancing lights and sparkling eyes — the night is just begun.
Beauteous night, O night of love! — Youth and joy are met.
Shine on our enchantment still! 'Sweet, your eyes are wet.'
'Dear, they sing for us alone!' Such the lover's creed.
— But the hired man on horseback is off with the stampede!

There is no star in the pit-black night, there is none to know or blame,
And a hundred yards to left or right, there is safety there — and shame!
A stone throw out on either side, with none to guess or tell —

But the hired man on horseback has raised the rebel yell!
He has turned to loosen his saddle strings, he has fumbled his slicker free,
He whirls it high and he snaps it wide wherever the foremost be.
He slaps it into a longhorn's eyes till he falters in his stride —
An oath and a shot, a laugh and a shot, and his wild mates race beside;
A pony stumbles — no, he is up, unhurt and running still;
'Turn 'em, turn 'em, turn 'em, Charlie! Good boy, Bill!'
They are crashing through the cedar mottes, they are skating the rim-rock slick,
They are thundering through the cactus flats where the badger holes are thick;
Day is breaking, clouds are lifting, leaders turn to mill —
'Hold 'em, cowboys! Turn 'em, Charlie! — *God! Where's Bill!*'

The proud Young Intellectuals, a cultured folk are these,
They scorn the lowly Babbitts and their hearts are overseas;
They turn their backs upon us, and if we ask them why
They smile like jesting Pilate, and they stay for no reply;
They smile at faith and honor, and they smile at shame and crime —
But the old Palo Pinto man is calling for his time.

The Hired Man on Horseback

For he heard old voices and he heard hoofs beat,
Songs that long ago were gay to time with drumming feet;
Bent back straightens and dim eyes grow bright —
The last man on horseback rides on into the night!
Cossack and Saracen
Shout their wild welcome then,
Ragged proud Conquistadores claim him kind and kin,
And the wild Beggars of the Sea leap up to swell the din;
And Hector leans upon the wall, and David bends to scan
This new brown comrade for the old brown clan,
The great-hearted gentlemen who guard the outer wall,
Black with sin and stained with blood — and faithful through it all;
Still wearing for all ornament the scars they won below —
And the Lord God of Out-of-Doors, He cannot let them go!
They have halted the hired horseman beyond the outer gate,
But the gentlemen adventurers cry shame that he should wait;
And the sour saints soften, with a puzzled grin,
As Esau and Ishmael press to let their brother in.
Hat tip-tilted and his head held high,
Brave spurs jingling as he passes by —
Gray hair tousled and his lips a-quirk —
To the Master of the Workmen, with the tally of his work!

— EUGENE MANLOVE RHODES.

Contents

Illustrations

The Novelist of the Cattle Kingdom

By BERNARD DeVOTO

To THOSE who study it professionally, an annoyance of literature is that it will not stay put. It is an impure mixture and does not behave dependably in the presence of reagents which are employed to test it qualitatively. Of fairness, of critical intention, it should be uniform. Let it be as rare or as obstinate as you please, it ought in simple decency to remain constant once it has been isolated — or how may the critic deal with it? His instruments of analysis and appraisal are forthright. He brings to his job a fervor partly moral and partly mathematical; equipped, if he leans toward the academic, with a kit of catchwords and categories which, like the wrenches of a mechanic, can be fitted to every nut in the machine. Or equipped, if he is the more elevating variety, the aesthetician or metaphysician, with a kit of right ideas which dovetail with one another and compose a logical, articulated, self-adjusted structure within which literature is to be penned and folded. Literature is what the wrenches fit, what can be accommodated to the categories and catchwords. Or literature is what the right ideas have required it, in advance, to be.

Which is perfectly all right. Both sets of instruments have been fashioned in relation to many books which you and I enjoy, and much literature exists in a mixture sufficiently like a pure solution to behave in an orthodox way when litmus paper is thrust into it. Working with such literature the critic is a happy man, sure of himself and of his competence to handle a known stuff which leaves no residue when heat-treated in a test tube. There is, however, a discouragingly large amount of literature which breaks in a sharp curve just as the critic swings at it. It will not behave, it will not order itself according to his requirements. Some of his wrenches will not fit, some of his taps and dies cannot take hold — or it leaves some of his right ideas hanging on air, moored by cantilever to the pier he has built at one end but with nothing more than blue sky to hold up the other end. What to do with it?

If none of his instruments take hold, if none of his ideas fit, the critic's procedure is obvious. Books are to be written thus and so, and if they are neither thus nor so, then the hell with them. Our journals do not lack examples of rejection and annihilation, and few critics choose silence when they perceive that something is in no degree whatever literature. The truly uncomfortable predicament arises from stuff which is clearly so but just as clearly is not thus — from the conglomerate, from the mixture which is not a solution. And much literature is like that — which, boys and girls, is why much literary criticism is irritable and unhappy.

The critic, you see, has been trained in pure substances and ideal forms. The water which you and I drink may serve to quench our thirst, but it contains various calcium salts and iodides and silicates, a dozen other mineral adulterants, and small forms of plant and animal life whose effluvia complete the frustration of chemically pure reagents. It is therefore not water to a chemist: his water is 11.186 per cent hydrogen and 88.814 per cent oxygen by weight, and it is nothing more. We may drink ours if we choose but we are not drinking hydrogen oxide. Or perhaps the critic is not so much a chemist as a crystallographer loosed in the natural world straight from his apprenticeship. On the laboratory table he has examined and committed to memory the cardboard models which show the fundamental shapes of matter. They are perfect to the eye and to the calipers. He has measured their angles and the slant of their planes. He can recognize them at a glance and identify them as the external expression of a definite and constant internal structure which has absolutely conditioned their shapes. But when he picks up a piece of rock chipped from a ledge he can find nothing whatever that corresponds to the eighteen-inch bits of symmetrical cardboard which were made for him by the laboratory technician. He sees nothing that looks like a crystal. There are few pure planes, there are few measurable or even recognizable angles; the forms bend upon themselves beyond identification and, what is much worse, they merge with one another. The fundamental shapes of matter flow into such a shocking amorphousness that, when an occasional blob bears some resemblance to a drawing in the textbook it seems, and usually is, a scientific paradox, a joke in nature.

So a critic who must encounter the mixed stuff of literature is commonly distressed. It trues foursquare with some of his right ideas, but it is dreadfully out of plumb with others. In some of its aspects it is unquestionably what literature ought to be, but in other aspects it is unquestionably what literature cannot possibly be. Thrust a piece of litmus paper in here and it turns blue, which is the behavior required by theorem, but repeat the operation a little farther along and the test-paper remains pink. And this troubles the critic. The world of categories and right ideas, of wrenches and reagents, can make nothing of mixed substances. In that world there may be rock and you are at liberty to quench your thirst, but literature is hydrogen oxide or it is nothing, and it must have identifiable crystals or critics will find security in silence.

That last, I think, explains why criticism has declined to examine the novels of Eugene Manlove Rhodes. They are troublesome and so it has been shrewd to ignore them. On the one hand, millions of people have read his stuff with pleasure, which should qualify him under a right idea of the moment, the idea that the taste of the multitude is sound provided you are careful to designate it as a folk taste. On the other hand, for many years there has existed a small coterie of people who fanatically admire his stuff and have made it all but unobtainable in second-hand shops, a coterie as select and discriminating as any that ever boosted a tenth-rate English poet into a first-rate reputation — which should assuredly qualify Rhodes under another right idea. The difficulty appears to be that the two ideas are themselves immiscible — that in right-thinking you must get a pure substance even at the cost of plucking out both eyes.

I find no other tenable explanation — and, as an admirer of Gene Rhodes, I have devoted much thought to this critical anesthesia. Back in 1931 or 1932 I wrote a short essay about his books. The first of them had appeared twenty-five years before that and the others had been appearing at fairly regular intervals ever since, but that was the first critical notice that ever discussed them as serious fiction. (So at least Rhodes wrote to me, and a conscientious search of the record bears him out.) There proved to be no room for it in the magazines devoted to the discussion of literature, and eventually his publishers — who it may be had reservations of their own about the propriety of treating a writer of horse operas as a novelist — ran a condensation of it as a paid advertisement. A blurb does not make the best medium for critical discussion but I got an astonishing number of letters from people scattered over the United States, thanking me for saying what they knew to be truisms and platitudes but what no critic had bothered, or it may be dared, to say before. When I began to edit *The Saturday Review of Literature*

I could make my own space and promptly (in 'Horizon Land') called Rhodes to the attention of its subscribers. Again a large mail greeted me as one endowed with grip and password and thanked me for elaborating the obvious. About a year later a broadcasting company made me a gift of six minutes on the air to use as I might see fit, and I devoted them to Gene Rhodes. Once more the letters came in thanking me for praising what many people knew ought to be praised but had not seen praised in the journals where the literary practice their trade.

Yes, people read Rhodes's books. Only the last two or three are in print and none of the others can be come by without effort. But they read those books, an astonishing number of sensitive and intelligent people, a voiceless and heterogeneous audience — and they remember them. If it be consonant with one of criticism's reagents that a book lingers many years in the remembrance of people who read it in the perishable pages of a five-cent weekly, then the number of my correspondents who refer to 'The Little Eohippus' must be a formidable argument, for that is not the title of the printed book. There is another consonance, if it rest only on my private experience. In twenty years whenever I have recommended one of those books to a person whose literary judgment I respected, he has returned a favorable verdict, and usually an enthusiastic one. I gave 'Pasó por Aquí' to a colleague in the Harvard English department; a week later it was on the list of required reading for one of his courses. I lent 'West is

West' to a Frenchman who permits himself only an abstemious admiration of our provincial literature; he returned it with the annotation, 'C'est épatant,' and I have known him to use that adjective, besides, only in relation to 'Green Pastures.' I suggested to Robert Frost that he might like Rhodes; a month later he was an addict. The three men make a considerable spread of connoisseurship; minds more unlike would be hard to find, but they are indifferent to categories and right ideas.

It is true that Rhodes does distressingly scramble the categories, aesthetic, moral, and intellectual. Thus, most of his work, practically all of it that counts, first appeared in *The Saturday Evening Post.* A right idea holds that only commercial tripe written by prostituted hacks appears in those repulsive columns, and that settles it. Again, all of it is set in the West (criticism, which is above geography, recognizes as Southwest only the Santa Fé school of eurythmics and confession), the West it is set in is wild and addicted to gunfire, and almost all its characters are what Ruggles described as cow-persons. Right ideas to take care of all that are immediately at hand. It might be possible to spare a few words for the conventions of popular art or even, if one happened to be exceptionally well informed, to inquire whether Rhodes followed the conventions of Alfred Henry Lewis or the simpler ones of Hollywood and *Cowboy Tales.* But even these few words would make plain that a cowboy story is a cowboy story, the merest refuse of stereotyped production, in short popular fiction. . . . Here, of course, we may speculate. Since Rhodes died a shift of rightness in ideas has occurred, and that part of popular literature has been legitimatized which sympathizes with the worker. Rhodes not only sympathized with him but championed him, apotheosized him, and warred on his exploiters. So Granville Hicks may yet bring out an annotated edition of, say, 'Once in the Saddle,' to prove that the Great Tradition had its upholders even among the desert individualists.

Or take those terms which trouble the intelligence of sophomores and their instructors. On the one hand, the man was a rigorous realist. Drouth is drouth in his pages, thirst is thirst, heat is heat, and dust, dust. When a remuda comes in, that is the way remudas come in. Water in barrels at a cook wagon stinks as water does stink when carried fifty miles and left under the desert sun. When a miner hits the hand of his helper with a sledgehammer (though they happen to be rescuing comrades trapped by a cave-in), blood and nausea are as conscientiously rendered as if this were one of Mr. Hemingway's books. More than that: Rhodes sometimes neglected to disguise the names of his characters. The reader will recognize Pat Garrett of something over a dozen I might mention. When he did change their names, he frequently left untampered with the literal history of their exploits. So that his stories, which might seem to the uninitiated the wildest kind of invention, were frequently just a log of what had happened, and it has been hinted that several of them so trod on sensitive toes that there were survivors in New Mexico, equipped with practicable guns, who would have admired to meet Gene Rhodes again. He sent me a number of his books with explanatory marginalia. (I should explain that, though I never met Rhodes, I corresponded with him for some years and could frequently spell out a fair half of what his indescribable scrawls in ink were intended to convey.) In all discretion I may quote this, from above the second chapter-heading of 'Pasó por Aquí': 'His name was Bruno Marquez [it is Rosalio Marquez in the book]. He died one week before I got back here. Ross McEwen's name was Ross McMillan.' (But I cannot be sure whether that last vowel is *a* or *e*.) So the gambler into whose mouth, as Mr. Orcutt says, Rhodes put his summation of an epoch's ideals, was a gambler from the annals of history, and the fleeing outlaw was fleeing from a robbery which you can read about in the newspaper files, and he fled from it as Rhodes tells. If Ross McMillan did not saddle a steer and did not pause in flight to nurse a family through diphtheria, why, the record shows that Rhodes himself did.

He was frequently a historian and always a faithful chronicler. If it is realism when Mr. Dreiser sifts the court records of a murder trial or when he heaps up authentic detail from the correspondence of bankers, the cant of revivalists, or the trade practices of building contractors — be informed that the whole archeology of the cattle kingdom can be recovered from Rhodes's books. His round-ups, his dry camps, his brand-blotting, all the details of habit and custom and the skill he so whole-heartedly admired, all the routine and adaptation of life on the range, in the mines, and in the little towns is absolutely correct. (It ought to be: Rhodes was twenty-five years a cowboy, a twister, a top hand, before he was a writer. He had guided cavalry in pursuit of Indians, he had homesteaded, freighted, mined — and washed dishes in a cowtown lunchroom. Legend says also that reasons which made it convenient to leave New Mexico gave him an additional authority.) What you read in his books you may, as an archeologist, depend on. And, as I shall be showing in a moment, he has a more important realism, for the pattern of thought and feeling in his books is that of the era he wrote about. It is the record of the deposit which experience in the range country left on the minds of those who underwent it. I am willing to let that define realism in fiction.

But the man was also, sometimes at forced draught, a romantic. The women in his books, for instance. It is only when they have reached middle age, when he can read from their hands and faces what life in the desert had cost them, that they are human or even credible. They are incredible, and the attitude in which they are approached, the lush and trepidant veneration, the tropical breathlessness in the presence of mysterious, mysteriously fine, and infrangibly virginal female flesh makes one wonder why an artist who could differentiate the colors of grasses under a five-miles-distant wind never bothered to observe what a woman looks like.

They are distillations of sweetness and exist merely to stimulate the hero to precariously gallant behavior, usually on occasions when good sense in a woman would have made it impossible, and to reward him when the complications have been worked out. There are no wives younger than middle age anywhere in Rhodes, no unself-conscious women, no prostitutes, only one girl whose behavior is indiscreet, only one tarnished virtue, and, I believe, only one threatened virginity (Bennie May Morgan's in 'West is West,' which is nearly betrayed by what is to be a false marriage, but a loyal servant shoots the betrayer and is shot by him). The typical Rhodes heroine is Lyn Dyer of 'Stepsons of Light,' who tremulously confesses to her fiancé that she has had a dream about another man. These girls are of a stuff that has been uniform from the Court of Love to Hollywood, though the historian is obliged to point out that there is a possible contagion in the literature that was accepted when Rhodes was learning to write.

In these women, in the reverence they aspire among hard-bitten men, in the conversations those men hold with them and the courtly quests that ensue, Rhodes is an extremely odd, and embarrassed, cowhand wandering under a property moon. He had a harder and even more romantic time with villains — for he has villains, and they are astonishing. The villain is never a 'bad man,' as pulp-paper and the screen have developed a Western bad man in obedience to Bret Harte and Alfred Henry Lewis. He is seldom, even, an outlaw: outlaws are more likely to be the heroes. He is (Mr.

Hicks may begin taking notes here) almost always a banker, a financier, a merchant, or a railroad-manipulator who has squeezed the little people in bad years and robbed them in good ones. Secondary villains may be cowmen who have gone wrong — and if so are distinguished by flagrant disloyalty and more flagrant cowardice. But principal villains are those who prey on the humble, the hard-working, the ordinary citizens who are the commonwealth, the predestined victims of privilege and guile. Rhodes, who belonged to the plundered province, could imagine no other kind of villain; and, faced with one, he could attribute to him no credible humanity. So little humanity shows through them in his books and they talk rather like their counterparts in Henry Arthur Jones and the early Owen Davis. They are furiously conscious of their own villainy, and they come down to the footlights and, like Iago, inform us that they are determined to prove it. They are conspirators to an offstage violin, they scheme like Chinese doctors in wood-pulp, and they spill sawdust at the ears. Usually they are craven but sometimes, backed against the wall, one of them shows guts, the bedrock of absolute courage. That one will be permitted a clean death or even, on occasion, a contrived getaway.

> 'I think maybe the sheriff won't come back, [Bill Doolin, who was bent on outlawry but led by circumstances and justice into righteousness, says of such a one at the end of 'The Trusty Knaves']. I think possibly that jailer or somebody might slip out and put a bug in the sheriff's ear. In fact, I know he will. Weak-

minded of me, I know. But I keep thinking about him standing up for the Carmody woman and the Carmody kids. Dave Salt, he's just a tool and a cat's-paw. But that dumb, pot-bellied old sheriff is some part of a man, even yet.'

'I know,' said Pres soberly. 'Elmer and me and the youngster, we hog-tied a real man today, and let him down that shaft like a calf in a crate.... What makes 'em go bad, 'Enry? Why can't they be straight?'

But if we were to say of Rhodes's heroines and villains only that they are romantic, we should be missing a point of fundamental importance. They are his flagrant weakness, but they are immensely true, not to life, but to the sentiment of the society he writes about. The significance to literary history of Rhodes's books is that they are the only fiction of the cattle kingdom that reaches a level which it is intelligent to call art. Now it must be clearly understood that the cattle kingdom (the phrase is Walter Webb's, and one who is unwilling to accept my assertions here, should examine the evidence in his memorable book, 'The Great Plains') was a social system. It was short-lived, it lasted less than a single generation, and it is so completely extinct now that it may seem like a legend, but it was a successful social adaptation to the conditions of the range country. It was the only successful one that has so far been worked out, as you may verify in the government subsidies, the social chaos, the newspaper headlines, and whatever else you associate with the 'Dust Bowl.' It was a social system: it had its own dynamic organization, its own culture, its own vital beliefs and myths which were essential to its successful functioning. All societies must have such sentiments, and it does not matter whether we call them social myths or social ideals. Rhodes not only shared but was immersed in them: he was of this society, they were the basic assumptions by which everyday reality was to be oriented.

I cannot further characterize them here — anyone who is interested may consult some half-dozen essays on the West in my 'Forays and Rebuttals.' But criticism must remember, first of all, that this society was both intensely individual in that it required a man to assume complete responsibility for all his actions, and intensely co-operative in that it required him to subordinate himself altogether when his interests conflicted with the group's. It was in the highest possible degree both 'solitary' and 'neighborly.' (The principal literary distinction of Owen Wister is that he recognized this fact at a time when he had no predecessors in fiction to instruct him in it.) Interstitial with this sentiment, inseparable and indivisible from it, were complex relationships with other sentiments that made a part of its force, and those we are considering highlight a similarity to all pastoral societies. That adjective, pastoral, must be allowed its literal meaning. The beliefs, the assumptions of the cattle kingdom may be found, *mutatis mutandis*, wherever men live in a sparse country, where the conditions of life are stern, and maintain themselves principally by grazing flocks or herds. The manners, the bonds and constraints, the basic beliefs, the virtues praised and vices scorned in the cattle country were strikingly like those of, for example, the Scotch Border in the eighteenth century. It is not by chance that the border balladry is quoted throughout Rhodes, that his cowboys sing it fully as often as they sing 'The Chisholm Trail.' Miss Lyn Dyer sings 'Kirkconnel Lea' and 'Jeanie Morrison' half an hour before she confesses to Hobby Lull that one night another man got into her troubled dream. Most appropriately. Jeanie Morrison and Lyn Dyer are distilled from analogous beliefs.

These inconceivably feminine girls supersaturated with sweetness and offensively chaste accurately represent a sentiment of the cattle country which was part of and essential to its adaptation. They had no relation whatever to, no bearing on, the girls a cowboy visited in town on Saturday night. They expressed a necessary social idea of the cattle country, and you may see how such energies work out in any treatise on sociology. There were probably as many bastards on Kirkconnel Lea as in the Panhandle, but the minstrel ignored them in the service of his people. He was, as the more excitable of us might say today, expressing an ideology.

The villains are even more directly from the social matrix. The West was, I have said elsewhere, incurably addicted to civilization. These people were bringing the country in. They were redeeming it from the desert, they were making human life possible there, they were building a society. You must remember that this was a hard job. All misunderstanding of the

West seems to derive from people's forgetting that it was a hard job, and that fact of a crushing labor is the key to the critical appraisal of Gene Rhodes. The conditions of life, of survival, in the high plains, the mountains, and the desert were so completely different from all others which American pioneering had had to face that both the culture and the technology of pioneering broke down under them. A new culture, a new technology, a new social system had to be developed—and with them a morality that would make them work. In that morality, whatever contributed to the new adaptation was good, what stood in its way was bad. The speculators, the bankers and manipulators, the mortgagees and monopolists, all the operators of the machinery by which the East systematically plundered its captive province, were public enemies. Whoever defeated these vermin or even scored a point against them, whether by skill, quick thinking, guile, chicanery, fraud, or even gunfire, was necessarily to that extent, if only in that instance, heroic.

If he were sometimes also an outlaw, why, a large part, perhaps the largest part, of the Western adaptation had to exist literally outside the law. Within it survival was impossible, and though a new social system implied the slow development of a new and radically different legal system, which is operative though uncompleted yet, the lag was necessarily great. Mr. Webb shows how futile, how damaging, and how asinine were the measures devised for the West, in all goodwill, by the national government. He remarks in summary that, down to the date of his book, not one intelligent measure bearing on the West had ever been enacted by Congress. And thus a common theme in Rhodes's stories is how both justice and necessity may require the breaking of statutory law. His peace officers, his sheriffs and deputies, are frequently from among the unrighteous, the exploiters; when they are not, they frequently connive openly at lawbreaking. The jailer and the judge in 'Stepsons of Light' are aware that Johnny Hines is being betrayed and exploited by people who can use the law as their instrument; so they extend to Johnny the consolations of illegality. At least a dozen other stories employ the same device more or less centrally, and in employing it express a sentiment of primary force in the cattle kingdom.

But when, in 'Pasó por Aquí,' Pat Garrett (please: this was the man who shot Billy the Kid) conceals his identity as sheriff from Ross McEwen, the man who had robbed the bank and store at Belen, and lets him go free, in fact escorts him to safety — he is symbolizing something even more profound and even closer to the core of this society's belief.

McEwen was an outlaw in flight. By the exercise of intelligence, endurance and indefatigable courage he had outdistanced the pursuit which had been organized; he had got beyond the posse and the telephones, and safety was within his grasp. But, coming to a little ranch for water, he finds a family stricken with diphtheria. He stops and nurses them through it — he plays out the string, he shovels on a little more coal. They need help and, being there, he gives it. So when Garrett catches up with him there is no question of arresting him. He will do to take along, he will make a hand, he has been a man, and Garrett, the sheriff, will go with him as a friend that no suspicion may gather... 'Why,' says Jay Hollister, the uncomprehending Eastern girl, 'they could impeach him for that. They could throw him out of office.' And Monte, the gambler, explains: 'But who will tell? We are all decent people.'

There is more of Monte's explanation, and some of it must be quoted here, for in it Rhodes sums up his belief. Monte who is, remember, a gambler remarks that his people came by Zuñi to El Morro, Inscription Rock, before any of Jay's people had crossed the Atlantic.

> 'Well [he says] eet ees good camp ground, El Morro, wood and water, and thees gr-reat cleef for shade and for shelter een estr-rong winds. And here some fellow he come and he cry out, "*Adios, el mundo!* What lar-rge weelderness ees thees! And me, I go now eento thees beeg lonesome and perhaps I shall not to r-return! *Buenos, pues,* I mek now for me a gravestone!" and so he mek on that beeg rock weeth hees dagger, "*Pasó por aquí, Don Fulano de Tal*" — passed by here, Meester So-and-So — weeth the year of eet.
>
> 'And after heem come others to El Morro, so few, so far from Spain! They see what he ees write there, and they say, "*Con razón*" — eet ees weeth reason to do thees. An' they also mek eenscreepción, "*Pasó por aquí*" — and their names, and the year of eet.
>
> 'I would not push my leetleness upon thees so lar-rge

world, but one of thees, Mees Hollister — oh, not of the great, not of the first — he was of mine, my ver' great, great papa. So long ago! And he mek also, "*Pasó por aquí*, Salvador Holguin." I hear thees een the firelight when I am small fellow. And when I am man-high I mek veesit to thees place and see him.

'And thees fellow, too, thees redhead, he pass this way, "*Pasó por aquí*" and he mek good here and not weeked. But, before that — I am not God!...'

Monte was not God and what the redhead had done before this was not his responsibility. McEwen had passed this way, and what he had done here was good and not evil, was done unhesitatingly and courageously, with manhood. He had done what had to be done, not considering himself.... He had been true to the need, the admiration, the ideal of the little people, the people on whose side Gene Rhodes had enlisted. They were the ordinary citizens building the commonwealth, living together. They were simple people and it followed that their virtues were simple: courage, loyalty, fortitude, helpfulness, sympathy, humor, endurance: the ability to disregard themselves when facing the need of others, the ability to work with others, an unconquerable decency and dignity, an unthinking but basic assertion of the worth of human life. They might be, as McEwen was, speckled with qualities not well thought of in themselves, but if the metal which they showed in the testing-fire was the right one — what matter? We have nothing to do, no commerce, with the sons of light — a part of the West's characteristic thought, Rhodes did not believe in them — but only with the stepsons.

Those virtues were what enabled society to exist and endure in the cattle kingdom. That is the important thing for literary criticism, not that Rhodes was making an affirmation of democracy. He was a realist not only of the externals of life in a vivid, brief era but a realist of the beliefs and aspirations that gave it vitality. And the historian must conscientiously point out that, during the 1920's when the more important part of Rhodes's work was done, it was not fashionable in American literature to assert the tenets of democracy nor to affirm the dignity of common life and the worth of native American ways and values. His work ran exactly counter to the main stream of fiction and criticism during that museum decade, which may be another reason why criticism ignored it. And not his fiction only. He hated the disparagement of the ordinary man and of the American heritage that was the current coin of our literature. He made violent war on it and its authors, though mostly in obscure places since there were few magazines, no magazines of discussion, that cared to give the other side a hearing. Some of that sword-play is magnificent, and all of it would seem strangely prophetic and of this moment if revived now. It will be a pleasure to collect it in a book some day and, for the instruction of the young, to display Rhodes's place in the small company of literary men who would not slander America during a time when slandering it was the highway to money, reputation, and the approval of the elect.

I have been discussing Gene Rhodes, writer of horse

operas, as a serious literary artist. Why, yes: literature is where you find it, literature is of its own kind alone, literature is what it is and almost never what it ought to be. It is of its own kind alone, though the vocation of critics is almost exclusively to reproach it for not being something else. You would be wasting your time to go to Rhodes's books in search of psychological subtleties, an impressive aesthetics, or any formulated philosophy of mankind, history, or the nature of things. Such qualities are not in his books. And it would be idle to pretend that, in their own kind, they are always of the best or that any of them is free of defects. There was as much flesh in him as in the next man, and he was not always at his best, and some of his contrivances fail, and some of his passages are flatted. If, for instance, he had stopped five lines or even one line short of where he did stop when he was finishing 'Pasó por Aquí' his masterpiece would have been a better job. All this is true. And yet, to come back to where I started, people remember those books, and they abide as something true spoken of their era, their society, and the people who appear in them.

That is the generalization about Gene Rhodes: that his books are the only embodiment on the level of art of one segment of American experience. They are the only body of fiction devoted to the cattle kingdom which is both true to it and written by an artist in prose. Surely that is a great deal: to have given fiction its sole mature expression of one era in our past, one portion of the experience that has gone to make up America.

The public, though it would use less solemn terms, would ratify that judgment, having ratified the humbler literature which Rhodes transcends. Out of what was no more than the business of growing and selling beef cattle it has erected a genuine symbolism, to which time has attached a greater glamour than any other business ever pursued by Americans has evoked. Out of the West, that ever-strange country, has come much glamour and many symbolic images: the long hunter, the trapper, the trader, the flatboatman, the Indian fighter, the scout, the cavalryman, the gold-washer, the nester, the sodbuster, the railroad builder. Yet only the cowboy has created a literature of his own, a type of literature with its own conventions, rituals, and graphic notation. It is a trivial literature, whatever poignancy of desire unsatisfied it may represent, and the mistake of the unthinking and of critics has been to confuse Rhodes's books with it. They are not a part of this cowboy literature, they do not belong, even, to the finer *genre* worked by Owen Wister, Henry Phillips (who helped Rhodes during his apprenticeship), and the remaining small company of the good but second-best. It was not pageantry to Rhodes, it was not glamour, it was not ritual and symbolism — it was the way of life he had grown up in, the life lived by the people whom he respected and loved in the country that had his heart. So, a fine artist, he broke through to the realities.

Too near the end of my allotted space to permit much remedy, I perceive that I have touched on none of the things that a proper critical study would take into account. Let me do briefly what ought to be done at length. Anyone who may go to his books from this essay need not take with him the sobriety I have employed in discussing them, for Rhodes was primarily a story-teller. That too was out of tune with his age, which not only preferred to take its sentimentality upside down but regarded the art of narrative with a loathing undisguised. He was a skilled craftsman. Whether spun on a pattern so complicated that its very expertness may have been one barrier to recognition, or whether told simply and straightforwardly, his stories are done with a sure touch, with a mastery of pace and effect which you will not too readily match elsewhere in the fiction of the Twenties. As stories they are all expert and the best of them are superb. Mr. Eddy Orcutt, whose fine article for *The Saturday Evening Post* I have read in proof while writing this introduction, considers 'Pasó por Aquí' the best. It is certainly the one which strikes the deepest note and shows most clearly what Rhodes was driving at. But there is an élan in 'The Trusty Knaves' that the more somber story never achieves. There are passages in 'Beyond the Desert' which I will remember fully as long — though if it comes to passages, I could quote all eleven of his books. A scrawl in one of the copies Rhodes sent to me indicates that he considered a chapter in 'Good Men and True' the best thing he had ever written. I cannot follow him there: the books he did after 1920 seem to me considerably better than the early ones.

Yet the one most often alluded to in the letters I get from fellow initiates is 'The Little Eohippus,' which was serialized in the *Post* in 1912.

His writing is simple, unmannered, in the tone of a quiet speaking voice, though on occasion he can make rhetoric serve his need. Twenty-five years of reading by campfire-light or in the dust of herds the paper-bound classics of English literature which the Bull Durham company distributed had given him objectives long before he began to write, and his simplicity is no more naïve than Huxley's and no more artless than Swift's. It is most striking in the dialogue he writes, much the best dialogue put in the mouth of Western characters since Mark Twain. The whole revelation of a man, perhaps the point of an entire story, may depend on the turn of a single phrase, and that turn may depend on an inflection which not the eye but the ear must catch. Yet the inflection is not missed: his Westerners tranquilly reveal themselves in authentic speech. It is an instructive exercise to place one of Rhodes's stories beside, say, one of Alfred Henry Lewis's. You will end by observing that, as I have said, Target or Salamanca is a community, whereas Wolfeville is just a set of painted flats against a canvas backdrop or one of Colonel Cody's twelve-sheet posters. But the first, the most obvious difference you will notice is that Lewis's characters speak a vaudeville argot assembled from Bret Harte's inventions and the comic press. You would not notice it, so fixed has the convention become, except that Rhodes's people talk like living men.

Yet it is not the speech of his characters but his rendition of the Western country that I for one most sincerely and enviously admire. Perhaps one must both have grown up in the mountains and tried to put their feel and appearance into words, in order to appreciate fully the sureness of Rhodes's pen. If you have never seen sunrise across a thousand square miles from such a ridge as the San Clemente, if you have never ridden in desert noon down such rimrock as Cienfuegos, it may be that you must miss something of a fine art. I think of one small scene, one of many, no more than two or three paragraphs: the moment when the dark changes at a camp high on the slope of a mountain, the stars still bright, the cook already at his fire, the night-wrangler coming in with the mount. Rhodes's hero wakes to that tremendous unreality, and in five inches of type the thing is done so that your very bones and lungs ache with remembered rock and cold, your eyes with remembered darkness where the roof-pitch of the world falls away below you, and remembered woodsmoke is sharp in your nostrils and drifts between you and the dimming stars — when some now dead squatted before the fire drinking coffee from tin cups and bringing in the day. Yes, the man wrote prose.

He passed this way. He lived in a hard country in a laborious time, loving that country and its people. In the fullness of his love he wrote about what he knew. So, like Monte's ancestor, he scratched his name on Inscription Rock. An honorable time will have passed before the wind and sand can erase it.

'When you ride up to that camp, you ride a-whistlin', real loud and pleasant. That Charlie Bird, he's half Cherokee and half white, and them's two bad breeds.' It is Bill Doolin speaking, in 'The Trusty Knaves.' Two bad breeds, and Gene Rhodes had had ample cause to know how bad. Yet the reason why someone not Bill Doolin must ride to that camp is that Bill and Charlie Bird were boys together, and the halfbreed remembers Bill and must not learn that Bill had got off the trail. If we must concentrate a man and eleven books in a single sentence, let that one do for Gene Rhodes.

The Hired Man on Horseback

CHAPTER I

Letters to a Poet

GENE and I resolved that to everyone who inquired how we became acquainted, we would give a different answer. We followed this pleasing custom for years. Toward the last, I think our devilish ingenuity forsook us, and we may have repeated ourselves.

When I had diphtheria, my sister came to take care of me. She recited poems to rest me. One that I especially liked had this stanza:

> Brown eyes, love-lighted and tender,
> My beacon pole star on the dark stormy sea where I sail.
> I am weary and sad. Through the storm and the darkness
> Shine softly tonight on the Santa Fe Trail.

(My eyes are gray.)

I bobbed my head from side to side on the pillow and murmured, 'A very beautiful poem.'

'Why don't you write and tell him so?' she suggested. 'He is a rising young poet and they like to be encouraged.'

Remembering this when she was gone and time hung heavy, I wrote him an appreciative little note. Nothing happened. The days and weeks went on as before. I grew enraged at such discourtesy, then finally forgot all about it. A good three months after came a big, fat letter, twenty pages or so, and it closed like this, 'With love, Jean.' I read this closing several times, tasting it over like a sweet morsel and said, 'H'm'm.'

He had been to a big round-up and had just come back. Round-ups were something new on my horizon.

There were more letters, many more, the most wonderful letters I ever have read. As soon as I was strong enough, I had started doing practical nursing to support my two small orphaned sons. Two years of this and then a course in Training School in Philadelphia. Still the letters came. I was graduated one April evening, and went immediately to Gloversville, New York, to officiate at the arrival of a new niece. The letters had grown perilously sweet.

Then came the news that Gene was heading East with a trainload of cattle from New Mexico. I fled home to Apalachin at the earliest possible moment, to fix the house a bit for such distinguished company. Mother was no longer young and a bit sketchy about her housekeeping. With my two offspring eternally under her feet, it was no wonder.

I had three days of grace. In one day I papered the kitchen, which was low, dingy, and dark. Then I gave slight licks and big promises to the rest of our little house.

Gene, meanwhile, went on to Gloversville, expecting to find me there. He made the acquaintance of a comely damsel on the trip up from New York City and helped her from the train with tender solicitude, all to impress me — and I wasn't there. He went to my brother's to stay overnight. Next day, he left for my home. Wild horses, my brother maintained, couldn't have kept him any longer.

We were to meet at the Spooky Bridge, down the hill from our house, and really haunted — I have the word of various old ladies in the neighborhood. Spooky Bridge was the beginning of one of the most winsome dells in the world, lined with poplars like slim young girls, laced with feathery willows, a tangle of raspberry bushes and wild clematis, watered by a silvery talking brook. A veritable 'Leisurely Lane,' as Gene and I named it.

There is no road now to Leisurely Lane.
Ah, God, we have wandered so far.

I heard the faraway train whistle. After sufficient pause, I craned my neck out of the little upstairs window, as Connie McMahon's shacking team and old canvas-covered stage ambled up the valley road. Yes, the stage stopped at the corner. A solitary passenger stepped out. I scudded down to the Spooky Bridge. There I met him.

A quiet, medium-sized man whose blond hair and mustache, he always insisted, were mouse-colored. Blue eyes, a face richly sunburned. 'Hard as nails and quick as greased lightning,' the cowboys described him. A man of strange contradictions, gentle and dreamy, who wrote exquisite poetry and had a superfine taste in literature, yet, in the twinkling of an eye, could be metamorphosed into incarnate rage. Of his temper, which made him both feared and respected in that lawless land, he once said:

> He should take who hath the power,
> And he should hold who can.

He had been in a big fight, and one ear was a bit torn off, his face bruised. He wore a cheap light suit he had bought of a Jew in New York City. 'I was a stranger and they took me in.' Because the Jews were among the best citizens in New Mexico, Gene wasn't prepared for our Eastern variety. From his arm swung a red *papier-mâché* telescope. We kissed each other, a bit timidly I'll allow, and hand in hand we paced slowly up the hill to the house.

That fight at Niagara Falls from which he came battered and sore, he described many years later in 'The Prince of Tonight.'[1]

> Across the unimaginable blackness mysterious lights signaled, winked and wavered like fireflies across dewy turf; over the black, empty silence dull rumblings and faint whistles spoke of busy trains afar. From its high standard the solitary yardlight picked out, blurred and uncertain, wave after wave of car-roofs — waves from an ocean of cars, pressing in and breaking upon that dim island of light.
>
> Cheerfully he waited, seated now on the end of the running board, with dangling legs and a mind conscious of its own rectitude. Along the side of Jimmy's string of cars a bobbing lantern appeared. It came nearer; it was raised and lowered. Plainly, one came who looked

[1] *Saturday Evening Post*, October 19, 1912. (Substitute Gene for Jimmy.)

with interest into every car of steers. Jimmy's heart expanded with hospitable anticipation, for the agent of the consignee was to join him here.

The lantern came nearer, still bobbing up and down to bear out Jimmy's fancy of a cockle tossed on a choppy sea.

'Boat ahoy!' hailed Jimmy, and swung the harbor light.

At this friendly greeting the lantern came on, swift and unbobbing; a man shaped and grew to substance. He stopped under the ladder and looked up, holding the lantern level with his face. It was a red face, under the billycock hat; and an angry face, with a prognathous jaw.

'By ——, are you supposed to be taking care of these cattle?' he bawled.

Jimmy leaned his chin in his hand and eyed the visitor gravely. 'Say sir to the ladies and yes'm to the men,' he prompted. 'Part your hair neatly, do not speak too loud or too much, and wipe your feet before you come in the house.'

'Why ain't you down here tending to these steers? You'll go no further on this train, you damned tramp!'

'Cattle doin' fine,' said Jimmy dispassionately — 'fine as silk. I looked after everything while we waited across the bridge — fed 'em, watered 'em, showed 'em the Falls and tucked 'em in bed. Left a call for six A.M. Come up and let your feet hang off. Sorry I ain't got no fan for you.'

'Get off that car!'

'Comin'!' said Jimmy. 'We aim to please.'

Obligingly he hurled his prodpole — not with the pointed end down nor yet with any great force, but formally — much as the olden peoples tossed a spear across the frontier as a declaration of war. The rounded end of it glanced from the billycock hat and so angled away across the next track. The lantern retrieved the damaged hat and fled into the murk, having no mind for solitary combat.

'Hi! Hi there! Wait a bit! I'm comin' as fast as ever I can,' cried Jimmy, halfway down the ladder. There was no answer; so he hunted up his javelin and went back to the car-top.

. . . .

Jimmy climbed down to the way-car. It was lighted but unoccupied. Jimmy draped himself luxuriously along two cushioned seats. As the train gathered headway, voices floated in from the platform. Entered a cap, the conductor; a slouch hat, which was the brakeman; and a billycock, Jimmy's friend of the undershot jaw, who in passing shot a sharp glance at Jimmy. A step or so along the aisle he paused and observed:

'I bet I fix them Kansas City guys so they don't send up any more bums with the cattle trains. By ——, they'd better send a nigger!'

With an effort Jimmy sat up, yawning.

'Ah-o-ah! — ugh! Are you the gentleman who was swearing at me back yonder in the yards?' he asked sleepily.

Billycock half-turned, twisting, and rested his undershot jaw upon his left shoulder. 'Yes!' he snarled, and added the word of insult. At the same time he crumpled up and pitched forward, his head striking the leg of the seat down the aisle. This act was not voluntary. Trained to cat-quickness among flashing hoofs and horns, the cowboy had swung all his lithe body into one crashing blow against that conspicuous jaw.

Billycock rose, a gash cut into his sleek, black head by the iron leg of the car-seat. He spat blood, paused to ascertain with precision which way was up and which down; he crouched and rushed.

Things happened then to Jimmy. A bronco pawed him; a steer hooked him; a mule kicked him; a house fell upon him; an automobile ran him down. He was a book-agent — an indignant householder kicked him downstairs; he was umpire — several thousand fans beat him with bats and pop bottles; he was married, and his wives rebuked him with hot flatirons; he was a forest — and lightning struck thick and fast; he was a ten-wheeled freight engine that had jumped the track on a foggy mountain-side and bounded riotously over the boulders, fire streaming from every wheel.

The fog cleared; he was himself — Jimmy McClosky, of Black River — dizzily taking a glorious licking. Fairly matched as to inches and age, he was all but helpless under the onslaught of a skilled boxer. Good stock, strong-hearted, the blood royal, years of clean living and hard work befriended him now. Wearied with his fruitless labors, Billycock relaxed for a moment and mauled less savagely, waiting until Jimmy's instinctive covering up should waver and leave an opening for a finishing touch — and in that moment Jimmy's head cleared; he felt his feet touch ground again; he felt strength come back to him.

He had staggered and reeled from weakness; he reeled now with purpose, his eyes half-shut — to all seeming helpless and spent; in reality watchful, strong, desperate, and dangerous. He swerved as a smashing blow shot by his head, missing him by a hair. Unbalanced, Billycock's body followed the missed blow; Jimmy's fist flashed up, caught squarely at the undershot jaw — and the fight was over. Jimmy had landed two good blows, the first and the last; Billycock, who had landed fifty good ones, lay senseless in the aisle.

The victor was in scarce better case. Dizzily he dropped into a seat, bruised, battered, and breathless, holding the seat-back for steadiness, and received the congratulations of the train crew — even in his shaken condition conscious of a depressing idea that these gratulations might have been equally fervid had the battle gone otherwise. His foeman, Madden by name, had been a third-rate prize-fighter in the city of New York, the trainmen informed him.

Gene brought me the *Seven Seas* by Rudyard Kipling and underscored

I sent the lightnings forth to see
  Where hour by hour she waited me,
Among ten million one was she,
  And surely all men hated me!
. . . . . .
Ah, day no tongue shall tell again!

Beside it he set the date, July 18, 1899.

He also brought a pearl-handled six-shooter with which he later taught me to shoot. His doubtful conclusion was that I might possibly shoot a man if he held still long enough.

In the evening we walked over the brow of the hill, watched the sun set and the long shadows creep across the valley where the shining Apalachin Creek lay. The evening star appeared as we lingered there.

'Always, from boyhood, I have had the feeling that I could write, if I ever had a proper chance,' Gene said. Then he told me that he had been offered a position in an office by a Wells-Fargo executive. 'A man might better be in the "pen" than in an office.' But the decision was mine to make. With such a lead I hastened to assure him that an office was no place for an out-of-doors man.

A week later Gene's exasperated comment was that if he ever wrote a book it would be entitled 'Courtship Under Difficulties.' He made for the boys small sail-boats to go down to the creek to play. They dragged them around the woodpile with strings until they were far past being seaworthy. He took them to the upper barn, taught them to play handball, and then ran down to the house. They were there nearly as soon as he. They endeared themselves to him in a number of similar ways.

We were married on the ninth of August. Four days later, Gene started back to New Mexico, leaving me 'to weep and to wail.' He stopped in Illinois to visit his mother's relatives, where his pretty cousin told him teasingly that if he had come there first, *they* could have come to New York on their wedding trip.

That winter in the West Gene worked for Charlie Graham digging a well. He dug days and at night wrote his first story, 'The Hour and the Man.' When it was finished, he sent it back to New York. I hired a typewriter and typed it. It was sold to Charles F. Lummis for his *Land of Sunshine* magazine for ten dollars.

Gene had to go to Engle to get his mail. He would get his letters, go to the hotel, stay a night or more, and read and digest his mail and answer it before he went back to the ranch. A pretty school-teacher (why are they always pretty?) taught the Engle school and boarded at the hotel. She was engaged to Gene's dearest friend. He wrote me one night that he and she were sitting at the big dining-room table, each writing to the beloved. They didn't put in their whole time writing, evidently, for after a while he sent me this poem which he had written her.

WHITE FINGERS

Her fingers stray along the frets,
Her fingers wander o'er the strings;
A little while my heart forgets
Its griefs and cares and petty stings.
The air is filled with rustling wings,
Forgot are folly, wrong, and sin,
And earth seems made for happier things —
She plays upon her mandolin!

Her fingers fly along the frets,
Her fingers dance along the strings . . .
Courage, my soul, though strife besets,
Stand firm whatever fortune brings,
Heir to the ages, peer of kings!
High over turmoil, dust, and din,
The clarion call of Honor rings —
She plays upon her mandolin!

Her fingers dream along the frets,
They linger lightly o'er the strings:
What spell is woven in the nets
Of meshéd melody she flings?
A burning tear unbidden springs;
Old hopes, loves, dreams — all dwell within

That dying music's whisperings —
 She plays upon her mandolin!

L'Envoi

Prince, at the Gates of Paradise
 I fear I scarce could enter in
If still without, with luring eye,
 She played upon her mandolin!

A beautiful thing, it was copied in *The Literary Review*, from the *New Orleans Times-Democrat.* I wrote back with some asperity: 'If you want to hang around outside and hear her play her mandolin, pray do. I'm going inside, and flap my wings and have a good time.'

Another time at his Triangle E<F Ranch, Gene was riding a wild horse with Lon Roberts's saddle. As he started up the mountain-side with this 'critter,' it reared up and fell over backward, landing on his leg. He yelled, 'Come quick and get him off before he scratches Lon's saddle.' Dora Cooper, who lived with her folks at the Triangle E<F Ranch at that time, told me of it, and how they helped him to the house. His leg was badly hurt, but all he said was, 'Now I can write a long letter to my girl.' 'That,' she said, 'is when he wrote you that long letter.'

This was not so enlightening, for he rarely wrote less than twenty pages, and once there was a forty-page one (perhaps that was the time).

The following June when New York State was at the zenith of its beauty, I took Fred and started for New Mexico. Eager Gene had flagged the transcontinental express near Engle, a short time before, and gone aboard to see if I was on the train. And I wasn't. It was hot as hot when we reached El Paso and changed to the comfortless little passenger cars of the El Paso and Northeastern Railroad. We crawled along the desert within two grim walls, the Sacramento Mountains on one side and the Organ and San Andres on the other, without the mountain green I had been used to in the Adirondacks. Midway of nowhere the train broke in two and we were forced to sit there in the blistering heat and watch the engine and baggage car vanish in the distance. They finally discovered their de-tailing and came back to get us. It was a usual incident on the railroad in those days.

Gene met us at Alamogordo, the first station south of Tularosa, and rode along with us. Alamogordo, where I did my poor bit of shopping, was only a little frontier town in those days, hardly three years old, a little ramshackle town with board houses and a big rooming-house that was kept scrupulously clean and dusted in spite of dust storms. It was a lumber town — houses made of boards instead of adobe, called 'box houses.' The town was built on the site of an old lake, just a huddle of houses baking in the sun when I first saw it, before today's shade trees had grown. A dreary enough little place it seemed to me. A thing of startling beauty when I came back, so many years after.

A rainstorm, in glistening sheets, hung over the San Andres Mountains as we came down to Tularosa. Gene whispered, 'It is not raining rain to me, it's raining silver dollars.'

Fred was industriously eating peanuts and throwing the shucks out of the window. 'I guess you don't remember me, do you, Fred?' Gene said.

'Oh, yes, I do!' said Fred. 'You are the man where Mamma and I are going to live.'

Then after that ominous desert, the heat, and the alkali dust, just as the sun was setting, Tularosa stood out ahead of us. I don't think the Garden of Eden itself could have looked more lovely. All that gorgeous green of wide branching cottonwoods with the light gleaming from their polished leaves, the fields of sweet-smelling alfalfa, the tinkling music of the water ditches, and the mocking birds that I heard for the first time.

'We'll go around the depot and get in a hack,' said Gene. A hack! Visions of luxury, soft padding, and beauty of stepping horses. But this hack was a two-seated platform wagon with a tipsy tilt caused by the heavy driver, and two as sorry-looking horses as ever were.

We went to the hotel, a long, one-story adobe building, run by a charming and motherly woman, Mrs. Saunders, who greeted me smilingly. 'It's quite some consolation to know that I won't hear Gene Rhodes's spurs come clankety-clank down the hall at two in the morning and he won't come and pound on my door to say, "Couldn't you get me a bite to eat so I could start for the mountains?" "No," I'd say. "Go back to bed." An hour or two later he would come clanking back and I'd have to get his breakfast just to get rid of him.'

Tularosa — what magic the name holds! Dreamy,

quiet, save for the thud of galloping horses' hoofs. Thick-walled adobe houses with majestic cottonwood trees shadowing deep doorways from the blistering sun. Mexicans wearing straw hats with high, pointed crowns, and brilliant sashes of purple or scarlet knotted around their waists. White shirts always, and nearly always blue overalls . . . A pack of playing cards flung down in the dusty street . . . Pretty Mexican girls tripping up and down in high-heeled slippers, and over all the matchless New Mexican sun. This was Gene's country, where he had lived since boyhood days.

CHAPTER II

Cowboy Years

BUT the beginnings were back in Nebraska. It is sixty-five years ago. Dick, the hired man on the farm, is washing his face and running his wet fingers through his hair. Eyeing him is little Gene, aged four, waiting to accompany him into the house for breakfast. Pressing on the end of his eyelids, Dick skillfully pries out his glass eye and washes it. Little Gene gasps.

'Huh!' Dick grunts. 'Don't you ever take your eyes out and wash 'em? You should.'

Little Gene obediently jams a thumb in beside his eyeball. He injured his eye for life.

The scene took place in Tecumseh, Nebraska, before the double log house with a covered porch between, where Gene had been born on January 19, 1869.

Gene early exhibited courage. One day when he was five or six, his father and mother went away, leaving him to care for his younger brother Clarence. The day was long, there was little to interest two small boys, and little Gene began planning. 'Come! Brother will carry you pick-a-back down to Crowley (two miles away) and see the new baby.' They started off bravely, but little brother got heavier with every step. At last, pretty tired, Gene sat down to rest a bit. Suddenly a movement behind. There he saw a big gray wolf. Gene picked little brother up again and traveled on as quickly as his little legs would take him. He reached the neighbors safely and told his story casually. A party of hunters went back to find that the wolf had gone, but there were the big prints in the dust, dogging the little barefoot tracks.

His father, Colonel Hinman Rhodes, fearless fighter and Colonel of the Twenty-Eighth Illinois Volunteers in the War Between the States, didn't want his small son to be afraid of anything. He hid one night in a bush in the dark, and made strange noises when the little boy came along, whereupon Gene began firing stones at the bush with all his might until his father said he didn't know but he would be stoned to death before he could get away.

The family subscribed to *The Prairie Farmer*. It was a red-letter day when it came.

I remember, I remember,
   A farmhouse in the West,
The day 'The Prairie Farmer' came,
   Of all the days the best;
Its magic pages opened out
   On faery seas forlorn,
While blithe and gay the hoppergrass
   Went surging through the corn.

I remember, I remember,
   Those dreams of loveliness,
The chromos and the wooden skates,
   'The Boy's Own Printing Press.'

But bolder, blacker, finer far
  The ad which did relate
The tale of far-off Binghamton
  And 'Jones He Pays the Freight.'

I remember, I remember,
  I used to fancy then
That Jones of Binghamton was best
  Of all the sons of men.
How good of him to pay the freight!
  How pleased my dad would be!
(He used to speak about the freight
  With some asperity.)

O, topless towers of Binghamton,
  And Susquehanna's tide!
I used to think the Mississip'
  Was only half as wide!
The scales have fallen from my eyes,
  And now 'tis little joy
To know the man who pays the freight
  Is father's only boy!

The Rhodeses were scourged by prairie fires, grasshoppers, and cyclones. One day during a terrific storm when they had taken refuge in their cyclone cellar, they discovered that Gene was missing. His father dashed back to the house and found him, without a care in the world, calmly eating bread and jam.

When Gene was still small, they moved to Cherokee, Kansas, where they built their houses of green walnut boards. As the boards seasoned, they would pull loose from the houses and curl up like shavings. Folks made a baby cradle of them, so Gene told me, and the sun shone on it till it warped so they couldn't get the baby out. Until the baby grew big enough to 'bust' its way out, they fed it through a knothole. Bonds were issued by this little mid-West settlement, bonds which they knew they could never pay. Nothing daunted, the entire community abandoned their dwellings and moved over to the next township where bonds were unknown and they could start life over again.

Gene's father had a general merchandise store. In this way Gene fell heir to an old account-book. He cut pictures from almanacs, magazines, whatever came in his way, pasted them in this book, and wrote the stories to suit himself, using the pictures as illustrations. Even in those days he was accounted an unusual youngster. Folks used to say, awed, that he had read everything in the Bible.

He wrote in his mother's copy of *Bransford in Arcadia:*

> I used to get the most fascinating plays from Uncle Solon, *London Assurance*, *The Stranger*, and the like. Also, from surreptitious channels, Munro's dime novels! I realized even then that some of them were trash — but I fancy that some of them were not half bad. . . .
>
> Altogether, counting the Nebraska homestead, which was hard for you but delightful for me, and father's stories and the perfectly wonderful times I used to have with him when he sold sewing machines and took me with him, and the New Mexico days which were like a never-ending story to me, I think I may say that I had about the best time anyone ever had until we left the Agency. The Mescalero Agency — not the sewing machine. I am telling you this because you always

seemed to think I was entitled to sympathy, as a boy. Sympathy misplaced — that was just a fit for my wishes.

With love
JEAN

In 1881, Colonel Rhodes went to New Mexico to the post of Indian Agent for the Mescalero Apaches. He, with Captain Tuttle and Lew Friend, took the first wagon through Cottonwood cañon, where 'they made no road. When they came to a cliff, they jumped off.' Gene's mother and his brother and sister, Clarence and Helen, followed in 1883, in the company of some of their old neighbors from Nebraska. Doctor Bailey, his brother, and their families settled in Mesilla Park, while Colonel Rhodes remained at Engle, but later took a homestead in the San Andres Mountains in a cañon adjoining the one where Gene was later to settle.

In the old days Socorro and Doña Aña Counties made the larger half of both Arizona and New Mexico — running from Texas to California. The east-and-west length was just a trifle over the distance from New York to Chicago, or from New York to Savannah, Georgia. In 1881 the east-and-west line of Socorro was a little larger than from Springfield, Massachusetts, to the battle-field of Manassas, a line on which we could put Hartford, New York, Philadelphia, Baltimore, and Washington at appropriate distances. Quite a yardstick!

They had a delightful home in their cañon, and started in raising horses and cattle on a small scale.

Gene described their sitting-room in 'Maid Most Dear' in *The Saturday Evening Post*:

> Lincoln's face looked from the wall — a steel engraving. A flag hung there — an old sword. Venice glowing through a thin drifting mist, crowding feluccas at the wharves, their sails furled to the tilling yards; a fezzed and tasseled Arab with a villainous grin squatted on the sand and proffered a Dead Sea apple to a skeptical camel.

He saw the girl, Eva Scales, who figures under her real name in this story, dancing in a shaft of sunlight in an old deserted mill, when he was a lad of possibly seventeen and she ten or eleven. He never saw her again. In vain he hoped by putting her in this story once more to get in touch with her.

Gene's mother was tall and very fine-looking, with a captivating dimple in her cheek. She was an exceptionally good manager, which was a help at all times. Once, when a number of army officers were at Gene's father's ranch, his mother had been on a visit to her people in Illinois. The Colonel, like his son, was fond of practical jokes, and before leaving for the station to meet his returning wife, he had told the officers that Mrs. Rhodes was a fine woman, never a finer, but she had one bad habit. In spite of all he could do, she would smoke a corncob pipe. She wondered, when she arrived, why all the men looked at her so curiously, but didn't learn the reason until three days later. One of the officers finally said, 'Mrs. Rhodes, if you want to smoke your pipe, don't hesitate on our account.' 'What pipe?' she asked, amazed. He then told her the Colonel's statement. She never revealed how she punished him.

Gene's father was accounted a first-class story-teller with a sharp wit. His courage as a soldier was undisputed; in fact, Congress allowed his widow a special pension for her husband's bravery. As an Indian Superintendent he was regarded highly by his charges. The Indians also thought much of his son, especially after Gene had by throwing a stone, killed a bull which was attacking a young Indian. Thereafter the Indians called Gene the Ox-Killer.

In New Mexico life for the boy began in earnest. Of one incident he wrote in his unfinished *Old-Timers* book:

> Soon after the railroad came, Johnny Martin and I were having high old times at Engle. Twelve-year-olds, we were: and a chief delight was to ride out with the section hands on the hand-car. A delight to us, I mean. After all these years I am beginning to suspect that we were something of a cross to the section hands. This idea first came into my head about sundown on a March day. We were seven miles north of town, and just at quitting time, the Irish section foreman said: 'There's a crowbar and hammer up to the second telegraph pole beyant there. Will yeez slip down there, like good lads, and fetch 'em down to us?' We slipped up there like good lads — and found neither hammer nor bar. And when we looked back, the hand-car was far on its way. We walked in.
>
> The next night, just before six, Johnny and I had business at the north end of the freight yard, with designs on that hand-car. A March gale was blowing and the side track was filled with cars. Doubly sheltered

by dust and freight cars, we slipped down there and placed a couple of spikes in the frog of the switch, and retired behind the freight cars to observe results. They were not long in coming. There is a little hill a mile north of Engle. Just as we saw the hand-car top the rise, pumping hard against the wind — bump — bump — bump — *crash!*

The north-bound passenger train was hours late — which we had not known. Unseen and unheard by us, because of the howling wind, it had slid over that spiked frog. It had not gathered speed as yet, and so, mercifully, was not derailed. Had the train struck the frog from the opposite direction, a wreck would have been inevitable. As it was, one of the tender trucks left the track and was dragged over the ties until the train was stopped. By that time two small boys were quite elsewhere.

The next day ominous red handbills appeared offering one thousand dollars reward for arrest and conviction of the miscreants who had attempted to wreck the passenger train; and for some weeks Engle was pervaded by obnoxious persons with prying minds. The fiends were never identified. During these weary weeks — and for long afterward — Johnny Martin and I conducted ourselves in so exemplary a fashion as to excite remark. Wood, kindling, sweeping the yard, errands, currying horses — we turned our willing hands to anything. Bright and smiling faces — washed, too. Since that I have always felt an uneasy distrust for notoriously good people, with private speculations as to what they had up and went and done, now.

At thirteen, Gene began as a horse wrangler, punching cattle for the William C. McDonald outfit at Carrizzo Springs. His saddle he bought with soap coupons.

He was little and unbelievably shabby. Every penny of his small wages he sent to his parents. When Dallas, the foreman, told the small cowboy he'd send old Florentino out to camp at Christmas-time to take his place so that he could come in to the dance, Gene said, with downcast eyes: 'You needn't bother. I ain't got no good clothes and I'm broke.'

To reassure his folks, he wrote glowing letters of raises in pay, all entirely imaginary. The cowboys were peeved at his very saving ways, thinking him a miser. By chance they found out the truth and then they made much of him. He wrote of the incident of their first praise for him in 'The Bar Cross Liar' for the Charles F. Lummis magazine.

By the time he was seventeen, he was acting as guide and government scout during the Geronimo uprising. Fighting Apaches necessitated endurance of the first rank and knowledge of every nook and cranny of the mountains and deserts. Those thirty-four Chihuicahui men, eight boys, encumbered with ninety-two women and children, who went on the warpath on May 17, 1885, had, up to April 1, 1886, killed between three and four hundred people in the United States and Mexico and had lost only two of their own number killed. Only loyal men of their own race with equal endurance were able finally to run them to ground. Gene in later years made light of his part in the army work. 'I was guide (not enlisted) for eighteen months. But I was east of the Rio Grande. Geronimo heard I was over here and prudently stayed on the west side.'

When Gene was about twenty-one, he borrowed fifty dollars from his father, left in his care the ranch he had staked claim to and started to school at the University of the Pacific at San Jose. So widely had he read that he had added enough to his few years of common school to meet the requirements. He studied at the University two years, 1889 and 1890. He and a couple of other students lived in a three-cornered room, which may have been a signal tower, beside the railroad tracks. When the trains passed, the building shook and the table on which he worked rocked. So hard was it for him to earn his expenses that he lived principally on oatmeal, earning money doing janitor work. But for all that, Gene began writing at college occasional bits of verse for the college paper. In his Class Book, *The Narajado*, published by the Class of '90, his name is in the Rhizomian Society as Critic.

Those were two happy years at school, helping Gene satisfy the intolerable yearning for an education other than the one he acquired for himself by incessant reading. With his money completely gone, he had to go back to New Mexico. I am glad he had pleasant memories of school to hearten him during the long days when he dragged mud-coated cows from quagmires, only to have them turn on him and his horse in a frenzy of rage when they were released. He had his memories to comfort him when he rode in the beating rain, round and round the restless herd, startled by crashes of thunder and lightning that gleamed on the cattle's rocking horns and rolled in balls of flame over the ground. At some deafening roar, the stampede was on!

Gene moved the family down to Las Cruces in order that Clarence and Helen could go to school. He himself had taught school near Fort Stanton at Eagle Creek. It was a tough school where the students had a little habit of putting the teacher out of the window. When Gene took his place at the teacher's desk, he pulled his six-shooter from the band of his pants, rapped smartly on the desk with it, and announced, 'The school will now come to order.' It did.

While teaching in this school, where many of the students were his age and some older, he used to go over the lessons each night to keep up with his classes. In arithmetic there was one particularly knotty problem with a catch in it. He worked on it nearly all night before he solved it. Next morning one of the big girls, with a sly smile at her comrades, came down the aisle and laid her slate on the desk in front of him. 'Mr. Rhodes,' she said in mock appeal, 'I just can't get that example.' Gene looked it over blandly. 'That shouldn't be hard.' He started working it, while she stood by, watching jubilantly for defeat. He worked along, purposely making the same mistake he had made for hours on end the night before. Just when she thought she had him, he suddenly erased it. 'No, this is the way it should be done.' And he brought it triumphantly to a close. She went back to her seat, quite subdued.

The rest of Gene's education he received in the school of life on the range. It was a hard life into which his father sent him with warnings and encouragement. 'Dear lad, you've a hard old row to hoe.' Many years later he recalled that statement in a poem published in *Sunset Magazine*.[1]

A SONG OF HARVEST

'For God in cursing gives us better gifts
Than Man in Benediction.' — MRS. BROWNING

Stern of mood was my warrior-sire,
Slow to laughter, and quick to ire:
Little he deemed that duty won
Praise, in doing — but shame, undone.
Loath, as with all of the Saxon speech,
To breathe the loving of each to each.
But once, as we two toiled, side by side,
  He said to me — gruffly, yet kindly so —
With something of sorrow, but more of pride,
  'Dear lad, you've a hard old row to hoe.'

A hard old row! Ere long, in sooth,
It seemed his saying was bitter truth.
With aching muscles and swelling heart
From all my fellows I toiled apart;
Toiled apart on my weary stint,
And hoed my row on the hills of flint!
. . . .

If I envied the favored few
That lightly loitered their light lives through,
I said no word as I watched them go,
But I set my teeth, and I hoed my row.

God, I thank Thee! My toil has grown
To me an Empire — and all my own!
. . . .

[1] June, 1923.

And back I look with both shame and pride
At that crooked furrow at eventide:
Though I have labored since early morn
To rid Thy reaping of all save corn,
Still with the grain must be garnered in
The tares of folly — the weeds of sin.
Thou — Who hast noted each thorn and stone,
And the blazing sun where I toiled, alone —
Alike my evil and good you know —
Master of Harvests: Accept my row!

Land lay idle in that big, new, raw country. Men staked claims for any and everything, dam sites, mill sites, lumber sites, and plain range. The report was that Gene staked claims all over the Panhandle, one bounded on the south by the equator, on the north by the pole. When he couldn't file on all these claims nor, for his dignity's sake, allow them to be jumped, he allowed his friends a welcome chance to claim them. His ranch was in the San Andres Mountains, a country that was, and is today, the wildest and most isolated section of New Mexico. 'For years I was the only settler in a country larger than the state of Delaware.' Alma, New Mexico, was known from the Gulf to Canada as 'The Outlaws' Paradise.' When Alma got too hot for the outlaws, they came over and stayed on the Rhodes ranch. Unfortunately for Gene, his land was most conveniently located for hideout with getaway points. The fleeing bad man nearly always departed for the lower end of Socorro County, whose 'bootheel' southern end touched on Sierra, Doña Aña, Otero, and Lincoln

Counties, into any one of which flight could be extended when the sheriff approached the ranch. If he knew of their presence, Gene put them to work and made them earn their keep. To oppose them was sheer suicide. With their getaway horses always saddled, they did their work as cowboys until warning of the posse's approach came. And when they left, Gene was in no position to say in which direction they had gone. Sam Ketchum, Bill Doolin, Little Dick, and two of the Dalton gang were among those for whom the Rhodes ranch was an asylum. Black Jack hid out there for some time. The Apache Kid, unknown to Gene, hid out for nearly two years on the roughest mountain in the pasture, said pasture being nearly twenty miles long.

The Apache Kid was a bad boy from the San Carlos Reservation. He was said to be the son of old Chief Nana. William Paxton at Elk rescued him from the back of his dead mother, who had been killed in a skirmish between marauding Indians and cowboys. The Apaches had captured two white girls and Mr. Paxton hoped to exchange the boy, but the Indians were unwilling and the boy was sent to an Eastern Indian school, where he learned to speak English.

Back in New Mexico and Arizona he began his career of gun and horse thievery. A lonely cowboy would be found murdered. A harmless old man who herded goats was killed in broad daylight. The man accused of his death avoided conviction and hanging only by the sheriff's quick decision to prove his alibi. When it was demonstrated that the accused man, who had proved his presence in two places at different times on the day of the killing, could not possibly also have been at the spot where the goatherd died, the murder was laid to the sly Indian. Five thousand dollars reward was offered for him, which testifies to his reputation as a deadly desperado, but the posse who killed him didn't claim it, for they were not absolutely sure that the Indian they had killed was the Kid. Two killings were solved, however, when this Indian was killed by the men in search of Charlie Anderson's treasured dun ponies. On a string around the Indian's neck was found the key belonging to a brakeman shot mysteriously. And the personal belongings of an old miner shot through the head were found among the Kid's possessions. Exactly who killed the Kid will never be known. According to the *Los Angeles Times*, the Kid's rope hangs in Bob Martin's house — but Bob was not in the posse. The Kid's wife and children returned to the Reservation but no disclosures would they make. Nor is it known how the woman made her way across sixty miles of plain plus the distance from Tularosa to the Mescalero with her little children. Gene's opinion was: 'There seems to be no doubt that there were two young Apaches who played a lone hand — one in northern Arizona and one in southern New Mexico. Their methods were identical: they played it safe, cutting off one man at a time from ambush; and it would seem that the deeds of both are accredited to the semi-legendary Apache Kid.' But there is evidence from Charlie

Graham and George Sweigert, and with it goes the story of Gene's uncomfortably close encounter with the Kid, in 1893.

Charlie Graham and George Sweigert were working the Three River country, when some Mexicans told Graham that they had just seen his roan workhorse, sweat-marked and jaded. Everyone knew that roan horse. He was almost one of the boys. As Graham lived eighty miles away, on the Jornada, he felt some curiosity as to what his horse was doing here. He went to investigate and George Sweigert with him. They found a young Indian sitting with a Winchester on his knees before a little Mescalero camp, and they asked him if he knew who had been riding Old Roan. The young man spoke good English and his reply was much to the point.

He said he had been riding the horse himself and that it would be wise of them to leave him alone; told them he was not in the habit of fighting white men unless he could take them at a disadvantage, but that he really didn't want to be bothered about that horse. He said he had picked up the horse at a ranch in the San Andres, and while he was in the house a cowboy had driven a bunch of horses down the cañon.

'He was out of sight before I was sure he was alone,' said this candid warrior, 'or else I would have shot him.'

That is the way the story was told to me. I worked with Charlie Graham ten or twelve years after that, but never remembered to ask him about this happening. And that was a curious omission, because I was the lad who rode into the ranch (which was my own ranch) and who was lucky enough not to stop.

Gene had been working at the Bar Cross round-up. As he had some papers to serve on a man in the San Andres, Cole Railston, the foreman, told him to take a bunch of sore-backed and lame horses to the horse camp on his ranch as he went by. When he came near the spring, he saw the tired, sweat-marked sorrel horse, which he found out some weeks later was Charlie Anderson's horse, stolen from the ranch in the Black Range to replace one of old man Cornell's from Anchor X Ranch. Old man Cornell had lost his life in the encounter with the thief. When Gene came down to the house, driving his herd before him, he discovered that the house had been robbed of every last thing he owned on earth. Said Gene, in part, 'Oh, bother!' forked his horse, and was away before the watching Kid had him.

> The day after Graham and Sweigert interviewed the Kid was the day he stole a young Indian girl at the Rinconada. She said that he took her to the San Andres first, where he had food stored. That was the stuff he borrowed at my place.... We (Hiram Yoast and I) followed our camp robber's tracks about twelve miles, over a mountain that we had always called impassable. We found a coffee mill and some other stuff of mine that he had lost or discarded. If we had followed up the trail to his cache, we might have interrupted his honeymoon.
>
> The girl said the Kid kept her chained at first, but that he made her a good husband. They reared five children. She added that he was not bloodthirsty, as people said; that he never killed anyone unless he was running short

of ammunition or grub, or needed a fresh horse or something like that. Only on his market days, in fact.

Those were exciting days which Gene so faithfully recorded in his stories in later times. Three fourths of the characters in Gene's stories were real people, and in most cases their real names were given. Gene listed some of them in his interview for the *Los Angeles Times*: 'The 'sclusively oldtime cowboy was not a murderer, thief, drunkard, gambler, wastrel, or weakling — but a man who would rank as good at any time, or at any place. Men like Will Rogers, Charlie Russell, Will James, Ed Borein, Andy Adams were not the exception. They were the rule. Bob Martin, Polk Armstrong, Cole Railston, Frank Bojorquez, Felipe Lucero, Frank Calhoun, Pete Johnson, Hiram Yoast, John Yoast, Gene Thorogood, Emil James, Frank Hill, Billy LeSeur, Tom Ross, Jeff Bransford, Tom Tucker, Johnny Dines — a hundred more who expressed themselves in deeds.'

Bob Martin, one of the Old West's finest and a lifelong friend of Gene's, was 'kid foreman' on the 7TX when he was twenty, married the daughter of the owner of the Bar Cross, with which Gene had worked before he took out his own ranch. Bob is quoted as saying modestly that 'he guesses he was made a foreman so young because cattle weren't worth much in those days.'

Francisco Bojorquez was one of Gene's good Mexicans who figured in 'The Star of Empire.' Frank 'was a cowboy at Hillsboro and became foreman of the Bar Cross there, and the long-legged, white-eyed Texans who were notoriously prejudiced against Mexicans were all proud to work for him.' Felipe Lucero was another of Gene's favorites. Because one could not succeed oneself as sheriff in Doña Aña County, Felipe and his brother Jose were sheriffs, turn and turn about for thirty years. In all that time they never killed a man. 'Jose was doubtless just as good a man as Felipe, but Jose was merely miller and sheriff — while Felipe was cowboy and sheriff. We counted only the cowboys.'

A cowboy Gene was for twenty-five years. He was known as a reckless rider with a mania for bad horses, and admitted that in all his years of riding he had been thrown but three times. The boys all said of him that he could ride anything that wore hair. Bob Martin tells a story about Gene and his pet strawberry horse which he called 'Vinegar Roan.' When the two arrived at the place where the cattle were ready for the morning drive, Vinegar Roan always fell sound asleep promptly, head hanging. But the instant a steer tried to slip out of the herd, Gene's heels were in Vinegar's side. As instantly the strawberry horse was pitching, Gene flying high in the air but always in saddle contact. Another of Bob's 'windies' tells how Gene stopped at the ranch of a friend to borrow a horse to replace the tired pony he was riding. The friend led him to the corral, saying, 'Little short on horses, but there's one you can have — that bay over there.' With considerable maneuvering Gene got his saddle on the dancing bay. 'Looks like he's kinda wild,' said Gene. 'Does he pitch?' 'Never has yet,' said his owner. When Gene got on, the fun began — but he stuck. 'Thought you said he never pitched!' 'Never did. Nobody ever rode him before.' Gene rode the horse to Las Cruces.

New Mexico was a 'wild and woolly' place. Gene had a special kind of enemy in the station agent at Engle. One day Gene had occasion to visit the telegraph office in hopes of getting an important telegram. The message hadn't arrived and an argument between the operator and Gene resulted. Words flew, until Gene, tiring of the argument, opened a newspaper and started across the street, reading. The operator, incensed at such casualness after all, dashed into his office, grabbed a Winchester, and took aim at the figure of Gene calmly walking across the street. No hits — and Gene didn't run. When he reached the other side, excited friends asked him why he didn't dodge. 'Dodge?' said Gene. 'Why, I was afraid if I dodged, the damn fool would hit me.'

But for all his riding prowess, Gene was most noted for his reading. Not that all the cowboys didn't find that a nice way to break the loneliness. But Gene was 'loco' on reading. Even when riding broncs he read. He carried magazines in his saddle pockets. For every time he turned a page, there was a probability the bronc would swallow his neck. One horse was given a special reading breaking. Gene's patience was exhausted to the point where he resolved to teach the ornery cuss a lesson. So when the bronc went over backward with an earth-shaking thud, Gene, having thrown himself clear as usual, raced to the animal's head before it could make a move to get up, and sat down on it. Sitting on the bronc's head, Gene pulled a volume of Browning from his jumper pocket and lost himself in communion with the immortal poet. Small wonder the man who discovered him thus engrossed spread the tale of dementia.

Gene drove up one day to the Bar Cross store at Engle to load up his wagon with barb wire. When it was time to go, the team, made up of a balky horse and a balky mule, decided to stay. The accepted procedure in this case would have been to beat up the team, usually futile so far as its influence on particularly the mule would be concerned, but vastly satisfying to the driver. Did the outburst come? No. Gene calmly put on the brake, tied the lines to it, dragged out his big scrapbook, and forgot the animals. There he read for two hours. At the end of that time the horse and mule were ready to go.

When books and magazines were not available, Gene read even the labels on cans, commending as especially enjoyable English the label on Worcestershire sauce bottles, which he read a countless number of times. He had a wonderful knowledge of geography, in large part due to his habit of covering the walls of his kitchen-dining-room with railroad maps which had been given him. When he sat at the table eating, he would study them. At that table he wrote 'The Hour and the

Man' and some poetry for *Out West.* But Gene took no credit for his persistence in study. The tall tales of his absorption in books with the endless changes to them disgusted him. 'I can ride horses that no one else could stick on, but they never mention that. They say, "He reads!"' — adding bitterly, 'I've learned my A B C's, why shouldn't I read?'

Such was Gene's education which flowered in his stories and novels. He was a cultured, talented man, this ex-cowboy with whom I had come to New Mexico.

CHAPTER III

Honeymoon in Tularosa

A NEWCOMER to the sunny Southwest, I would think each morning, 'Well, the sun will surely not shine today.' But up it came. Three hundred and sixty sunshiny days a year is New Mexico's proud boast. I used to get up at four in the morning to do my washing.

We rented a small adobe house a quarter of a mile or more out of town. The house had two rooms separated by a hallway with a door at either end. Before the kitchen's only window there was a big blood spot on the floor. However much I scrubbed, it would not come out. I never found out how it got there, but evidently somebody had been shot there.

Gene hired a woman to help me clean the place, for it was horribly dirty. Then before I had even begun to unpack my barrels that I brought from home, I was taken down with tonsillitis. In later years Gene said that I couldn't stub my toe without its resulting in tonsillitis. He called 'Doc' Tomlinson, who figured in Emerson Hough's *Heart's Desire*, to treat me. Gene was rather embarrassed at the idea of Doc Tomlinson seeing me in only my nightdress, but I seemed so unconcerned that he was reassured. I grew worse, and when Gene saw the doctor trying to scrub the cankers off with some sort of bottle brush, he was disgusted and got another doctor, the only other one, who was a throat specialist and soon had me well again.

At Tularosa I had my first riding lessons. My only previous experience as a farmer's daughter had been riding a fat, black, farm horse down to the creek to water. That didn't fit me for the life of a New Mexico ranchwoman. Gene's mother was a superb rider and had won a number of trophies, riding at fairs, in a silk hat and sweeping habit. He said that all the Rhodes women were good riders, so it was up to me to do my best. I managed with one notable exception to stick, and above all, never to hang on to the saddle — 'claw leather,' they called it and judged it the height of ignominy.

Gene led a hectic life at this time. He had brought in two wild range cows so we could have some milk. They kept trying to jump the corral fence, hanging by their hind legs over the *arroyo* that bordered it. Time and again he had to rescue them. Fred, left to his own devices, was not much better. He blackened the stove, which was not yet set up, with axle grease. He discovered that the roll of wire screen for the doors and windows was nice and springy and proceeded to flatten it out. He ranged the window sashes side by side and was using them for a sidewalk for his little bare feet, when Gene discovered him. Gene told me that he didn't know whether to kill Fred or himself.

When I got the place settled and more or less homey, a young man from New Orleans, Lewis Fort, who had been out at Gene's ranch, came to stay with us. He took his meals in the house but slept out in the yard in his blankets, beautiful red wool blankets.

Then Fred was lost. Remembering all the scary stories I had ever heard of lost children, I was frantic — all that vast expanse of bushes to hide him, and he so little. Gene was an expert tracker and trailed those little, light, barefoot tracks for half a day, sometimes losing them and then finding them again, or seeing a wisp of blouse on a bush. When Gene finally reached him, Fred's dusty, dirty little face was furrowed with tears, but he was not crying. His blouse had been torn when he climbed through a barb-wire fence. He had killed a snake and was dragging it by the tail. Seeing Gene he remarked casually, 'See this snake I killed.' Gene used this episode in his story 'Lubly-Ge-Ge and Gruff-and-Grim' for the *Land of Sunshine* magazine.

A celebration like a big country picnic was held in Tularosa shortly after we moved there. Girls in their prettiest dresses and the cowboys in vests and shirt-sleeves, often finished off with leather cuffs. The Indians were to dance, but at the last moment the Superintendent wouldn't let them lest they become excited. Here I saw my first Indians. I could hardly distinguish them from the Mexicans, as interesting and not at all bloodthirsty.

Gene introduced me to thousands of people, it seemed to me, and I couldn't remember one of them five minutes. As we started into a dance hall, we passed a very lovely girl standing in the doorway. Milk white was her skin, with red lips (not drugstore ones), magnificent red hair, and, yes, a perfect form. Gene reminded me many times not to forget to mention her form.

He stopped and said, 'Laura, this is my wife.'

She swept me up and down with coldly appraising eyes, and said in a voice so cool that in spite of the hot day, I all but shivered:

'Are you sure you are his wife?' and turned away.

I went home with spirits very much soured. A country where you had to carry your marriage certificate around with you! I assured the listening world (in this case comprising my husband and the young man from New Orleans) that if I ever saw that girl again I'd scratch her eyes out.

So life in Tularosa was gay and social, happily remembered when we moved to the ranch, out where mail had to come from Engle, thirty miles away. It was a matter of weeks, sometimes of months, once almost two months, before we had our letters. I sorted them over in sequence, but even then they hadn't the same zest as when the news was new.

I went with Gene out on the desert with a team and lumber wagon to get mesquite roots to burn. This was a strange land where you had 'to climb for water and dig for wood.' While the mesquite bushes themselves are not overly large, the roots are in most cases good size, burn like hickory, and last nearly as well as coal. Gene grubbed them out with a pick — they lay quite near the surface — and chopped them off. I found a quantity of smaller ones lying on top of the sand, and added these to the load. We took a lunch along, pickled tongue, sandwiches, and boiled eggs, but when we were ready to eat, we found that the cover had jarred off the salt-shaker. There was salt over everything. We wiped it off as well as we could, and being hungry, we ate most of the food. And drink! That canteen of water vanished in no time. Then thirst came in proper fashion. We were several miles out with a slow team. When we reached the edge of town, a man was letting the water down a ditch he had just built. It was thick with mud, but it was wet, and the way I drank it!

Gene was continually singing. His favorite at this time was

Hello, my lady, hello, my baby,
Hello, my ragtime gal.
Send me a kiss by wire
Honey, my heart's afire....

He would come in a day or two later and say, 'I have an entirely new song.' I would look up quite interested and ask, 'What is it?' And he would sing:

If you refuse me,
Honey, you lose me,
Then you'll be left alone.
Why don't you telephone
And tell me you are my own?

When I first went out there 'Lorena' was his favorite. He doted on 'Lorena,' always either singing or humming it.

I often wish that I were dead
And laid beside her in the tomb.

This was hardly flattering, and I was grateful when he switched to ragtime.

Meanwhile I worked away at making the house a home. I had brought my cherished dishes from New York. They were a creamy brown, with sprays of brown flowers on them, but most appealing of all was their shape — square. A young man asked me if I got the dishes with the house. When I told some of the girls from the village of this, they said I should have told him that I bought the dishes and they threw the house in. My kitchen had the good cookstove from the ranch which Gene brought in, leaving a most disreputable makeshift out there. He also brought a big wooden cupboard, in addition to which I had a food cupboard with panels in the doors of perforated tin. This was called a 'safe.' A small work table completed my kitchen — that is, complete with my trunk, which I kept there. Gene had bought a pretty oak bed, a dresser with a long mirror on half the top and a cabinet on the other half, where I kept the medicines, St. Jacob's Oil, Chamberlain's Cholera Cure, and others, and, to complete the set, a washstand. From home I had brought my washbowl and pitcher set, gilt-edged and decorated with pretty gray thistle heads. A small bedroom rocker, a home-made desk, and a couple of chairs completed the living-room-bedroom.

When Mr. Fort first came to live at our house, I

made the comment that it was strange Gene couldn't see what a dreadful place New Mexico was. He answered that Gene saw it through rose-colored glasses. 'Take this yard, for instance,' I said. 'He wrote me that "There was a large lawn, but it was somewhat neglected." It's large, all right. It reaches from here to the San Andres Mountains, sixty miles away, and there isn't a spear of grass in it, with the exception of the small plot where our landlord's beehives are located, so it must be neglected.' The bare ground in the grassless yard scorched my feet. Lizards that seemed as large as crocodiles scuttled from one wild gourd vine to another.

Yet strangely, the lure and enchantment of the grim and hideous desert can get into your blood like a microbe and make you wholly its own. I found that the clean and freshly washed desert after a summer rain has a fragrance unrivaled. I came to delight in this desert with all its changing moods.

When Gene came to town from the ranch, I coaxed him to go to church with me, to which he consented after much persuasion. There was no 'church house,' so services were held in a hall. We put on our best togs, took Fred, and departed. I have never heard such a sermon and hope never to hear another like it. The preacher dragged us through the nethermost depths of hell and poured hot pig iron down our backs. At the close of this lurid discourse, the preacher said that all idiots would be saved. Gene said it was astonishing how that congregation brightened up. Never again did

I want to go to church there. This preacher finally gave up preaching and went to work on the railroad; he said there was more money in it.

But I took Fred to Sunday School. The Sunday School Superintendent was a little man with a spike beard. The story goes that not long before we moved to Tularosa, he had an altercation with the Water Boss, Randolph Reynolds. He wanted to turn the water in his alfalfa and Randolph, claiming it was not his turn, shut the water off. Although Randolph was nearly twice his size, the little man raised his shovel and knocked Randolph out cold. I had great respect for that Sunday School Superintendent.

Another round-up was due to which Gene had to go. He hated to leave me alone because I had been in the country only about three weeks, and thought he might leave Mr. Fort, the man from New Orleans, with me. Mr. Fort spoke Spanish and had been out there some months. The matter came up as we were eating breakfast. I spoke up quite promptly and said I thought it should be left for Mr. Fort to decide. Immediately he was on his feet, his hand on his heart, and bowing deferentially: 'It is for you to decide, Madame. I am as dough in your hands.' Gene, who had been in the kitchen to get himself another cup of coffee from the stove, came back just in time to hear this. Smilingly he said, 'I hope I'm not intruding?'

Gene gathered up his belongings and left for the round-up with its grueling hard work and scanty rest. He was his own man now, not somebody's cowboy.

He had his own horses, from four to six of them, and had his camp bed packed on a pack-horse. The bed with its bulky blankets sheathed in tarpaulin was put on the pack-horse's back and roped on with an N-hitch. It looked, with the horse's head sticking out of one end, and its tail out of the other, like some strange sort of sandwich.

Life for Mr. Fort was no bed of roses. We had a very obstreperous cow that broke out of the corral and charged madly down into our landlord's patch of cane. It was Mr. Fort's job to look after this beast. How he loathed her! Fourth of July came and he announced that he was planning to go to Alamogordo to the celebration. When I said plaintively, 'Who will water the cow?' he declared vehemently that he didn't care if that cow never saw another drop of water while she lived, and went on his way. It wasn't so bad after all, for it wasn't necessary to milk her. Her calf was in the pen and could attend to that chore itself. Mr. Fort would be gone only overnight.

Fred and I were miserably lonesome and homesick that Fourth of July. I told him that first we would water the poor cow and then we would fire off his package of firecrackers. The cow was chained to a big post that supported the scaffold where the alfalfa was stacked. I led her down the lane and across the flat to the irrigation ditch. Fred trotted along for company. On the way back, my shoe came untied. While I stopped to retie it, she waited patiently. When I told this to Mr. Fort, he was more furious than ever, and said he had to drag her every step of the way to water by main force, and then drag her all the way back again.

Fred and I sat on the woodpile and fired off the firecrackers, lamenting that we had no more. Then we saw some riders out on the flat, and went to see what they were doing. They were racing. We perched on the bars and watched them. A young man on a gray horse seemed to win all the races. When they were over, he rode up to the bars and swept off his sombrero, bowed, and said: 'I am your husband's foreman, Steve Jackson. I wanted to see him and thought my chances would be better here than at the ranch.'

So we all waited for Gene to get back. It was a long wait. Several weeks, in fact.

We all went to a picnic one day, Steve on horseback, Mr. Fort and I with Mr. Cooper, one of the Tularosa neighbors, in a lumber wagon, with chairs instead of seats. We posted a sign on the door, 'We have eloped!' But we had only the pleasure of taking it down when we came home, for Gene still hadn't come.

The rains were late that year and set in with a terrific downpour. Mr. Fort went out to close the wooden shutters on the two front windows (the rear of the house had no windows, to ensure more safety in case of Indian attacks) and got his hair full of adobe mud from the rivulets coursing down the walls. Adobe mud is stubborn stuff to get out of one's hair. No sooner had he come in than we heard a loud 'Woosh!' and the mud roof over the kitchen caved in. Mud and water in horseshoe formation like Niagara Falls deluged the kitchen floor. He looked at me from under his thatch and grinned. 'Don't you wish you were back in New York now?'

'That isn't all,' I retorted. 'I'm going! I'll pawn my diamonds tomorrow.' (I had none.)

My six weeks' honeymoon was long gone by when Gene returned. I told him I had never thought of spending my honeymoon in the company of a man not my husband, but it seemed to have happened.

Gene was considered wild, even in that time, 1900. The ladies of Tularosa, with two or three exceptions, left me pretty much to myself. One woman said I had six husbands living back in New York. Gene went to an auction one day and saw this woman over on the edge of the crowd. He held up his hand to attract her attention and called, 'Mrs. Hearst! Mrs. Hearst!' She raised on tiptoe to see what he wanted. He shouted: 'That was a mistake about my wife having six husbands back in New York. There are only five of them.'

Midsummer of my first year in New Mexico. Gene had gone back to his ranch in the San Andres to work, again leaving Mr. Fort as guide and counselor, an invariably cheerful and gay one. One morning, Mr. Fort came rushing into the house, shouting, 'Where's the carving knife?' He snatched it and dashed out again, with me at his heels. The cow had thrown herself with her head doubled under her so that the prong of one of her long horns had gone through the front of her udder. The only thing to do was to cut the udder and release her. Mr. Fort did so quickly. When the landlord came past, he told me to wash it off with dishwater and the grease would keep the flies from blowing in it. My dishwater was never any other than greasy after my first thrilling experience using a soap-shaker in it. It caused a tarry deposit on the entire panful of dishes, and I had to use ashes to scour it off. I depended on keeping my dishwater as hot as possible after that, and soapless. But the cow got worms in the wound after all. When Gene came home, he had some special preparation for such things and she recovered.

There was never any telling what Gene would do. I sent him up to the store to get a pound of butter one day, so we could have it for dinner. When he didn't come back, I was uneasy. I asked Mr. Fort if he supposed somebody had shot Gene, to which he answered that he had never known a man better calculated to take care of himself than my husband. We ate our dinner without butter, jerky gravy, tomatoes, potatoes, Mr. Fort's most delicious corn bread, oyster pie from canned oysters which were all we could get in that line then, and coffee. In those days we always used Arbuckle coffee, from which I religiously saved the coupons to get books for Jack and Fred, Hans Christian Andersen's *Fairy Tales*, *Alice in Wonderland*, and the like. Toward night Gene came home, stopping from time to time to double up in fits of laughter. He could hardly tell us why he was laughing so hard. He had been to some little twopenny trial. They had a Mexican interpreter and he interpreted all that the witnesses said, and any chance remarks the bystanders made. A young girl with her hair braided down her back had been one witness. She stood up, her eyes flashing, and pointed an accusing finger at the Judge, '*You are a liar, Judge Parker.*' Incidentally Gene had forgotten the butter.

Then Mr. Fort went out to the ranch and Gene stayed with me. Late one night we heard the *thud-a-te-thud* of a galloping horse. A few minutes later Gene's foreman, Steve, burst into the room with the news that a deputy sheriff had just been shot in the corral at Gene's ranch. Deputy Hamilton had come to arrest Barbee, a desperado, who was staying there. Barbee got Gene's gun, by some means, and shot the deputy — in cold blood, shot four bullets into him. Then he jumped on one of Gene's horses that had been caught to take him away a prisoner and dashed down the cañon.

Gene exploded, 'Why in hell didn't you stop him?'

Steve said he had been just too scared and Barbee still had a bullet in the gun. Steve caught a horse that had been bridled only once or twice, left the ranch at four P.M., and reached Tularosa at eleven over unworked roads through mazes of mesquite bushes and sand hummocks.

Gene notified the sheriff, Pat Garrett, where he could head Barbee off. In Gene's own words: 'I had never seen Barbee. But I knew his connections and how his mind worked. Roused from slumber by this news, I at once wired to Pat Garrett (ninety miles away) that if he would take the train to Rincon, forty miles north, and then ride briskly to Worden's Ranch, another forty miles to the northwest, he would get there just before the murderer did. Garrett didn't go, but Barbee arrived at Worden's within half an hour of the time I set.... Timing Barbee's trip to Worden's was easy. He was riding my *palomino* horse, fine-looking, but the slowest horse in the Territory. I knew just how long it would take him to go sixty miles. The same time it would take any other horse to do a hundred. Barbee had no chance.'

The coroner said it was useless to go out to examine the body of the deputy. Mr. Fort and a friend of his, two city lads, were left there with that dead man, the nearest neighbor being twenty-five miles away. They sawed some of Gene's wooden water troughs up and made a coffin, put the dead man in it, and dug a grave outside the corral as best they could on the rocky slope. A man told me he came by after a heavy rain and the dead man's feet were sticking out. He threw rocks and what dirt he could get over them. The cloudburst that later destroyed Gene's homestead scooped the entire coffin and all out and carried it down the cañon. Nobody knows to this day where 'the hand of God' buried it. It never came to light again.

Some time after this when Mr. Fort and his friend were in town, something had displeased me, and I threatened to kill myself.

Mr. Fort looked at me imploringly. 'Please don't, Mrs. Rhodes, it's such hot weather to dig graves.'

'I don't care whether you bury me or not,' I retorted.

Mr. Fort announced impressively: 'You would be

buried. We left a man unburied for two days at your husband's ranch, and we bitterly regretted it.'

Then they were all away. Just Fred and I were left. It was getting late in the fall. At election time Gene came in town, bringing me as a great treat, some *enchiladas* a woman in Tularosa had made. The Mexicans always celebrated special events with this delicacy, but I had never eaten any. I started in with gusto. Then, dash for the water pail! I didn't know but I would die before I reached it. Steve, who witnessed the scene, said I should have used hot coffee instead. It took the burn out.

On Thanksgiving Day, Gene boxed with six picked Mexicans in Tularosa. They saved their strongest man till the last, but he out-boxed them all. An all-round athlete, was that man I married. He was passionately fond of baseball and organized a team the first summer we were living in Tularosa. On the way to a ball game at Alamogordo one Sunday morning, he left me to hold the team while he went down after his first baseman. The horses were poorly broken and didn't like to stand. I expected every minute that they would run away. After a very long time, Gene came back.

'What in the world kept you so?' I asked.

'Oh, my first baseman didn't want to come,' he replied cheerfully, 'and I had to lick him. But he's coming now.' Gene made a home run to win the game for Tularosa that day.

CHAPTER IV

We Move to Gene's Ranch

IN EARLY December of 1900 Gene sent one of his cowboys, Arthur Douglas, who had been one of Roosevelt's Rough Riders, to bring Fred and me to the ranch. Douglas came with his wife and four-months-old baby daughter in his big prairie schooner. The wagon had two stories with high sides. All the stuff was stowed on the first floor. Upstairs were put the bedsprings and mattress. Fred and I rode on that. Mrs. Douglas with Sophia, the baby, and Mr. Douglas rode on the spring seat. He had a team of big gray draft horses that never went faster than a walk that entire interminable trip. Idiocy, Gene called it when he heard of it later.

The first night it was long after dark when we camped. Mrs. Douglas and the baby and I slept on the floor of an abandoned adobe house in our camp bed, and Fred and Mr. Douglas slept in the wagon. We had come twenty-five miles that day.

Next morning I saw the most marvelous mirage, the first I had ever seen. Out across the plains, cool and frosty in the morning air, appeared before my eyes a beautiful city with courthouse, church spires, and all.

THE WHITE SANDS NEAR ALAMOGORDO
The San Andres in the background

WHITE MOUNTAIN, RUIDOSA
'This mountain is the center of New Mexican myth, legend, and life,' Gene wrote

I gasped in amazement. 'I didn't know there was a city near here.'

Mr. Douglas explained.

We drove near a round-up the second day just as the cowboys were branding a calf. The poor little thing was bawling piteously. The smell of burning flesh made me suddenly nauseated, as I was pregnant, and I shut my eyes not to see. There were no comfort stations along the route, which I found quite a hardship. When I explained about this to Gene afterward, he was surprised and said: 'Why didn't you tell Douglas to stop? I have grown so used to girls getting out to pick wild flowers, often with two or three inches of snow on the ground, that I shouldn't have thought anything of it. Neither would he.'

The second night we were in the foothills of the San Andres Mountains, and stayed in the Douglas tent. I felt something uncomfortable in the bunk where I slept that night, and found that I was sleeping on a rifle. The middle of the next forenoon we reached a big gateway, with massive posts at either side. 'This is the entrance to your husband's ranch,' said Mr. Douglas.

'Thank heaven we are there!' I said with fervor.

'Not yet,' he answered, smiling. 'We have sixteen miles yet to go.'

The ranch house which was to be home was a *jacal*, big poles set upright side by side, with one end firmly bedded in the ground, the sides daubed with mud. It was at the bottom of a steep mountain-side, and before the poles were firmly set, the pressure tilted the house forward. The cowboys' joke was that 'it has started south to spend the winter,' but Gene was sensitive about it. He wanted all his work to rank as A Number One. The rocks and soil from the mountain-side slid down against the back of the house until it was buried almost up to the two small windows on that side. I had never seen a *jacal* house before. I thought it, with its tipsy tilt, about as unprepossessing a habitation as I had ever seen.

But the yard with the splendid live-oak trees, that was something else again. The grassless red dirt yard sloped down to the cattle pens with their shining troughs of clear water. Clear blue it seemed to me, after the muddy irrigation ditch water of Tularosa.

Several years afterward when Gene told a man about taking me out there, he admitted candidly, 'It would be flattering to call it a hovel.' To which the man had replied, 'Well, call it a kennel, and let it go at that.'

The house had one room and a bedroom. I went in and sat down, too tired to take off my sunbonnet. Charlie Graham, one of Gene's favorite characters, was there, a well-to-do man, long past the 'cooking stage' of his career, but he felt so sorry for me, he told somebody afterward, that he cooked our dinner. I have remembered him gratefully for this all these years, though I saw him but once after that.

There was, at the time, a party of hunters at the ranch. Looking back, I wonder if they were not outlaws. They disappeared, anyhow, and Gene came in directly. So shy of any demonstration before people, although we hadn't seen each other for weeks, he said casually, 'Oh, you got here, did you?'

The Douglases set their walled tent up next to the house so the door in the end of the house opened into the tent. They had brought some wallpaper with which we set about, one snowy day, to paper the board walls. Gene said I exhibited more enthusiasm over the project than he had seen since I had come West. We also set up the Douglases' big airtight heater into which they would put a sotol to start a fire in the morning. The resinous leaves of this yucca-like plant started as if by magic.

At the ranch I baked yeast bread, which was fairly good in spite of the altitude. But the cowboys didn't like it. They wanted 'sour-dough' biscuits three times a day. When there was a cowboy available to manufacture them (and they could make them to perfection), I handed over the job.

The stove I had to cook on was a worn-out old thing with an oven door that had to be propped shut with a stick of wood, not to mention a big hole between the firebox and the oven where ashes could sift in to flavor the bread. Mr. Stewart made a cement of salt and ashes and mended the hole for me. Heaven knows how long the cowboys had put up with it in its makeshift state. I made tarts and pies, and fairly good cake without eggs, which were, of course, never obtainable there. Only one other woman lived out there. And ranchers couldn't raise chickens and go to round-ups too.

Before our first Christmas, Gene had to go to Tularosa, leaving me at the ranch with the Douglases until he came back late in January. We didn't have even Christmas together. Gene sent a man out with a wonderful box of Christmas things from Mr. Fort for Fred, to my great joy, otherwise the child would have had none. That winter I developed a terrific cough. Before I had left town, I had asked the doctor how much he charged to go out to the ranch. 'A dollar a mile.' (They still charge that.) 'I shall take care not to get sick in that event,' I answered. But I coughed and coughed till Mr. and Mrs. Douglas were worried. But they got some wild stuff, steeped it, and gave me the tea. I was much better when Gene came back. Most important of all, I saved the sixty dollars we didn't have. My life was anything but drab and lacking in surprises.

Poor as we were, we controlled an empire, for Gene had homesteaded all the water. He had miles on miles of barb-wire fence; from one nook in the mountains one could see ten miles of fence. It is his land he described in *Stepsons of Light* when Johnny Dines came riding through Moongate Pass where led the road, branching on the summit to five springs: the Bar Cross horse camp, Bear Den, Rosebud, Good Fortune, Grapevine. 'At the summit he came to a great gateway country of parks and cedar mottes, gentle slopes, and low rolling ridges, with wide, smooth valleys falling away to north and south; eastward rose a barrier of red-sandstone hills.' If it had been properly stocked, he would have made a fortune. He gave away two springs, Bear Den and Rosebud. He had named these himself.

In 1901 Gene wrote 'A Blossom of Barren Lands,' published in *The Land of Sunshine*, in which he celebrated the beauty and spirit of his country.

A flower grew in old Cathay
Whose blood-red petals ease our woes;
It lulls our haunting care away
And gives your weariness repose.
When tortured heart and fevered brain
Long for black slumber, dull and deep,
The poppy's charm can ease our pain
And bid us — sleep.

And subtler Egypt's fabled bloom,
The lotus of forgetful breath,
Brings to remorse oblivion's doom
And gives the shameful past to death.
When bitter memories, fierce and fell,
Scourge our dark hearts with wild regret —
Oh for the flower whose languorous spell
Bids us — forget!

But dearer, more divinely born,
Amid the deserts desolate,
The yucca blooms above its thorn
Triumphant o'er an evil fate.
Brave, stainless, waxen miracle,
So may we with our fortunes cope,
Who in life's burning deserts dwell,
You bid us — hope!

I rode with Gene at times, but he generally rode some outlaw horse that nobody could do anything with, which wasn't overly conducive to my peace of mind. Gene had his work horses and saddle horses named Strawberry Roan, Teddy Roosevelt, Coalie, Hammerhead, Monte, his private saddle horse, and Ida, named for a pretty girl, but when Gene was vexed he called her 'Bug-eye' (Ida's eyes were buggy).

Gene bought me a very pretty *palomino* saddle horse named Gypsy. She was kind but lazy. He had raised her himself, and wanted a gentle horse that I could mount and dismount from comfortably, if I happened to be out on the desert alone. One morning Gene took me for a ride, evidently against the wishes of my horse. The horse promptly started for a tree with the intention of scraping me off her back. When I engineered her away from that, she started back for the corral. I shouted to Gene, 'This horse is no good.'

'Yes, it is, too. She isn't bridle-wise. I caught her up for you because she was so gentle.'

A newcomer was expected in the house of Rhodes, and for me to mount a horse at all took considerable maneuvering. But that made no difference in my riding. Years after Gene lamented, 'How could I have been such a fool?'

At one time Gene, another man, and I had gone to get some horses, up on the mountain-side back of the ranch. The trail was so steep it seemed nearly straight up and down to me. We were going down the mountain-side and had just crossed a fissure that looked as if it might go down to China when Gene looked back at me and called, 'Do you see that mountain behind you?' Perched none too securely on the horse, I nearly dislocated my neck craning to see it. I said 'Yes.'

'Well,' he said cheerfully, 'that mountain was there when I first came out here.'

He loved practical jokes, that child of the wind's will I married. So Zeke, a negro he had working for him, was to discover. Gene was on the mountain-side cutting a tree down for wood when he saw Zeke on the trail with some horses he had been sent to the cañon to get. When the tree was felled, Gene noticed a hollow under it into which he could crawl nicely. To Zeke, coming down the mountain, it looked as if the tree had fallen on Gene. Zeke dismounted with great outcry.

'Oh, my pore Massa Gene! Pore boy! Pore boy!'

Gene looked up casually. 'Got a match, Zeke?'

Zeke jumped on his horse and rode down to the ranch, gathered his belongings, and lit out. Only with great trouble did Gene restore peaceful relations between them.

Gene had a singularly worthless bronco buster, Jess Locton, an uncouth, ignorant, and wholly undesirable fellow. Gene had picked him up in Tularosa at one of his poker and boxing bouts. He had been instructed to saddle horses for and to accompany either Mrs. Douglas or me whenever we wanted to ride. But we didn't like him, so we didn't go often. Although it was probably wholly braggadocio, he repeatedly said that he felt he would have to kill Gene some time. He would hate to do it, but if Gene ever crossed his path, he was a dead man. And when Jess himself died, he said he wanted to be buried on one of the sugar-loaf hills on the ranch and have the American flag waving over him. I told him it was a frightful use for the American flag.

That was but one of the offshoots of Gene's love of boxing and fighting. Clovis Aguilar told me of an incident when he, Gene, Selko Vanages, John Walters, and twin boys from La Luz, and Frank Balt were in town on Christmas Eve. The week before the twins had broken up a dance at Knouse Hall. Now the cowboys decided to break up their dance. Walters had been drinking. He was fighting with Aguilar when Gene pulled him away and said: 'You can't fight, you are too drunk. I'll fight him myself.' He told Clovis to rest a bit till he got his breath and then he would take a hand. He broke Clovis's nose and they had quite a satisfactory fight. Then they went in Tobe Tipton's saloon, and he washed Clovis's nose and mended it with adhesive plaster. When it was all over they parted on the most amiable terms. No more dances were broken up.

The men had three tame bears at the ranch to which they fed the scraps from the table. The big beasts used to fight and tumble around the yard. One day when Gene and the hands were gone, some men passed by and stayed overnight. In the morning one of the bears put his paws on the window sill and looked in, as was his pleasing custom. The man put his six-shooter to the bear's ear, saying, 'Have you used Pears' soap?' and shot him dead. Then they shot the other two. It was a long time afterward that Gene heard of this address to the bears.

Gene used to tell a story of a pet bear, Susie, that he

once had. Susie was very friendly, even allowing Gene to ride her upon occasion. Then Susie went away for a time and returned with two delightful cubs. All went well if Gene didn't try to correct the cubs. Susie wouldn't stand for that. But he found that if he could make Susie understand what he wanted, she would train the cubs herself. Gene had loads of fun exhibiting Susie and her accomplishments. One day on the way up the cañon with Susie and the cubs shacking along for company, suddenly ahead of them around the corner of a rock appeared a big and surly wild bear. Susie charged him immediately in defense of her cubs, who ran whimpering to cover. Gene didn't dare shoot for fear of wounding Susie. Finally the bears separated a bit and he fired. He disengaged Susie, who was in a highly excited and truculent mood, and with greatest difficulty mounted her and engineered her down the rocky trail. It was so narrow that there was practically no way to go but ahead. By kicking her in the ribs and whacking her with his gun, he finally reached home. There the bear reared up and faced him. To his horror he discovered that he had killed poor Susie and ridden the strange bear home.

He told this story at a banquet in Los Angeles at which John Burroughs was present. Gene said he didn't think John Burroughs ever forgave him.

After three months on the ranch, the Douglases returned to town, leaving me to the care of Jess, the bronco buster. When Mr. Douglas came back for his last load of goods, negligent Jess saw an opportunity to break a bronc left for his training.

'If I could hitch a bronc in with each of your horses and drive over to Salt Creek with you, the broncs would be broken.'

'Yes,' said Mr. Douglas, 'but Mrs. Rhodes would be left here alone overnight. If anything happened to her, you would have to hit the high places to keep out of Gene Rhodes's way, I'll tell you that.'

They argued about it at some length and then left it for me to decide. I agreed to let Jess go if Mr. Douglas would leave his big army six-shooter with me. It was a bold thing, my asking for it. He wore it constantly. But I promised I would bring it in when we came to town, which was to be very shortly. He consented graciously and they set out after dinner. I washed the dishes and tidied up the house. At three o'clock in the afternoon the sun was setting in our cañon, veriest gash in the mountains, that cañon.

The light glimmered on the water and the shiny new galvanized steel troughs that had replaced the wooden ones used for coffin material. The cows that had been lying chewing their cuds contentedly around the water pen under the big live-oaks moved leisurely up the trail to the summit where the sun was still shining. Then it was quiet. I remembered how Apache Kid once had his hideout not far from me, how he had come and robbed the ranch. I remembered the grave of the murdered deputy. I remembered that my nearest neighbor was twenty-five miles away.

Then I stopped scaring myself to death and called Fred to go out with me to pick up a pan of chips to build the fire in the morning. We were just about to light the lamp and settle down to playing dominoes when I heard a frightful hullabaloo. Rushing out, I was just in time to see a herd of horses being herded into the corral. I ran down and was rewarded with a large smile as Gene swung off his horse. He laughed and kissed me.

'This is the first time you have ever been glad to see me come!'

'What nonsense,' I retorted.

'Well, it's the only time you ever came down to the corral, anyway.'

A woman who had moved out to the mountains with her husband sent word that she would like to have me come to see her, or if I were very conventional, we could arrange a trysting place halfway between ranches. Gene and Fred and I started out to travel the twenty-five or thirty miles through rocks, gullies, and washes, where there was no road. We drove as far as we could, and then took the saddles out of the wagon, which we left in a group of trees, and saddled up. Gene took Fred on the horse with him. The trail was narrow, winding up the mountain-side in a veritable stairway of rock, ending in a floor as slick as glass. My horse actually skated. Long years after when Gene was writing his *Hired Man on Horseback*, he groped in the air vaguely with one hand. 'I want a word to describe the rimrock.' This expedition flashed through my mind. 'Skated,' I said promptly. 'Yes,' he said, relieved. 'That is just the word I wanted. "Skated the rimrock slick."'

When we reached the Henry ranch, Mr. Henry was mining. I had taken my feet from the stirrups for Gene to help me down. It wasn't necessary. Mr. Henry set off a charge of dynamite. The next thing I knew I was sitting on the ground; my horse was galloping away. Mrs. Henry was a charming and remarkable woman; still is, for that matter. She lived in a one-room adobe house which her brother had floored for her with trough planking. In it she had constructed three of the cleverest rooms with white muslin for partitions. Her table had a pretty white oilcloth — I thought of our well-worn red one. She even had butter, a luxury I hadn't tasted in long weeks. The bedroom wall was the head of a high square bedstead; a rod hung with pretty portières went from this to the wall. A tiny washstand stood at the foot of the bed, as cosy and dainty as could be. The tiny living-room had a corner fireplace in it.

The visit was wholly delightful — except that we talked ourselves nearly to death.

CHAPTER V

The Arrival of Alan

On a ride up a sugar-loaf mountain my horse slipped and skidded frightfully on the loose shale. On the way down, I pleaded, 'Let me get off and lead my horse down.' Reflectively Gene answered, 'I suppose you can, but I would hate to have my son a coward.' I rode down.

On another ride he said: 'I would have a son that would stick with dogged perseverance to whatever he undertook. If it was to drive a bunch of cattle to some certain place, then no matter how many times they broke away, he would stick persistently to the job until the last one was rounded up.'

He had that sort of a son. Back in New York, Gene would exclaim wrathfully: 'You can't tell that boy anything. He gets an idea into his stubborn head and all hell can't drive it out.'

I would chant softly, 'I would have a son who would stick with dogged perseverance to whatever he undertook ——'

At that point Gene would generally begin to laugh.

In March we were ready to go back to town. We had a light lumber wagon with, as usual, a 'raw' bronc to hitch in. Gene hesitated to let me ride in the wagon because one could never tell what crazy thing the wild horse might decide to do. Instead he had one of his cowboys accompany me on horseback down to the entrance of the cañon, eighteen miles or more, to give the wild horse a chance to be 'gentled.' As the cowboy helped me to mount, he remarked: 'John L. knows well that a woman is going to ride him. When any of the boys try to mount he whirls three times before we can ever get our feet in the stirrups. Just look at him now.'

Gene and I camped that first night on the flat alongside the mountain range. It was nice to camp again; the food tasted good, the stars were bright and near and friendly. Even as I watched them, I wakened and it was morning. But Gene did not like to camp on the plain. He had a deep-seated prejudice against it, an ingrained fear of prairie fires, perhaps, or Indians or lawless white men.

We visited some folks up in the mountains on our way in to Tularosa. The woman hadn't seen another woman for a year, and her daughter, aged fifteen, simply ran away and hid. Our bed that night was made of poles laid across the bedstead instead of slats, not nearly as comfortable as sleeping on the ground.

When we reached Tularosa next day we were quite disconcerted to find that we would have to move. The landlord wanted to sell the place we had rented the summer before.

Gene rented a house in town, and with the help of the men, moved our belongings there. My neighbors were all Mexicans, but it was so glorious to waken in the morning and know there were people all around me. The Mexican women were beautifully neat, swept the street in front of their doors for half the width of the street, and always had flowers growing somewhere. This house was a big advance over the first one. Its white-plastered walls made it quite presentable. The bedroom had a square place up in the wall opposite the street window, which had window screen on it but no window. Gene suggested that he buy four geraniums for a dollar and a half. I had a vision of four scarlet geraniums on that white wall, but then I remembered that money was so scarce. I said 'No.' Poor economy, I think now.

There were four rooms, a cute little corner fireplace in each of three rooms, and although the kitchen, bedroom, and storeroom had dirt floors, there was a nice floor in the living-room. We tacked white muslin sheeting to the ceiling of the living-room. It looked white and pretty, but it was funny to see the little undulations when a mouse would scamper across it. I put matting on the dirt floor of the bedroom. Over the screen door leading from bedroom to yard, I hung a calico curtain so I could have the fresh air.

Diagonally across the street, I had a very pleasant neighbor, the wife of the grocer. She had a very attractive home and marvelously well-behaved children. Her husband had the best stock of supplies obtainable. One thing I especially enjoyed was raspberry jam. I used great quantities of it. I knew it was raspberry by the seeds. But, alas, the pure food law was unheard of then. When it went into effect, I learned that my cherished delicacy was timothy seed, dyed with aniline dye.

All this time the day of my confinement drew nearer. Gene, after seeing that I was comfortably settled, had gone back to the ranch and his work. My friends and neighbors were manifestly uneasy. One friend sent her young daughter to stay with me when the moon changed, because, said she, you could never tell what would happen when the moon changed. The only thing that happened was that when I was frying eggs for breakfast, one of the eggs that I broke into the frying-pan had a chicken in it. I didn't seem to care for eggs that morning.

At last Gene came back to town. Albert, the husband of my friend, said it didn't look right. The minute he returned from a freighting trip, he was met with 'Albert, you must start right out again.' But when Gene came back, Albert would hear his wife say, 'Gene Rhodes, don't you *dare* leave this town!' 'It shows,' said Albert, 'which one she is partial to!'

The lady was hastily summoned one evening to help the doctor. At 8.30 P.M. June 12, 1901, the Rhodes heir appeared. The neighbor washed and dressed him, settled me for the night, and then she went home to her brood. I took care of the baby that night myself. She came mornings and straightened me for the day, cooked my breakfast, washed the baby, and then went home till the next day. When Alan was five days old she couldn't come any more, for one of her youngsters was sick. I sat up in bed and gave the baby his bath, Gene getting the water and clean clothing. Gene cooked my meals. He was an excellent hand to devise good things for a lagging appetite. It was *so* hot when the newcomer arrived.

The morning after the event Gene went up town, where whom should he meet but Bob Martin, his one-time fellow cowpuncher. 'Hello, Bob,' said he. 'I'd invite you down to the house, but we have distinguished company.' Bob turned on his heel and went into Tobe Tipton's saloon, and cursed round oaths, I have no doubt. 'As if I wasn't good enough to associate with any company *Gene Rhodes* might have. Why, I've killed men for less than that.' Fortunately they hastened to enlighten him ere he had occasion to cut another notch on his gun.

The kitchen floor of our house had to be sprinkled to lay the dust before it was swept. It was not a bad-looking floor when it was clean. During my illness Gene sprinkled the floor so assiduously that, as the lady expressed it, 'It's plumb boggy, and there is a hummocky trail all across your sitting-room floor.' The adobe mud dries almost as hard as concrete. That trail bore silent testimony to the trips he took to my room. In later days when the old-timers were inclined to patronize me, I told them that my son was born in a bedroom with a dirt floor. They became human immediately.

On the Fourth of July for the Tularosa celebration, Gene invited his cowboys in to dinner. He hired a neighbor woman to help me. Together we cooked a chicken dinner for about ten hungry men. The little kitchen was hot and stuffy and I got overheated. As I was nursing the baby, it reacted on him and he was frightfully sick. For days I held my breath each time I weighed him. He never gained and sometimes he even lost.

Alan had been sick a couple of weeks when Gene went to Alamogordo, to be gone several days. The baby was lying on my lap one Sunday; he was waxen and his eyes were dull. The grocer's wife was worried. 'I don't think that baby is going to live. You should send for his father.' I wrote a little note which her son took up to Mr. Douglas's blacksmith shop to ask him if he would go down to Alamogordo. He sent back word that he would go as soon as he closed his shop for the night. There had been heavy rains, and as Alamogordo was located in the bed of an ancient lake, in those days unprotected by dikes, the water stood all over it. Mr. Douglas had to go through water a foot deep the last three miles of the trip. I expected Gene sometime next day. It was with no small surprise I saw him come in around one o'clock in the morning. In amazement I asked, 'How in the world did you ever get here?'

'I *had* to get here. I went down to the railroad yards, fired up the switch engine, and came up on that.'

I learned later, that the water stood a foot deep in the railroad station, and that the tracks were under water. How he could turn the switch under roily water is still a mystery.

'How did Douglas find you?' I said.

He grinned and replied, 'Oh, he knew where to look.'

I had childishly made Gene promise not to play cards on Sunday, and he was sitting watching the clock for midnight when Douglas found him. He sent Douglas to his room to go to bed, and lost no time in getting home.

With cooler weather Alan improved, and at six months was a very healthy baby.

After Alan's arrival I had no further time for horseback riding, so Gene sold Gypsy to a man from La Luz. I waited a long time for the money. Not getting it, I wrote a mild reminder to the man. No answer. I waited, more or less patiently, then wrote again. Still no answer. Then I wrote a series of letters, each more imperative than the last. No answer.

As I was kneeling by my bed one night saying my prayers, Gene came and knelt softly beside me. When I finished, I looked at him inquiringly. 'I have a confession to make,' said he. 'I wish you wouldn't write any more letters to the man who bought Gypsy. He paid the money and I spent it.'

Mrs. Dieder, an old friend of Gene's, had come up to her ranch just out of Tularosa for the summer. She brought her lovely daughter and a son. The daughter and I grew to be great friends.

We were sitting visiting one day when Gene burst out laughing. 'Do you remember the girl whose eyes you were going to claw out?'

'Indeed I do,' I answered.

'Well,' he said, pointing to my friend, 'there is the girl; now claw!'

I rushed across the room with both hands extended. She raised protesting hands. 'Wait a minute, and let me explain! During the diphtheria epidemic,' she went on, 'when forty people died in one week, my mother donated her home for a hospital, and your husband volunteered as nurse. I was fifteen and greatly taken with him. He told me about his wife and two children out in the San Andres Mountains. The boy was Ernest; I don't remember the girl's name. They were out there alone for months on end. He would happen to think of them sometimes and go out to see if they were all right and cut some wood. My heart was just broken for that poor lonely woman. Then one day I told one of the cowboys that I thought it was dreadful for her to be out there alone and he said: "Why, good heavens! Gene Rhodes isn't even married!" Now can you wonder that I asked you if you were sure you were married?'

Gene pleaded his case. 'Well, Laura, I had to tell you something or you would have made off with me bodily.'

'I would at that,' she avowed.

Laura was devoted to Alan, took him out by the hour in his carriage. She called him 'the little usurper.'

Mr. Fort visited us for a day. He and Laura were chatting together with great animation. She wore a white mull sunbonnet with embroidered ruffles — there can be no more alluring headgear — to frame her bewitching face.

When Alan was six months old, my neighbor across the street took Laura and me in her surrey to Alamogordo to have Alan's picture taken. There was no picture studio there at that time, but a man had fitted up a railroad car as one. It was a windy, blustery November day. I hugged Alan to my breast under my coat to keep him from getting chilled. After the pictures were taken, Alan was hungry and needed changing. There was apparently no place to go except the rooming-house where Gene and I had once stayed. The long hall we went into was unpainted, unpapered, not a chair, not a soul in sight. I sat down on my heels like a squaw, swiftly changed Alan's pants, and served his refreshments. Laura and I were nearly in convulsions over anything so unceremonious.

While he was still quite small, we took Alan out to the ranch. When we joggled over a section of Gene's cañon road, which the cowboys had forgotten to clear of the boulders that had fallen into it, Alan hung to the edge of his bib with one hand and to his cap string with the other, quite as if he realized the gravity of the situation.

The wife of John Christian, one of Gene's cowboys, had a baby, too. Gene went down to see John and took me along. In the one-room adobe house, dreary and dark, the young mother was sitting listlessly with the baby in her lap. I went over to see it and called to Gene, who lingered by the door.

'Come over and see the baby!'

He came clanking across the floor, glanced at the

little mite, and said in a deep, throaty voice, 'Where's John?'

Going home I told him that was no way to address the mother of a new infant. He must ask how much it weighed, how old it was, whether a boy or girl, and its name. He seemed quite docile and memorized it nicely. I had him recite it over and over, and finally felt that I had accomplished something.

Shortly after this the doctor's wife, who lived in the square just back of us, gave birth to a baby and we went over to call. My pupil went through his lesson proudly. I was purring with contentment when I heard this.

'What is the baby's name?'

'We named him Cecil for his father.'

'What is it, boy or girl?'

I gave up and let him go his own wild way.

CHAPTER VI

Gene Writes Again

IN TULAROSA I kept my pearl-handled six-shooter loaded on my dresser. The other women of the town had neighbor women stay with them, when the men were away mining or on business trips. I stayed alone. Mr. Douglas told me not to open the door if anyone came around the house at night, but to shoot through one of the thin panels. Luckily I never had occasion to do that.

By and large I enjoyed my pioneering efforts. We women lived as any small-town housewives would, visited, made patchwork quilts. I made several myself out of big patches cut from men's worn-out suits — 'breeches quilts,' they were called. We also canned quantities of fruit, which was unusually fine in Tularosa. Gene planted a splendid garden for me, making ridges like inverted V's and planting the seeds along the sides. I had a lot of vegetables from it. Feeling sorry for the cowboys out at the ranch, forced to eat beef, veal, and venison, mixed with beans, coffee, and sour-dough biscuits, I sent them a big gunny sack full of cabbages, cucumbers, onions, and everything. The next time they came to town I asked Steve how they had liked them. Instead of being in transports of joy, as I had fondly imagined, he faltered: 'Well — really — Mrs. Rhodes, we didn't eat them. You can't go back on your raisin'.'

Water came down once a week through the *acequia madre*, the big ditch, from which a little ditch branched off to water my garden. To get to the big ditch I had to cross the road in front of the house and go down a steep bank. My drinking barrels stood just at the edge of the stream. In this water ducks swam, dogs paddled and drank thirstily, splashing water gaily over themselves and scampering up the bank. I prophesied a certain epidemic of typhoid, but it never came.

Remembering that the water, which was apportioned us in rotation, was due to come to me in a day or two, I asked Mr. Fort, who spoke Spanish, to ask the Mexican across the street to irrigate for me. The Mexican was agreeable. After a while, to my dismay, I saw the Water Boss and the sheriff ride up. I went out to see what the trouble was.

Anyone caught stealing water was arrested and fined ten dollars. That was more money than I had seen in many a long day. I assured them I hadn't stolen any water. They insisted that there was even then a Mexican irrigating my garden with stolen water. Then I understood. I explained that he had misunderstood me, that I had wanted him to irrigate when I was entitled to the water. They called him off, but he stopped so slowly that he finished the garden before the water stopped running altogether. He would never irrigate for me again. The sheriff cautioned me not to let it happen a second time and rode away.

We had the horse, 'Teddy Roosevelt,' a fine-spirited creature, with us. I rode him sometimes, but he was too flighty for me. He adored Fred. Fred, now six years old, would go out to the pasture, put a soap box in front of Teddy's front legs, climb up on the soap box, from there throw a rope around Teddy's neck, and lead him to the house to saddle and bridle. One afternoon I sent Fred to the grocery store. He came riding home with his arms full of bundles. The houses opened directly on the street. As he rode up a gust of wind caught the screen door and flapped it open and shut right in Teddy's face. Teddy never flinched.

'Teddy never batted an eye!' Gene cried exultantly when he told a friend about it. 'That boy can ride!'

'As I understood it,' said the friend with a twinkle, 'he never batted an eye, but his chin quivered just a little.'

We had such sandstorms that March was almost unlivable in New Mexico. It was not only the dirt that penetrated everywhere, but the demon howling of the gale that drove one almost insane. When Fred was taken sick during one of these storms, I had to go to the doctor for medicine. The wind blew so hard it hurled me time and again against the adobe walls that bordered the street.

Gene came home in one of the fiercest of these storms. I remarked sarcastically that it was fine weather for traveling. He said he was at the Mal Pais, twenty-five miles away, and it was impossible to buck such a storm as that, so he had just drifted along with the wind. I was glad that a peculiar twist had landed him right in Tularosa.

All this time we were struggling along on the meagre sums Gene received from the sale of his steers. There was practically no money in Tularosa. I have been without money in the house for days at a time. We bought groceries on credit and paid when the steers were sold. Then we had the idea that teaching school might help out our finances. Accordingly Gene went to Alamogordo to try the teachers' examination. There were a number of subjects he had never studied, political economy and the like. But he sat there and reasoned them out by rule of thumb and won a first-grade certificate with the highest rating. But alas, he was refused a certificate because his 'moral conduct' was not such as to warrant it.

Gene had always wanted to continue writing, but somehow he had no time or mood, though plots for more stories came swarming to his brain after he had finished 'The Hour and the Man.' Whether it was the advent of his son that encouraged him or some other moving force, Gene settled down in the little Tularosa house and began to write in earnest. We went to Daddy Moore's blacksmith shop for a plank bench with sturdy legs of two-by-fours. The smith sawed it off until it was the right height, hammered the nails down, and there we had as solid a table as heart could wish. We rented a typewriter of the Mexican postmaster, and we were ready for business.

Gene worked assiduously on the story-writing, now that it wasn't necessary for him to write at night. As he wrote, he ran his fingers through his hair as if to stir up the sleeping ideas. With good plots to work on and the stories moving smoothly, we were deeply gratified. Here at last would be satisfaction for Gene and an income without help from the ranch or the school-teaching, which had rankled deeply in my haughty soul.

'His Father's Flag,' an intensely dramatic story of the Boxer Insurrection in China, went to New York to my brother George, who took it to *McClure's*. He left the manuscript with the managing editor. When he went back the editor told him regretfully that when they read it, they found a mistake in it. The story mentioned 'Dixie' played on a bugle. Everyone knew that one can't play tunes on a bugle. If one mistake was evident in cursory reading, they were reasonably sure that the writer had made others. They just couldn't afford to print a story full of errors.

My brother asked to be allowed to read the story to a friend of his who was an ex-naval officer. George felt sure that the story must be correct, because a month before he had organized an out-of-doors political meeting in his little town, and hired a bugler to play McKinley's favorite tune. George carried the story to his friend, Lieutenant Commander Rittenhouse, whose business it had been to organize the band music on board a man-of-war. He explained to George that a bugler carries several different instruments, among which is the French-keyed bugle, on which complete tunes can be played. Perhaps the bugler my brother referred to had really played a cornet. He suggested that in the manuscript we add the letter 'r' to the word bugle, so that instead of the bugle sounding out Dixie, a bugler did the act.

My brother took the story back to *McClure's* with this added information. They took it. And paid us forty dollars for it. Joy! Our fortune was made. 'The Ragged Twenty-Eighth' was written for *McClure's* also. Gene's father was Colonel of the Ragged Twenty-Eighth. He would have been pleased with the story, perhaps knew about it, although it was printed long after he died.

In 1903 or 1904, Agnes Morley Cleaveland of Berkeley, California, read several stories in Charles Lummis's *Out West* by a writer, to her unknown, named Eugene Manlove Rhodes, and was much excited over their portrayal of the life she had been brought up in. She, too, had been a New Mexico pioneer. Cowboy stories were generally grotesque distortions of the more violent side of western life, at that time as now, and the deep insight into cowboy thinking revealed in these stories in *Out West* impressed her greatly. Oddly enough, she did not connect the author's name with a certain 'locoed cowpuncher down round Engle' who was becoming a tradition in her section of the country.

> Countless tales of the locoed cowpuncher of Engle were [Mrs. Cleaveland writes] familiar to me, but for

some perverse reason, I did not connect the 'Gene' of the stories with the impressive name, Eugene Manlove Rhodes, who wrote the stories in *Out West*. Who ever heard of a bronco buster writing stories?

Then one day in 1905 or 1906 I received a surprising letter through the mails. It was a very small envelope, about the size of a child's party invitation, and there were three double sheets closely covered with a fine handwriting and postmarked Socorro, New Mexico.

Afterwards it was a joke between Gene and me that some day when he was rich as well as famous, I would demand large tribute for destroying this. Alas, the Berkeley fire wiped out my hope of illicit gain from this source.

I had been publishing a few cowboy stories in Eastern magazines for which I was paid money. It seems that *Out West* did not pay money, and Gene wanted to know how I managed to make my writing of some pecuniary benefit.

The letter was quizzically humorous but with an undercurrent of apology for the intrusion of an unknown cowpuncher upon the attention of a literary person, one who had attained the dizzy heights of receiving seventy-five dollars for a tale of cowboys and sheepherders. I started to laugh aloud and then broke off——

For the first time, it dawned upon me that Eugene Manlove Rhodes was the locoed cowboy of our round-up wagon tales.

Humble before the spark of genius I had detected in those early stories, I wrote Gene a long letter and explained how I had crashed the gate into the sacred purlieus of paid authors. This, as was the case of many another young writer, was by way of tutelage on the part of the great Bob Davis, then editor of the Munsey Publications.

The same mail that bore my reply to Gene carried a letter to Mr. Davis in which I proclaimed a genuine find for the cause of literature.

Mr. Davis probably smiled when he read my glowing words, for he undoubtedly was overwhelmed with similar proclamations. Anyway, he wrote back, tolerantly, and told me not to worry about my own laurels. I had prophesied — ah, how truly — my eclipse in the heavens of Southwest literature through the brilliance of this new portrayer of that life.

I recall the closing sentence of Mr. Davis's letter (also lost in the fire). 'Do not be too discouraged. You may find that all Rhodes do not lead to ruin. Anyway, tell the young man to send something along and I will take a look at it.'

That was Bob Davis, always helpful to the unknown writer. He went even farther and wrote to Gene before Gene had time to get a story ready to submit. Bob Davis had an uncanny sixth sense for ferreting out talent.

But Bob Davis never bought a story of Gene's for his own publications, because, he said, there was an 'essay-like quality' in Gene's stories that did not fit into the type of Westerns the Munsey Publications were then using. But he did give Gene a needed boost at a critical moment in Gene's career.

Later, when Mrs. Cleaveland met Gene for the first time, after months of joy-bringing correspondence, he told her that that first letter to her from Socorro had been his toss of a coin. He had been quite serious when he had said in the letter that he felt he should probably stick to bronco busting, but that the desire to write gnawed at his vitals and gave him no peace. On her reply to that letter would hang his fate (so he imagined). If from her Olympian heights she deigned to reply to the locoed cowpuncher of Engle, he would take it as an augury that his choice was to be letters. But if seventy-five dollars should have removed her so far above mortal approach that she remained haughtily silent, then he would take it as an augury that he should dedicate himself to a bronco-busting career.

'I think this was kindly fiction on Gene's part,' Mrs. Cleaveland says. 'It is undoubtedly true, however, that Bob Davis's letter did reach him at a critical moment of indecision and turned the scales in the right direction. Ultimately, of course, they would have turned that way, for Gene could no more have helped writing than the sun can help shining, but he might have postponed his serious efforts a while longer and some day when the horse went over backwards, his foot *might* have caught in the stirrup! It happens to the best of them!'

In the spring when Gene had to go back to the ranch, I decided on a trip back home. I was increasingly overjoyed at the prospect as the weeks passed. Though I hated to leave Gene, he was out at the ranch so much of the time anyway that I saw him only at long intervals. Just before I left we had a distinguished visitor. An aristocratic cousin of mine, Ralph Boyce, was summering at some fashionable resort in the Adirondack Mountains and had told a young man acquaintance of his to visit me when he went West. I was about all packed up to go home, the curtains were down, the pictures packed, and the typewriter had gone back to its owner. Only the unplaned plank table was left. When the young man arrived, he was frankly horrified from the start. He sat staring at the offending table, which was behind me and which I had forgotten all about.

To make polite conversation the stranger asked, 'Do you ever go to Alamogordo?'

Before I could answer that we did our shopping there, Gene spoke up.

'Yes, we did go there one time. They had the darndest little lights. You turned a contraption and they lit, and you turned it back and they went out!' The young man rose weakly, bade me a wan good afternoon, and went on his way.

I am loath to close this chapter of the book. Fred and I with the baby started for New York in May for a three-months' visit. I didn't come back for twenty-five years.

As we entered Missouri, the conductor said, 'Doesn't this green rest your eyes after Arizona and New Mexico?'

I confessed that it did. Rank grass grew green right up to the railroad tracks. If Missouri was as lovely as this, how much lovelier New York would be! Picture my dismay when I saw in the New York fields, not the lush grass, but weeds and sorrel. At Buffalo I boarded the home train. It was nearly twelve at night when I reached my native village. A light rain was falling. By merest chance, the station agent was still at the station. He informed me that the road was all washed out and recommended that I go to a hotel till morning.

'Not much. I'm going home!' I caroled blithely.

'Well, if that is the case I'll get you a driver, but I warn you that the man won't know the way.'

'I can tell him,' I almost shouted. I wanted to climb out and hug every weed along the road. My driver had to get out and strike matches to see how he could get his horse out of the holes the swirling water from a cloudburst had made. A narrow single track was all that was left of the Spooky Bridge. The winsome dell was a rubble of stones.

That joyous reunion, with my little boy, my father, my mother, and my brother's wife who was visiting them! My mother said, 'I want my child,' and folded me close.

CHAPTER VII

'Snowed in Back East'

WHEN I had been East three years, Gene started on his way to join me. His mother had come to New Mexico from her home in California and had helped round up and sell the stock on Gene's ranch. There was not a great deal and she owned part of that. Gene went to work in Oro Grande, laying a pipe line to carry water to that settlement. He was keenly interested in any constructive work, especially road-building, which he claimed was 'the most fascinating and romantic work a man could do.'

He described this incident of his last morning in the West.

> I got up in the morning, ate breakfast at Johnny Coleman's restaurant which was in Hilburn Brothers' saloon. Heard laughter in the back yard, went out. A lot of men shooting craps under the kindly sun — old abandoned crap table out there. Walked up and sezzi to 'Tex,' who was in possession of the bones, sezzi, 'I've got you — hands up!'
>
> Then this coon jerked his gun — I had never seen him in my life — hadn't even looked that way when I spoke to Tex. He was mighty drunk. His gun was pointed exactly at the pit of my stomach. It was a big

gun — .45 with a six-inch barrel — regular old hog-leg. And he was just across the short diameter of the crap table and he began cursing me in the vilest terms then current. Then Jeff stuck a gun in his ear, as I told you before. Colored gentleman dropped his gun and I left. He went across the street and into the fenced yard back of the 'Brown Palace' Saloon. In about two minutes, as soon as I could steal away unobserved, I went over after him — alone; went in the back yard and told him I had come to make an adjustment for all those sons-of-bitches he had been calling me. I didn't feel ashamed of the beer bottles. He was a big man. However, they were an afterthought. There were a dozen barrels of empty beer bottles out there, and after I had knocked him down twice with no perceptible results, I took to the barrels.

I will say for the nigger that he was game. I punished him fearfully but he kept bearing in. Didn't throw bottles, held 'em in my hand and hit him on the head and sideways too. I tried to catch him on the point of his jaw. He never did hurt me any, and (except that he finally passed out from loss of blood), the bottles didn't seem to hurt him any. Broke six bottles on him and cut him up horridly, then Baker did the arrest stunt and I faded away.

Sequel is even more amusing. Johnny Coleman is a very small man — over 125. Very early next morning this darky's brother came down looking for revenge; went up to Johnny's restaurant counter and demanded breakfast.

'Gus,' said Johnny, 'you come around inside and eat — no offense, but my customers won't like it to find you here.'

'Like hell,' said Gus. (He weighed about 180.)

'Now be sensible,' said Johnny. 'I'll eat with you, if

you think I'm trying to insult you. But you know there's sure some hard cases here — and if one of them comes in half drunk, he'll break a stool over your head, and you know it.'

Gus then began to cuss Johnny. Well, Johnny had better luck than I did. You know those little thin pepper-sauce bottles — corrugated? Johnny reached back on the shelf and threw a new unopened pepper-sauce bottle. It caught poor Gus exactly on the temple — the corner of the butt end — and Gus heard the birdies sing.

Johnny came and dragged Gus to the door. They hauled water there — and a nice new barrel of water stood there by the back steps. Mighty hard for Johnny to lift so big a man, but he got Gus's shoulders on the edge of the barrel rim and then grabbed him around the hips, and then up-ended him, head first into the barrel. Poor Gus was about drowned before his struggles upset the barrel.

'Them was the days.'

Local history has it that Gene left New Mexico in a hurry with two posses on his trail and lived in New York until the law of limitations ran out. His friend, Harrison Leussler, described it as follows. 'It was over a question of being "near-sighted," while reading a brand on a yearling which he killed to feed a stranger whom he had picked up on the road. In those days, it was common practice for any good citizen never to eat his own beef. In this case, Rhodes followed common practice, but the stranger, violating all the rules of Western hospitality, informed the proper owner, who happened to be a purist. The warrant was issued because Rhodes "convinced the chief witness for the State he ought to leave the country."' Gene himself has given this some credit. And I know that, many years later, while we were living at Three Rivers, a sheriff came through Alamogordo and sent his regards to Gene by a mutual friend. The sheriff said he was sorry he couldn't come up to see Gene, but he had a warrant for his arrest that he had carried for twenty-five years or more.

Gene reached my home the twenty-third of April, 1906. He had my guitar, a rug of which I was very fond, and three dollars. I welcomed him with joy. There was so much to tell, so much to listen to; we sat till late in the night and the kerosene lamp burned low. It snowed that night, and when Gene wakened in the morning and saw the ground white, he thought he was ruined for life. He didn't ever like springtime in New York. He had told someone he never did *live* there. 'He just went back and got snowed in for twenty years.'

We were all very happy in the little house — Father, Mother, Gene, Jack, Fred, Alan, and I. Gene had always insisted that his mother was a good cook, when she had the materials at her command, but he now admitted that he had never had really good food until he came to New York. It was a revelation to him. Farming was new too. He knew nothing of the rotation of crops or the use of fertilizer, but he attacked the problems of the farm with the same fury he displayed in everything that interested him. My father was glad of every bit of help he could get. Gene devotedly learned from him, as my mother had in her youth when he was schoolmaster and she among his pupils.

Gene loved to plow, and could make a surprisingly straight furrow. He bought a young gray horse to use as a saddle-horse and to put beside our old black Prince, for farm work. The gray horse, named Dick, was a good all-round horse, but he had one besetting sin. He would run away on the slightest provocation. In one instance when Gene had been to the village for some groceries with a little phaeton he had bought for my mother, Dick started running, threw Gene out, slung groceries all over, and broke every spoke in one of the wheels. Dick went past the turn to our house and on to the blacksmith shop, just a little way past the turn. He was not at all frightened, the blacksmith told Gene, 'just cussed.' Gene was very fond of Dick but he finally decided to sell him. The man who came to look at him liked his looks very much until Gene revealed his honesty. 'It is only fair to warn you that this is a very dangerous horse, and if you don't watch out he will kill somebody.' The man didn't buy.

Gene was at the blacksmith shop one morning when Henry Sempleton, a worthy farmer from Pennsylvania, came by with a herd of cattle. He drove his horse up in front of the door of the shop, where Gene stood. Sempleton looked Gene over.

'Stranger, hain't ye?'

Gene nodded.

'Where do you live?'

'Up the hill.' Gene nodded his head in that direction.

'Live in these parts?'

'Yes.'

'Married?'

'Yes.'

'Who to?'

'Lucius Davison's daughter.'

'Huh.' He cleared his throat. 'Well — ain't he — what you might call an odd fellow?'

'Why, no,' said Gene doubtfully. 'I think he is a Mason.'

'I didn't mean that. I meant he was kinda queer.'

Gene was reminded of the old Quaker — 'and sometimes I think thee is a little queer.'

At this point Sempleton started up his horse. Gene put his foot on the hub and laid a restraining hand on the reins.

The farmer waited.

'Whose cows are these?'

'Mine.'

'Did you get trusted for them or pay for them?'

'Paid for them,' explosively.

'Are you any relation to Eddie Sempleton?'

'Uncle,' he snapped angrily.

'Well, don't you think that Eddie is a little queer?'

(He was notoriously so.) For answer the man struck the horse a sharp cut with his whip, as the boys in the shop started laughing.

At about this time Henry Wallace Phillips, famous for his Red Saunders stories, invited Gene down to his home on Staten Island. Gene got a room near by and for six weeks wrote stories with him. Henry Wallace Phillips's aid, encouragement, and instruction were beyond price. He collaborated with Gene on 'Check,' 'The Punishment and the Crime,' and 'The New Numismatist,' all of them Gene's stories, all sold to *The Saturday Evening Post*.

It was a proud and happy day when he sold his own first story to the *Post*. As he drove in our yard back from the village post office, he waved the envelope proudly in the air and shouted, 'They took it!'

My father was so happy when he came in from the field and heard the news that he tossed his cap up in the air. Even so, it didn't equal the thrill of the forty-dollar *McClure* story. That thrill comes but once.

Gene was tremendously fond of cards, in all righteousness claiming he was the only man alive who ever made any money gambling. He had his special way of doing it, however. A poker game figured in a *Post* story. It seems they play poker differently in the West than in the East. Consequently the editors of *The Saturday Evening Post* questioned some of Gene's plays. Gene took a big sheet of paper and worked the game out, play by play. Then he wrote, 'Now if this isn't sufficient, gentlemen, I'll come to Philadelphia and demonstrate.' They wrote back, 'Come down to Philadelphia, by all means, but you don't get to play with us children.'

For all his love of the West, Gene was charmed with the scenery of New York State, especially with the lingering twilights and the fireflies. It was a very lovely valley that our house overlooked, perched a little way up in one of the cushiony hills. He described it some years later in *Copper Streak Trail*, calling Apalachin, Abingdon.

'The hills send down a buttress to the north: against it the Susquehanna flows swift and straight for a little space, vainly chafing. Just where the high ridge breaks sharp and steep to the river's edge, there is a grassy level, lulled by the sound of pleasant waters; there sleep the dead of Abingdon.

'Here is a fair and noble prospect, which in Italy or in California had been world-famed; a beauty generous and gracious — valley, upland and hill, and curving river. The hills are checkered to squares, cleared fields, and green-black woods; inevitably the mind goes out to those who wrought here when the forest was unbroken, and so comes back to read on the headstones the names of the quiet dead. . . . Something stirs at your hair roots — these are the names of the English. A few sturdy Dutch names and a lonely French Mercereau; the rest are unmixed English.'

With the hot weather, Gene and I adopted the upper barn as a sleeping place. Big folding doors opposite the big barn doors opened out over the underground basement, part of which was given over to the cow stable. We put a big board across this opening and in the draft of these doors, our bed, a clean tick, on the floor, filled with bright oat straw, was most delightful. To look over Apalachin Creek valley from here was magic.

Alan, still the baby — he was only four — slept beside us on a little pallet. Jack and Fred slept up in the haymow. Being of a more or less inquiring nature, Alan leaned out over the retaining board one evening to see what he could see, lost his balance, and fell out. He missed hitting the iron-tired lumber wagon wheel by a few inches and landed head foremost on the wooden pail in which we fed the calves, knocking the bottom completely out. It frightened him but didn't hurt him any. The boys came rushing down to the house and we to the barn to inspect the casualties. Far from being disconcerted, Alan seemed to be quite pleased at being the hero of the occasion. He was his father's son. Gene loved the limelight, although he liked to pretend that he didn't.

The second summer, 1907, Gene was greatly interested in threshing and went with the machine for some time. It was probably a pleasant change to be with a crowd of men once more. But I think the dust from this, added to the dust from round-ups, laid the foundation for Gene's bronchitis.

Always homesick for New Mexico, in New York and later in California, Gene dreamed almost nightly of being back there and herding cattle and horses. Patiently he waited till I would be free to go with him. Meanwhile he made the best of it. We belonged to a reading club which exchanged books every two weeks, we subscribed for a number of magazines, and Gene borrowed books from the Binghamton Library and the Coburn Library in Owego. He read so rapidly that his brother's wife used to say he read the left page, the right page, and the page over the leaf, simultaneously. It almost seemed so. With tenacious memory, he stored away in his mind all this accumulated reading from books, magazines, scraps of newspapers, old tales told by the campfires, to be produced at unexpected moments, amazing quotations to fit any occasion. He was an eloquent and interesting conversationalist. And he loved to talk, to pace back and forth with his hands in his pants pockets settling the affairs of the universe.

Gene claimed that it would take a battering ram to dislodge the women from the Apalachin church door, but he did enjoy the preacher McAllister, an athlete so outstanding that Gene used him as a character in 'The Man with a Country.' McAllister, his wife, and their youngsters were our guests at dinner one day. So pleasant was the visit that they stayed on for supper. Gene and Mac were deep in the intricacies of a game of checkers afterward, when all at once Mac started: 'It's prayer-meeting night!'

Off he rushed for the barn and his horse and out of the gate at record speed. He was only a trifle late, but as he went up the church aisle, my aunt Eliza, who was deeply religious, looked at him with cold disapproval.

Aunt Eliza had always drifted through life, with the pleasant things coming her way. Her corn was always shelled, you might say. She lived quite alone. As she was about to go to bed one night, she fell by the bedside and couldn't get up again. She managed to drag the bedclothing down to put over her, and lay there until the next day, when her cries attracted the neighbors and they came in. At once when this was reported to Gene, he went down and read the riot act to the Ladies' Aid. All her life, Aunt Eliza's one idea had been religion. Now they had better get busy. They made her some wrappers.

Because the children were sick with whooping cough, and I couldn't get away to look after my aunt, Gene found a place for her to board, notified the relatives, who most of them contributed to her keep, and looked after her amazingly. When the place he had found for her didn't come up to his expectations, he found another and better place, where she lived till she died. Although she was a terrifically heavy woman, they moved her on a bed. The day was hot. Gene walked beside the wagon the entire distance holding an umbrella over her to keep the sun out.

A New Mexico woman told Gene he never met a stranger in his life. It was largely true. He had a way of always meeting people as friends. A man who had come to Apalachin several years before Gene told me that he was not spoken to except as Mister So-and-So, whereas they called my husband Gene almost from the moment he landed.

Gene had some remodeling done on the little house, the sitting-room and pantry and bedroom ceiled with Georgia pine, a door cut in the western wall of the summer kitchen, an extra window, from which we could see sunsets of rare beauty, and another window in the kitchen. The north window looked to the woods. A bower of T-vine sheltered the new door.

We entertained a number of dignitaries at this little place. One of them, Agnes Morley Cleaveland, the writer, who had been visiting her aunt in Berlin for six months, met Gene personally for the first time. She had acquired all sorts of lovely clothes in Paris. Alan, with childish curiosity and awe, inspected the Gladstone bag. Mrs. Cleaveland, having a son of his age that she hadn't seen for half a year, warmed to him. She sat down on the floor and he squatted Indian fashion beside her, while she exhibited the contents of that bag to his admiring gaze. That morning when he was ready to start to school — I had started him in at four to get him out of his father's way — he came flying in to where she was drying the breakfast dishes for me, and put up his arms to hug her and give her a good-bye kiss. He was very like his father.

When the time came that she had to leave and Gene was ready to take her to the train, this slight, graceful, and vibrant lady standing in our little sitting-room made the surprising statement, 'My children will venerate me as one of the pioneer mothers.'

It was difficult to associate this stylish, pretty woman with our ideas of pioneer mothers. Mr. Fort had told me that when he had first come to Glorietta Ranch in New Mexico, the daughter of the people in the big house had a college chum home on a camping trip. He held that girl up as a shining example to me. Now here was that model in our own home.

CHAPTER VIII

'How to Drive a Husband Distracted'

I EXPECT I drove Gene almost mad by asking him to do something and then asking him to do something else, before he had a chance to finish the first job. He broke me of it very thoroughly by writing the following playlet. It wasn't really as bad as he makes it in the play. He never cleaned a stove for me. I never asked him to, for he had the utmost horror of getting his hands soiled with gudgeon grease, or anything of that description. I am all too afraid the rest of it is pretty accurate.

How to Drive a Husband Distracted

THE HOUSE THAT JACK BUILT

A FACT

BY

EUGENE MANLOVE RHODES

DRAMATIS PERSONAE

Mrs. R., a lovely lady.
Mr. R., husband to above.

SCENE. THE MILKHOUSE. AND ALSO OTHER PLACES.
Morning. Birds sing. Cows low. Hens cluck.

Enter Mr. R., laden with harness

He whistles. Goes to tool chest, gets out hammer, punch, straps, knife. He sings. Drops box rivets on floor. He swears. Looks around cautiously. Gets on hands and knees and picks up rivets. He seats himself à la Turk on the floor, punches hole in leather, inserts rivet, and feels for hammer. He sings:

'Oh, once in the saddle I used to go dashing.
Once in the saddle I used to go gay.'

He raises the hammer.

Voice (*without*). Jeannie!

Mr. R. Here I am.

Voice (*nearer*). Oh, Jean!

Mr. R. Here! What is it?

Mrs. R. (*appears at door, smiling*). Dear, can you get me some hickory wood? I want to bake a cake and this chestnut isn't good for baking.

The clock strikes eight.

Mr. R. (*with alacrity*). Sure.

He drags sawbuck from under wagon shed, goes back into milkhouse after saw. To himself:

'Now, why didn't I know enough to fetch that saw when I was in there?'

He puts hickory stick on sawbuck and picks up saw.

Voice (*behind scenes*). Oh, Jean!

Mr. R. lays down saw.

Enter Mrs. R., smiling.

Mrs. R. Won't you run upstairs and take down Mother's bed and carry it to the granary? I can't mop up there till it is moved.

Mr. R. (*cheerfully*). Why sure.

He pinches Mrs. R.'s cheek. He goes upstairs and takes side boards out of one side of bed.

Voice (*below*). Oh, Jean!

Mr. R. (*calmly*). Well, what is it now?

Mrs. R.'s head appears at head of stairs, smiling.

Mrs. R. Boy, can't you clean out the stove? It is all full of soot, and I can't get it out without getting down on my knees and Doctor Stiles says ——

Mr. R. Why, certainly, dearest. I'll fix it.

Goes downstairs. He begins to clean stove. Whistles.

Voice (*down cellar*). Jean!

Mr. R. starts nervously, dashes hand over forehead. A broad, black smudge appears on his face.

Mr. R. What is it, pet?

Mrs. R. (*at head of cellar stairs, smiling*). Oh, before I forget it, can't you put up a shelf right here? And fix that screen so the cat can't get in? I just came down to get cream and eggs for my cake and happened to see this. I've been wanting to tell you all this week and I never think of it.

Mr. R. (*gravely*). M. Louise, really — hadn't I better clean the stove and saw the hickory wood first, if you want to bake a cake?

Mrs. R. (*tenderly*). Bress its old heart, did I tell it so many things to do and get its poor old head all mixed up? (*Mr. R. brightens.*) Never mind. It's a dear boy. Didums!

Mr. R. (*grins*). That's all right, girl. *Exit Mrs. R.*

Mr. R. (*looks after her*). She's a dear — but ——

He saws wood and takes it in kitchen. He cleans stove. Sings:

'Dice Macario Romero!
No liase que seas casado
Es mucho lo que te queiro
Estoy muy apasionado —'

(*No matter if you are married*
I loved you very much.)

Voice (*without*). Jeanibus!

Mr. R. Hello! Oh, I say, May, just wait till I get this stove finished, will you?

Mrs. R. (*at door, smiling*). When you've done there, gather the eggs, will you, and I'll cook eggs and cheese together the way you like it so.

Mr. R. You're a fine girl.

He finished stove and goes to gather eggs. As he opens the henhouse door:

Voice (*without*). Jean! Oh Jean!

Mr. R. (*with some asperity*). Madam, pray remember that I am not twins. Can't you let me do one thing at a time?

Mrs. R. (*with dignity*). Very well. Mr. Griffin's cows are in the corn. I thought I would call your attention to it. I shall not trouble you again.

Mr. R.'s jaw drops. He looks after her. Raises his eyes toward heaven. Shrugs shoulders.

Exit.

Without, a tumult and a shouting. Calves bawl. Watch, the dog, barks. A crash. Enter Mr. R., flushed.

Mr. R. The fence is broken!

He procures hammer, nails, and board. As he starts to leave:

Voice (*without*). Oh, Jean!

Mr. R. (*throws hammer away, turns box of nails upside down on ground. Stamps on them. Spreads hand out palm up*). Coming up!

Mrs. R. (*appears smiling*). Hadn't you better put in those broken panes of glass while you think of it? (*She pats his head.*) Wasn't I the goodest girl, to wait till you had driven the cows out? You ain't cross wif' me, is you? Didums!

Mr. R. (*sheepishly*). Of course not. (*He gets glass and goes in front room.*)

Mr. R. (*thinks*). She is the finest girl — but ——

Voice (*without*). Jean!

Mr. R. (*goes to door*). Your servant, madam.

The clock strikes eleven.

Mrs. R. (*smiling*). You forgot to gather the eggs, dear.

Mr. R. (*with ghastly grin*). Why, so I did! The cat began to chase the rat, the rat began to ——

Exit.

Mr. R. (*enters with eggs*) — gnaw the rope, the rope (*he carries out bed*) began to hang the butcher, the butcher began to (*he puts up shelf in cellar*) kill the ox, the ox began to drink the water; the water began (*he mends the fence*). Oh, suz! I forgot to fix the screen down cellar. Where did I put that hammer? May! May! Have you got the hammer?

Mrs. R. enters smiling.

Mrs. R. You left it where you fixed the fence, I guess.

Mr. R. I put up the shelf since then.

Mrs. R. Why, no, you didn't. Why, there it is. Why don't you put things up, dear?

Mr. R. (*keeps silent with an effort. He mends screen*). Where was I? The water began to quench the fire, the fire began to burn the stick (*hastily*) the-stick-began-to-beat-the-dog-the-dog-began-to-bite-the-pig-pig-jumped-stile-and-old-woman-got-home! There!

He goes to milkhouse, takes up harness, puts in rivet, feels for the hammer, sings:

Sam Bass came from Indiana, it was his — now where did I put that hammer. May! May! O May!!

Mrs. R. (*appears at door, smiling*). Well?

Mr. R. Woman, have you got my hammer?

Mrs. R. (*sweetly*). You left it down cellar, dear.

Mr. R. glares at her. He goes out and returns with hammer. He seats himself on floor à la Turk. Puts rivet in harness. He raises the hammer.

Voice (*without*). Oh, Jean!

Mr. R. rises. An expression of crafty shrewdness comes over his face. He swiftly removes lines from harness, fastens them to rafter. He hangs himself.

Voice (*without*). Jean!

Mr. R. smiles malignantly.

(CURTAIN)

CHAPTER IX

Our Barbara

About this time it was evident that a new voyager was making for our port. Gene hired a neighbor girl to help with the endless amount of work there was to be done on the farm. Neat, swift, light-footed, soft-voiced, capable — that girl Leona was a prize. She had to go home nights because Gene's mother had come to visit us, making nine under the small roof. But our girl was always back in the morning in time to bake us buck-wheat pancakes, served hot from the griddle.

Being anxious that the newcomer should be a girl, we invoked the law of contraries and called her Hezekiah, invariably speaking of her as 'he.' We engaged the nurse who had cared for me when Fred arrived. When a doctor came to engage her for a patient a day or two later for about the same time, she told him she was already engaged for that date. He said it was impossible for a woman to know that far ahead, but she insisted: 'Not this woman. She is a graduate nurse and knows what she is talking about. She is very orderly, and if it works out so in this case, I can go on your case immediately afterward.'

I was 'orderly'!

The baby girl came on Jack's birthday, February 18,

1908. A heavy snow had fallen, followed by sleet, which made of the countryside a fairyland of beauty. Gene had to get the woman doctor who had been engaged and take her back home. About sunset as he was driving his horse and cutter home from the second trip, a man ahead, playfully inclined, would drive slowly till Gene was almost abreast of him, and then start up his team so Gene couldn't get by. The road was broken well for only one track. Gene lost his temper, gave his horse a cut with the whip that sent him plowing alongside the other sleigh. Putting his foot on the reins, he stood up and brought his whip down with all his might across the offender's shoulders. Once! Twice! Thrice! The man dashed for his own side of the road or, as he later admitted, Gene would have killed him.

Gene and I were so happy over our baby girl, so proud. Our darling one wish had been heard. With a son and a daughter what more could his heart ask? As Gene expressed it:

Whoso cometh desired into life
Is of immaculate conception.

She was a frail little mite, looked more like a little old woman. We named her Barbara Antoinette, Barbara from Stevenson's *Kidnapped* (for whose Alan Breck our Alan was named) and Antoinette for my beloved sister, who died so gallantly after nursing during the bubonic plague in Honolulu.

Gene wrote to Laurence Yates triumphantly: 'It's a girl (since yesterday). Mother and said girl doing excellently. Have a cigar.'

It was too crowded at the little house. In the spring we moved down to the Barton place, a few minutes' walk from the village and across the street from one of the kindest and most thoughtful of neighbors. In July Barbara and the three boys were taken ill with whooping cough. We closed the house and went back to the farm to get her out of the dust. She barely lived through the summer. Time after time I thought she was dying. She apparently grew stronger as the cool weather came in the fall, but the whooping cough left her with diabetes.

Gene wrote the account of Barbara's charming babyhood in 'The Brave Adventure.' He worked seven years on that story. Then *The Red Book* cut it back to almost nothing.

'The talking progressed but slowly. She was too busy to give it much time, that bold explorer. What need, when she could convey the finer shades of meaning with tone and eye and eloquent hand? She wanted to talk but the other things were more important. Accordingly she devised the plan of doing her language lessons after her merry, splashing bath — most methodical and economical of babies! While Mam-ma dried and dressed her, she chattered her scant vocabulary over and over with breathless rapidity, sometimes in the most unfavorable attitudes, thus effecting a vast saving of time.

'Her voice was a glad crow, silvery, exultant, her brief sayings ended ever on a rising, triumphant note. The vocabulary consisted almost wholly of cheery nouns, arranged on a system of her own, based upon relative importance: Mam-ma, Dad-die, Gamma, gamma, Gack, Ped, Ay-yun! The second and uncapitalized gamma was polite recognition of an existing husband to the first and greater Gamma; the last three ejaculations were Barbaric for Jack! Fred! Alan! — always delivered in lordly and commanding tones. People tried to impose upon her the word Pa-pa, a word musical enough in itself, but mythical, uninteresting, as lacking an attached entity; but the willful linguist firmly closed her incredulous lips and would none of it.'

I used to wheel her in her carriage down to the village, but these rides were uneasy things for her. She wanted to stand in the carriage, she wanted to ride backward, she wanted to see how far she could lean out without falling. Then one day I dressed her up in a charming Easter bonnet with blue satin ties that Laurence Yates had sent her. She rode along very quietly, in exemplary fashion. I was delighted. When I reached the store and came around to lift her out, I found the cause of all this good behavior. She had put one of the satin ties in her mouth and was chewing on it industriously.

Barbara died on Fred's birthday, October 24, 1910. She was Gene's idol. I really thought he would lose his mind with grief. He never completely recovered. We stood beside her wasted, colorless form in the dimness of the small bedroom where her body had been placed in front of the open window with the blinds closed. Gene turned the slats of the blinds and let the pale October sunshine fall on her.

'She will be shut away from the sun so long,' he said, his voice hoarse with grief.

He wrote a little letter to God, telling Him her favorite games, that she liked to help, and would He put her in the care of some very motherly angel. Dry-eyed, we both signed it. We were too crushed for tears. Then Gene placed the letter in her tiny hand, shrouded with smilax and pink rosebuds.

The morning after she died, an exquisite poem by Marjorie Pickthall appeared in the paper.

THE LAMP OF POOR SOULS

BY

MARJORIE L. C. PICKTHALL

Above my head the shields are stained with rust.
The wind has taken his spoil, the moth his part.
Dust of dead men beneath my knees, and dust,
Lord, in my heart.

Lay Thou the hand of faith upon my fears.
The priest has prayed, the silver bell has rung,
But not for him. Oh, unforgotten tears,
He was so young!

Shine, little lamp, nor let thy light grow dim;
Into what vast dread dreams, what lonely lands,
Into what griefs hath death delivered him
Far from my hands?

Cradled is he, with half his prayers forgot;
I cannot learn the level way he goes,
He whom the harvest hath remembered not
Sleeps with the rose.

Shine, little lamp, fed with sweet oil of prayers;
Shine, little lamp, as God's own eyes may shine,
When he treads softly down His starry stairs
And whispers, 'Thou art mine.'

Shine, little lamp, for love hath fed thy gleam.
Sleep, little soul, by God's own hands set free.
Cling to His arms and sleep, and sleeping dream,
And dreaming, look for me.

Gene wrote to Laurence Yates:

> Excuse me that I forgot to express my sympathy and good wishes for your father. Ralston, the Texas man, was telling me of it but I forgot to ask. You will know why.
>
> Laurence, please get today's *Binghamton Republican* and cut out the poem, 'The Lamp of Poor Souls,' and keep it safe in memory of our dear little girl. She was afraid of you, but she was so young.

Laurence Yates wrote in his paper, the *Owego Gazette*:

> Now that the book of life of this baby girl, sunny, winsome, and dear, is sealed, we can only wonder what would have been the story written on its fair pages had not the Angel of Death stretched forth an untimely hand and closed the volume. Surely the promise was rare, and sweet, and lovely.

Marjorie Pickthall said that the letter of thanks we wrote to her was one of her most precious treasures, and she would keep it as long as she lived. The poem was written about her little brother. To the day of his death Gene couldn't read that poem without a break in his voice. I used to ask him: 'Why do you read it? Why torture yourself so?' But he seemed to have to.

At Christmas-time we took a holly wreath to the country cemetery where she was buried. It was a cold winter with deep snow. A drift lay across her little grave. I can see now that Mother Nature was covering her with an extra puffy quilt, but it didn't seem so then.

CHAPTER X

Mutton Hill

GENE decided that the house, with those boys and a baby in it, was too noisy a place to write, and went back up to the farm with Father and Mother where he could write in peace. Up there he wrote *Good Men and True.* He experimented with the Morse code on the typewriter and used it in this story.

Gene also worked assiduously for the statehood of New Mexico, neglecting nothing. Passages from an article for *The Saturday Evening Post* in behalf of it, to which he gave the title of 'Stung' but which they discreetly changed to 'The Barred Door,' he was told, were read in Congress. A brief extract:

> THE BARRED DOOR
>
> Swinging round the circle has become a fixed Presidential habit. It is an innocent and harmless amusement — strikingly like the merry-go-round of blessed memory, both as to motive and result. The children have a good time and the cost is trifling. As a slight drawback a merrymaker sometimes gets dizzy; but that is not serious — quite the contrary.
>
> In October, 1909, President Taft, swinging round the circle, paused for refreshments at Albuquerque, New Mexico. There was the inevitable sound of revelry by

night: New Mexico's capital had gathered there — also her voluptuous swells and some few rough-riders — and bright the electric lights shone over the usual thing. Among the inevitable speakers was the only A. B. Fall. Ever hear of Fall — Fall, of New Mexico — cowboy, miner, lawyer, judge, gunfighter, able editor, rough-rider, farmer, private, chevalier, and brevet-captain of industry? Well, you will; in fact, you shall.

Fall is unique in one respect. He can, with equal ease and nonchalance, carry a safe Republican county for the Democrats or a safe Democratic county for the Republicans. And then do it all over again. From this you will infer that he is not a bigoted partisan. You win. He is simultaneously a Roosevelt-Democrat and a Fall-Republican. He has no acquaintances. Every New Mexican is either his steadfast friend or his bitter enemy; and they are all his admirers. Perhaps his best claim to distinction, however, is that he is the only rough-rider who has never been garnished with the decoration of the double cross for conspicuous carnage on the field of battle.

Pardon this digression and we will go back to our banquet, where all went merry as a marriage bell until Fall rose to say his little speech. Then there was — or were, when the construction calls for were — hurrying to and fro, and gathering tears, and tremblings of distress, and cheeks all pale which but an hour ago blushed at the praise of their own loveliness; for Fall wandered from his welcome to our fair city and tactlessly referred to the late passionate promise of immediate statehood for New Mexico. 'Perhaps,' said Mr. Fall, 'this time the promise will be kept.' Whereupon, says the associated press dispatch of that date, Mr. Taft 'rebuked him.'

Time has shown that the rebuke was richly merited.

That promise has not been kept. Mr. Fall should have known better. There was no excuse for such credulity....

I am pained and grieved that New Mexico was not admitted. The small boy's benefit in the change from skirts to knickerbockers is less from the actual and potential service of the new garment than from his own pride and pleasure; but to keep a boy in skirts for sixty-three years has a tendency to make him conspicuous. If you see a gray-bearded boy in skirts you surmise that all is not normal beneath the gray hair; you infer and say, in the classic phrase of Ambrose Bierce, that there are flitter-mice in his campanile. It does not command your confidence. You do not hasten to enter into business relations with such a one....

Arizona and New Mexico will get in — not yet, but not soon. If we are ever admitted it will not be for the justice of our cause or for our importunity, but because some party or faction needs our votes.

Addenda

I cannot close without calling upon you to share the admiration which I cannot withhold from my own moderation. 'The hardest test of a gentleman,' says Robert Louis Stevenson, the well-beloved, 'is to bear with fortitude the unspoken slights of the unworthy.' There is a harder thing: to bear with fortitude the unspoken slights of the worthy.

Nor have I been mealy-mouthed.

And I trust you will not charge me with any tactful effort to ingratiate myself with you. Such endeavor was not needful to the accomplishment of my purpose, which was, if you remember, not to enlist your sympathies for the New Mexican statehood but to enlist your aid in protecting us from any further promises.

Will you do that? No — don't promise to make no promises. Just don't make them.

When New Mexico was at last admitted as a state in 1912, did they give him the pen as a Reward of Merit? They did not. He probably didn't care, but he would undoubtedly have been pleased with this mark of gratitude.

Gene often said that for good or ill, he followed some set course, that he never drifted. But from our side, it seemed that he was like the wind's will. Over and over again he said he couldn't endure living on even a small farm and try to do literary work. Then one day, without my even knowing it, he bought a big farm, so large we had to keep a hired man all the time and sometimes two.

The farm was almost at the top of a hill. Legend has it that a man who had a sheep stolen started up the hill to make inquiries. No one had seen the lost sheep. But nearly every house where he inquired they were cooking mutton. It has been called Mutton Hill ever since. I named our place Tip Top, but it never was called that. But when we came home one day and found all the men drunk, Gene named it the Stagger Inn. That name has stuck to the place to this day.

Gene had the house remodeled, had everything done to it that a fertile imagination could devise. It was a rambling sort of a house that everybody who had lived there had added to until there were fourteen rooms. I had always loved casement windows and put a diamond-paned one in Mother's room. Gene had the living-room, dining-room, and bathroom trimmed in cypress at a dollar a foot. Some of the dining-room was in the old part of the house and had a low ceiling; the new part had a high ceiling. When strangers commented on this, Gene delighted in telling them strange tales, the most whimsical perhaps that the low part was to eat the regular meal in and the high part to go to for dessert.

My pride and joy was the new kitchen with windows on three sides and the sink and draining board under wide windows that looked down on the majestic sweep of the Susquehanna River. A wide screened porch along the length of the dining-room and kitchen was a pleasant place to sit. In the basement there was an elaborate water system of huge cisterns and a gasolene engine, which ran the churn, the milking machine, and the milk separator and also pumped up the water pressure for the bathroom. The house was painted a glossy white and shone like a cameo for miles away.

We had visitors constantly. Robert Frothingham, H. H. Knibbs, Charlie Van Loan of *The Saturday Evening Post*, Doctor Denyes, who was in college with Gene, and a large collection of writers came. An ex-editor of Scribner's, a superlatively gifted Southern lady, came to see us. Gene simply never stopped for breath all the time she was there.

'Stevenson, Kipling, and Barrie, "Cousin to Merlin"; here are the great. Stevenson is the most loved — and, as I think, has used the English tongue more skillfully than any other man, living or dead. His essays are better than his novels — his letters are better than his essays — and his novels — very uneven in quality — are high in any possible company of best. Father Damien's letter is the most eloquent thing English. *Pulvis et Umbra. The Lantern-Bearers* — here is wisdom. *Kidnapped* and *David Balfour* are my favorites, then *Dr. Jekyll and Mr. Hyde*; for stark power, *The Ebb Tide. The Bottle Imp* and two scenes in *The Wreckers* show the same gripping power. *The Master of Ballantrae* for seven-eighths of the way was his most enthralling tale. Fell down in disaster at the last of it. Sickness, perhaps — financial trouble.

'Curious! Kipling wrote two marvelous tales, his best — that make your hair to stand and your eyes to weep — and they are *never* mentioned. "Marlake Witches" and later, in the same volume, a tale of the Plague during the wars between Cromwell and Charles. I have forgotten the name. Both stories deal with sickness and with doctors and with valiant hearts.'

As we were taking her to the train, she said plaintively, 'I could have scintillated had I been let.'

Gene asked me why I didn't shut him off, that he didn't *mean* to take the center of the stage that way. I hadn't the heart, he enjoyed it so. Moreover he was *starved* for some intelligent companionship other than the talk of the farmers about their crops and taxes.

Gene took great interest in the place while we were having it fixed up. Then it promptly lost its charm for him and he looked wistfully over to our little farm on the other hill.

But the new home was an inspiring place for a writer. Gene wrote to Laurence Yates:

> *Feb.* 4, 1911.
>
> Sir:
>
> I am now on page 33 of the most ludicro-humorous-fantastical tale, 'A Number of Things,' concerning the comparative youth of John Wesley Pringle. And it is my intent to finish it today, copy tomorrow (Monday, the first seven pp. already all ready) that the wife may type it on Monday and Tuesday, that it may be mailed (to the *Sat. Eve. Post*) on Wednesday. Received on Thursday. Read on Friday. Taken on Saturday and paid for on Tues. the 14th, that therewith I may take up a note due on the 15th of Feb.

It was in the good old days when *The Saturday Evening Post* accepted or rejected a manuscript in a week. We had *just* time to get this story in, and get the check for it before a note fell due. How Gene piled into it! He would write a page and hand it over to me and I would type it while he was writing the next page. At last it was finished. We looked at each other, grinned, heaved deep sighs of relief, put on our hats, got in the buggy, and drove down in haste to get the story in the afternoon mail. As we were entering the village, two and a half miles from home, we discovered we had forgotten the story. A swift whirl around and breathless climbing of the big, steep hill. Snatched the story and hustled back, were still in time for the mail. 'Bregenz was saved!'

I had an endless procession of hired girls. When Alan and I lacked for amusement he would say, 'Let's remember our hired girls.' We would start in, but there were always one or two forgotten in the list. Gene came home from town one day and announced that he had a new one. I would have to teach her for she worked in a factory. He had brought home one of the prettiest girls I have ever seen, whom he had met at Laurence Yates' when they had been writing a story jointly.

One Saturday evening after she had come to us, Gene was going down to see Laurence. The girl sat on our front porch sewing rosettes on a skirt she planned to wear to a dance that night, and told Gene she was going down to Laurence Yates' with him. Gene said frankly that he didn't want her to go, that he had none too good a reputation in the community anyway, and he wouldn't have a shred left if she persisted in going with him. This did not 'faze' her.

Whenever Gene was going away anywhere he always reminded me of a big bumblebee. He couldn't find *any*thing. She nevertheless called to him, 'Mr. Rhodes, I'd like to get you to clean my white shoes.' Instead of telling her where she could go, as I expected he would, he said in an exasperated voice: 'I simply haven't time. You will have to get Fred or Alan to do it.'

The team and carriage were already waiting. He and Fred sat there impatient to be gone, for a thunderstorm was coming up. He shouted impatiently, 'If you are coming with me, come along.' She answered evenly: 'If you are in such a hurry, go along. I'm not going.' He said, 'Thank God!' and drove swiftly away.

This girl was the inspiration for 'A Rag-Time Lady,'

which he and Laurence Yates wrote for *The Saturday Evening Post.*

She kept to the grassy bank; the gay refrain lilted to her lips:

> 'Hurry up! Hurry up! with your violin!
> Make it sooner — don't stop to tune 'er,
> Fid — fid — fid — fiddle in the middle
> Of your ragtime violin!'

Quick hoofs plumped in the dust, drew eve, held up sharply.

'Hey, ghost! Want to ride and rest your wings?'

'Won't I, just?' said Martha, for the voice was a good voice. She fluttered down from the bank. 'Nix on that Sir Walter thing! You hold the jumping-jack horse — I'll get in . . . Home, coachman!'

'I don't believe you're a ghost at all,' said the voice, doubtful and rather aggrieved. 'You make the springs creak.'

'Hundred and thirty-eight in the shade,' said Martha complacently.

'Well, I'm going to look, anyway. You hold these reins.'

A match grated and flamed. She was a tall girl, but she had to look up, which she did with admirable composure.

She saw a well-shaped head, rather small for the broad shoulders; blue eyes, at once quizzical and puzzled; good ears and mouth; a puggy and much freckled nose; and dark auburn hair, curling willfully despite its shortness. The match nipped his fingers.

'Ouch! — and so forth!' he remarked in some haste, and added gloomily: 'Girl — shucks!' Then he sighed.

'Ever tried cold cream?' said Martha sympathetically.

In the starlight she saw his hands rub the freckled nose thoughtfully. He took the reins from her.

'Cold cream won't do freckles any good — they just won't spread and I can't make 'em,' he answered dismally. 'But even these few are some help.' He sighed again.

Martha required a little time to digest this.

'Oh, I see! The girls persecute you, poor dear! Do they call you Curly? You ought to buy a dog.'

'No use — they'd poison him!' said the disconsolate voice. 'This fatal gift of beauty' — with a manly effort he fought his emotion down and began anew: 'Smooth, oval face ——'

'Smooth, oval fiddlesticks! Why, your face is as round as an apple.'

'Yours —' said Curly, undisturbed. He went on in a dreamy monotone: 'Complexion good, but dusty — a little too white — looks like the tired kind of white; ripping hair — also rippling — brown and heaps of it — blacky-brown; a ki — competent mouth and chin; dark eyebrows — passable!'

'My eyelashes are considered rather good. Did you notice them?' said Martha anxiously.

'Lashes; big eyes, wide apart, golden brown. Why are they little skipping lights?'

More work done. Letter to Laurence:

And it please you, sir, I sat me down at 11 A.M. last Monday and wrote what was an editorial — in all but name — on a subject the which I know absolutely nothing about — which you will admit was considerable of a handicap. However, I wrote down my thoughts on straight lines, I hope — on this subject about which I know nothing — finished it, typing done by the missus, of course — and got it off on the 5.25 P.M. and for it I received $200!!! I am more elated over this essay sale than I have ever been over stories. For I like to preach, to exhort, to say how very intelligent I am — And, to deal plainly with you, writing stories is a particularly excruciating martyrdom with me. .

One of Gene's literary favorites was Cyrano de Bergerac in the ringing music of Rostand's romantic drama. 'I have fought better since.' In his imagination the unbuckled catches on his arctics made a pleasant jingling that reminded him, he said, of spurs. He would clank around in his like one of Cyrano's cadets, no doubt feeling a little like that Gascon swashbuckler himself.

As I was brushing my hair one evening preparatory to going to bed, our neighbor, Louise Alger, came running to beg us to come to her house and stay all night. Her father and her husband had killed a beef and taken some of it to Binghamton to sell. They wouldn't get back until the next day. We invited her to stay with us, but she said she couldn't, for half the beef was hanging in the barn and she was afraid someone would steal it. We finally put on our galoshes and went over.

Mrs. Alger gave us her room upstairs, cold as the tomb, and she slept down in the sitting-room on a bed couch. The last thing before we went upstairs to bed, Gene said to me in her presence, 'Now sleep as late as you can in the morning, and I will go over home and see to the fires.'

It was my habit always to waken early. In the gray dawn I suddenly remembered that I had set bread the night before, and pictured it all over the kitchen floor.

Rising ever so softly, not to waken Gene, and dressing with shaking fingers, for it was bitterly cold, I crept down the stairs and put on my arctics — and for the only time in my life I didn't fasten them. I slipped into my coat and stole outdoors with jingling feet.

A misplaced bedspring in the couch had been prodding the little neighbor in the ribs all night. She was roused by this pleasant jingling of 'spurs.' 'There goes Mr. Rhodes. I guess I'll go up and get into my own bed with Mrs. Rhodes.' But she was so drowsy. 'You can imagine how I congratulated myself,' she told us later, 'when I saw Gene come downstairs at nine o'clock, with his pajamas under his arm.'

Four things were uppermost in Gene's mind in those days: (1) baseball; (2) baseball; (3) baseball; (4) his literary work. Receiving a letter from Arthur Train asking him to meet Train at his country place and help dope out a story — 'big money and easy work' — Gene sent back a telegram that staggered Train, just ten words but it told the tale: 'Can't possibly get away. We play Warren Center Saturday. Sorry.'

It was up to Gene to organize the baseball team for the village.

Putting the town skinflint at the top for ten dollars, he went out with the list to get subscriptions. To each one he approached, he said, 'You'll have to come across good, of course, with Blankety-blank subscribing such a sum as that.' They all subscribed handsomely. When he had been the rounds he erased Blankety-blank's name and taking the list to him, spoke thus: 'You really can't afford to put down anything but a generous sum when you see what your townsmen have given.' B. B. looked it over carefully, and taking the stubby pencil wrote ten dollars and his name.

Gene's zeal in playing baseball was exceeded only by my energy when rubbing him with Sloan's family liniment. He was black and blue where he slid bases and he hurt the ligament of his leg. But all that was insignificant. He was having the time of his life. It was soon an accepted fact that the story-writing would be done only from the time that baseball stopped in the fall until it started in the spring. At one time when a city team came to play Gene's team, Gene found his catcher's mitt was missing. The visiting team was all loaded up in a truck to go home when Gene came over to ask if they had seen the mitt. They didn't know a thing about it! Nothing daunted he swung aboard, light and agile.

'Somebody here has that mitt and I want it.'

The resolution in his voice was unmistakable. The mitt was produced. Son Jack said afterward that they could easily have eaten Gene alive if they had dared to.

I had always wanted a dog. When a woman in the northern part of the state advertised pedigreed collie pups for five dollars, I sent for one. He was a cute little rascal, but the inevitable question of a name came up. Gene announced that the pup should be called Clip. Hadn't he been paid for with the five dollars Gene had wanted to send for the press clippings of his new book? A few days later Gene's publishers sent him the press clippings. I was at liberty to name the dog as I chose.

Ellis Parker Butler had a story in *The Woman's Home Companion* entitled 'Booge.' That became the dog's name. Gene wrote tersely to Ellis Parker Butler: 'Congratulations. My wife has just named her collie dog Booge.' Mr. Butler wrote back: 'Thanks. I can go you one better. I just named my first baby boy after myself.'

To help out with expenses we made butter to sell. Before we had the gasolene engine, Gene with a book in one hand, would work the barrel churn in the shade at the back door. We sold some of the butter to the man who lived just below us, a man who worked at odd jobs by the day. The man told the neighbors that it was 'rotten butter.' Gene heard of it and, a few days later, met the man and his father in a lumber wagon just outside the village.

The man was nearly twice Gene's size, but Gene climbed up on the lumber wagon beside him and said, 'You apologize to my wife for saying her butter was "rotten" or I'll punch your face in.' The man apologized. He didn't buy any more butter.

April, 1917! Fred enlisted. Gene felt the war overpoweringly. On the wide screened porch he put up a big war map on the wall of the house, and with a string and black-headed pins he traced each day's movements. We put forth strenuous efforts to raise food for the soldiers. The place was farmed day and night. The spiritual toll was heavy. Gene could hardly eat or sleep.

He lost all power to write. Only at the earnest solicitation of the Government was 'The Battle of Mutton Hill' produced and sent to the printers.

THE BATTLE OF MUTTON HILL

There are ten thousand Mutton Hills. We shall need them all. The fertile farms of the West are not enough. We need every stony acre of the East. The decisive battle of the war may be won or lost on Mutton Hill. Will you leave it to be fought by grandfathers?

What is wrong with Mutton Hill is wrong to some extent with every farm. The difference is in degree and not in kind. The young men have gone away. We have advertised them away, we have bribed them away, we have sneered them away, we have lured them away. The big wages have got them; the bright lights have got them; the white-shirt jobs have got them. This situation was serious before the war. It is now — in the plain and literal meaning of the words — a matter of life or death. If you prefer the military phrase, it is a question of victory or defeat. Our Allies must have food from us, or collapse.

The farmer is in the trenches. He clodhopped into the trenches four minutes after war was declared. He needs reinforcements.

... Let me take you into my confidence. I have been continuously and freely abused as a literary slacker, because I have abstained from writing war articles to advise this nation. There are two things about advice for which I have a constitutional dislike; taking it, and giving it. For three boiler-shop years it has been my solace and my comfort to say no word to swell the hideous din.

It is a mistake to think that farming is not a skilled

industry. The questionnaire which you and I got out the other day made this mistake. An unskilled locomotive engineer is one who cannot run an engine. An unskilled farmer is a farmer who cannot run a farm. If the engineer gets the engine's duty and the farmer gets the farm's duty, they are skilled workmen. If a young man raised on a farm, who can operate and repair all sorts of complicated machinery, who can doctor a sick cow and keep her from getting sick, who can cure a horse's galled shoulder or prevent it from galling, who can plow and sow and reap and mow, thresh, churn, milk, make garden, spray, graft (fruit trees), raise hogs and chickens, butcher, shoe horses, mend harness — if he is not a skilled laborer, there is no meaning to words. A man can learn to run a linotype machine in five months, he may become a skillful mechanic in five years. I defy him to become a skillful farmer in five years. The men with fifty years' experience on a farm are still learning.

... Every farm on Mutton Hill lost money. I do not think one hill-farm in five hundred, within one hundred miles in each direction from here, cleared one dollar on the year's work and investment. Those were the lucky ones who broke even. The valley farms did a little better, not very much better.

It must be said that the farmers of Mutton Hill kept a stiff upper lip, and came up smiling. They are a stubborn pack. I suspect that farmers are wonted to hardships; it is possible they are not so soft and effeminate as certain magazine writers — who admire Prussian militarism and would have us outdo it — would have us believe — that all Americans are the ignoble and peace-loving Americans.

For myself, I am lost in admiration of the cheerfulness of Mutton Hill. Except from one man, I heard no word of complaint. This one person was of an imperfectly patient disposition, and he frequently made four-minute talks which were worth going miles to hear. So I am told. I am that man.

When our neighbor across the field received word that her son, Archie, who had grown up with Jack and Fred, had met death in the Argonne, Gene suffered almost as acutely as she.

The years of the War saw only 'No Mean City,' a *Saturday Evening Post* story, finished. It dealt with a German attempt to blow up the Elephant Butte dam. But in the time between the Armistice and Gene's departure for California, he wrote *Stepsons of Light.* We had some good times before we had another of those 'vacations' which Gene said made our marriage so successful.

A writers' club was organized in Binghamton, fourteen miles away. The members came to our house for a picnic on the lawn. While the party was in progress Gene's dog Gus, who used to show his teeth in a fascinating grin, came creeping over a little rise of ground and had the whole party convulsed. Mary Brecht Pulver, a writer for *The Saturday Evening Post,* was mistress of ceremonies. When she was reading a collection of reviews put out by publishing houses, she read a caustic one about Gene, referring to him as Miss Rhodes, an incurable romantic. Gene wanted it, and after some persuasion she took from between the leaves of the pamphlet the review she had written herself. He was thoroughly teased.

A number of the professors from Cornell University came to visit us. One of them came in full dress one evening. Gene's dog nearly ate him alive. Westerner that he was, Gene told the professor that it was probably the silk hat that enraged Gus. The professor countered with a statement that Gus was no proper dog and would follow some tramp off one day.

Jules Livingston, who ran a daily column in *The Binghamton Press* in which a number of Gene's poems in lighter vein appeared, spent a week-end on Mutton Hill. He had come dressed in white flannel trousers and blue coat, groomed to the last degree. When the umpire that Gene expected for his ball game failed to appear, he asked Livingston to act in his place. Jules had to put all those dirty balls in his white pockets — and did it without batting an eye.

CHAPTER XI

The End of the Eastern Interlude

I STAYED on at the Mutton Hill farm the winter after Gene left for California, although I had never liked it for its constant associations in my mind with endless work and startlingly little play. Then Alan got a job in the city. In the springtime I took Mother and some of our belongings back to the little farm and the little house 'where her heart had ever been.' I was as fond of it as Gene was of his ranch in New Mexico.

I found the little house dirty and bedraggled. The door stood open and the dead leaves lay in drifts along the floor. The men who moved my furniture had been told to set up the heating stove for me but hadn't done it. It was nearing sunset. I tried to set it up myself with a post for lever and stones for cribbing, but it nearly fell over broadside. I had to let it go and warm Mother's room with a Rochester lamp. But we cared for none of these things. We were home once more. I wrote Gene that disheveled as the house was, you could almost feel the brooding sigh with which she gathered her wandering children in.

With a wonderful garden and Alan coming home for week-ends, with a horse (Dick, now worn and old) to get such provisions as we needed, we were getting along beautifully on the little farm when Mother fell and broke her hip. She was entirely helpless for four years.

Out in California Gene was having a terrific struggle. The movie people were driving him mad. None of his expectations of selling manuscripts to the movies materialized. Once he sent back a good printed contract to cheer me up with the thought that he would soon have some money to send me, but the deal didn't go through. Worse yet, he had all kinds of trouble with the first company that published his books.

He was so torn between all these conflicting issues in Los Angeles that he wrote only one story which he didn't sell for several years, until after he came back East. When one day he picked up a pencil, someone came in and said, 'Thank heaven! at last you are going to write'; he laid his pencil down and went to town and played pool all day. He wrote only reviews that he didn't get paid for and letters to the editors. Time after time he planned to come home, but always there was some urgent need for the money where he was. It was due to Olive Carey, bless her, that Gene finally started. She paid him the money for a story Harry Carey wanted to dramatize, bought his ticket, and headed him straight for the railroad station.

He wrote to Paul Eldridge, of Oklahoma University:

> *Dear Paul:* Am all shot: nerves used up by trouble. Going back to New York to help my wife bear more trouble. No writing finished for two years — a few articles, that's all. Hope to get straightened out, now. Have had hard time: deserved it.

> Write to me in New York. After I find Uncle Ben and hear rain on the roof, I may get so I can write a letter.
>
> ... Let me recommend as the best Western book I have read *Recollections of a Western Rancher*, New Mexico, 1883–1899, by Captain William French. It is written at first hand, with humor and insight — lacking the lurid headline sensational touch. It is surprisingly accurate. This was my own country — so I know what I am talking about.

Alan met Gene in Owego, eight miles away, because the midnight express didn't stop in Apalachin.

'I heard a voice like a bell. It was my son!'

In Gene's absence I had worked on the farm. From my dozen hens, I built up a poultry flock; I had a nice new hen house, made out of our old horse barn, and two hundred hens. Gene sailed into the chicken business with his usual enthusiasm. He had a natural aptitude for it. It was a funny thing that when he sold a story he spent the money like a hired man scattering grain to the chickens, but when he had the money for a crate of eggs sold in Apalachin, it was real money, to be doled out with the greatest care.

We had lengthy discussions on what to name our poultry farm. Gene favored 'Pip Passes.' I voted that sacrilegious. We finally called it 'The Cross Rhodes Poultry Farm.' It *was* on a crossroad. Alan was indignant. When the mailman said, 'Which one is the cross Rhodes?' I said promptly, 'I am.'

We had two breeding pens in the hen house, with

tiny doors in the back just about big enough for a big hen or rooster. We let our big flock out every day for exercise, unless it was storming. After we had put them in early, Gene would let out the breeding pens, one by one. He had a little switch, and handled the chickens like a herd of cows. I couldn't do it. When he put the first lot in, he would let the second pen out and handle them the same way. I have a picture of him doing it. What would his old cowboy friends say to that?

An undersized Englishman who preached at the Baptist church at South Apalachin and who was ever thoughtful about coming to see Mother while she was a shut-in, was coming up the hill one day to make one of these calls. He was walking backward that he might admire the view of the valley below him. Gene, who apparently never outgrew his boyhood, began walking backward down the hill until he collided with the minister. They both laughed and when he had come in the house, Gene passed his poem, 'The Immortals' over to him to read. The minister read until he came to the line, 'Thrust it in Joan's hand.'

He caught Gene's arm. 'No, no,' he protested. 'Don't torture that poor girl any further.' Gene was charmed. 'The man grew to heroic size,' he said. He changed the line to, 'Gave it to Joan's hand.'

That was what he meant in the first place.

THE IMMORTALS

Who, of the English stock,
Who would you be?

Richard in battle shock,
  Drake on the sea?
Look how they crowd and cling,
Yeoman and knight and king,
Warrior and sage and seer —
Choose from them, far or near —
  (Nelson at Trafalgar?)
  Which would you be?

Nay, but the soldier who
  In Rouen square,
Breaking his spear in two
  Made a cross there,
Past archer, priest, and squire
Pressed forward to the fire,
  Gave it to Joan's hand —
  Him would I be.

There, groping through the flame
  Those two hands met...
For that shared crime and shame,
  Heavy our debt.
Yet — for that soldier who
Brought love and tears to you
  In your last agony,
  Joan — forget!

Gene built a platform over the little creek that bubbled under the maple trees in front of the house. It was lovely out there with that gorgeous view of the valley below us. We placed chairs and a table there.

'And often after working, sir
  When it is bright and fair
I take my little porringer
  And eat my supper there.'

Leaving Alan to take care of his grandmother, we set out to collect some money owed us by a man in Cohocton — someone was always owing us. Gene looked at the map, decided it wasn't far, and off we went. We traveled and traveled. Night came on, but still we hadn't reached the place. It was long past suppertime when we stopped at a hotel, had something to eat, and registered. In the morning I suggested that we wait for breakfast until later when we could find some nice place in the country. Again we drove and drove. Finally smoke began curling from the chimneys. Gene asked repeatedly, but couldn't get any coffee. This was near calamity, for we almost lived on coffee. At nine in the morning near Lake Hamilton, we met a hunter who said we might be able to get some at Nut Lodge, which hadn't closed. As we came up the drive, Gene was jubilant.

'Yes, they have some. I can smell it!'

Son Jack said later that was a brutal statement, that you could just see the poor souls hustling the demijohns under the counter. What we got for coffee was horrible stuff!

A few miles farther on a drizzling rain set in and turned to snow. Gene phoned and phoned but couldn't find any trace of Beam, the man who owed us the four hundred dollars. We turned around and headed homeward. The mountains were beautiful and strange in the rain. The mist, like ghosts, climbed up the mountain-sides, clutching with 'boneless fingers' at the tree trunks, and the river rushed by in the sodden valley, as gray as the sky. When we arrived home at six o'clock Alan had a roaring hot fire for us to warm our chilled hands by, and a pot of hot coffee. Believe me, it seemed good.

Imagine our chagrin when we found that we had been going in the wrong direction. It was to Cohocton in the northwest Gene had taken us. We should have headed for Cochecton. Worse yet, we never did get the money. It was the first night in four years that I had been away from Mother.

Gene was always reluctant to press a debtor, but he would go out and move heaven and earth to raise money to loan a friend, even to borrowing it himself in order to pass it on.

Gene's first seven novels had been written in the East. But always his heart and mind had been in the West whose voice he was. His penmanship may have been execrable, but the meaning of his words was clear.

His handwriting had been a great source of difficulty to me as his typist and even to the other members of the family. When Jack and Fred were attending school at Owego and were entrusted with lists of things for family use, they had all the merchants on Front Street out on the sidewalk trying to decipher the writing to see what should come from each man's store. Henry Herbert Knibbs with much wit describes it in his Introduction to *The Proud Sheriff*: 'His handwriting was peculiar, to say the least, often all but indecipherable. There were words which looked as if an ant had got into the ink and then had begun his travels across the page in the erratic fashion common to ants. Other words were often a mere horizontal wave, with a possible dot above one of the crests to indicate that an "i" was concealed somewhere in the surf. As an illustration of his penmanship: He had written glowingly of "faith and honor." It was translated by a not unintelligent reader to "filth and horror."'

Not so indecipherable was his feeling for the West. He was an incorrigible romantic but his stories were realistic, and recognized as such in New Mexico. In fact so great reliance was placed on them that after 'Once in the Saddle' was accepted by *The Saturday Evening Post* but before it was published, the erstwhile owner of the identical spring mentioned in the story wrote to Gene asking help. Did he know precisely where one of the cornerstones of the Adell homestead was, for floods and stock had moved or erased them — and the ranch had been jumped by George Henderson, on the ground that Adell had mixed up the section numbers and proved up on a piece of hillside, not on the spring, exactly as it was recorded in the story!

'A thousand handsomely printed books have said, not casually, but shrieking and beating their breasts, that life in the western half of the United States has been all sodden misery, drab and coarse and low. If those books tell the truth, then any and all my stories are shameless lies. What I remember is generosity, laughter, courage, and kindness; kindness most of all; kindness from wicked men and worthless men as well as good men.' So Gene wrote years later for *The Trusty Knaves*. It was his opinion of the cowboys and ranchers with whom he had spent his life. And it was accounted correct by his Western co-workers, among them Frank Dobie, who wrote: 'They [Gene's characters] talk in a blithe way that no other fiction writer has made cowboys talk in, unless O. Henry be excepted. Mr. Rhodes knows literature, and while he will not have one of his cowboys sacrifice fidelity to his own speech in order to say a good thing, only O. Henry and Alfred Henry Lewis among fictionists of the West can vie with him in the grace of literary allusion. It seems perfectly natural for Pres Lewis in *The Trusty Knaves*, after biting off a chew of tobacco, to say: "You keep your voice down, brother. If you bellow at me any more I'm liable to prophesy against you.... When you got any communications for me, I want 'em sweet and low, like the wind of the western sea."'

The stories of accurate Western writers, Gene recognized as valuable documents in history, unrecognized because they seemed so common. 'You want to remember that in a thousand years, or some such, historians will publicly offer their right eye to know what you can see now, at first hand; just as they puzzle and stew and guess about Harold the Saxon nowadays. Heavens to Betsy, how they'd raise the roof, them sharps, if they could lay hands on a few anecdotes by Little John in his own handwrite, about Robin Hood and the proud Sheriff of Nottingham! But if they'd found those same letters while Little John was alive, they would have lit the kitchen fire with them.' Defending and appreciating Western authors was his passion and soul. 'Oh, yes,' he wrote to his publisher, 'writers of Westerns are supposed to turn out trash anyhow; s'matter of fact, they have as much conscience and pride of work as writers of Metropolitan or Parisian stories, "Eastern" or Asia Minorican stories. Depends on the story and the writer — not on latitude or longitude.'

With Harrison Leussler of Houghton Mifflin Company, Gene had put forth Herculean efforts to put across Charlie Siringo's last book, *Riata and Spurs*. As he told Alice Corbin Henderson, 'We want to give Siringo a bright sunset.' For *Sunset Magazine* he wrote an article on Siringo, whom he ranked with Daniel Boone, Davy Crockett, Kit Carson, all of a kind. In the article he told of Siringo's adventurous life, fifteen years a cowboy-detective, and how he once caught a murderer whose kidnaped victim had suffered mutilation. To the father, the murderer had threatened to cut off the kidnaped boy's hand if the money was not paid, and if not within thirty days, the boy would be killed. In thirty days the boy's body was shipped to his father, a corpse lacking the right hand. Siringo plunged into the Virginia wilderness, alone. Within a month he brought the crime home to its perpetrators and secured confession. Such was one of the 'Western writers.'

In *The Literary Digest* 'International Book Review' for November, 1923, had appeared a criticism of Emerson Hough's *North of '36* written by Stuart Henry. The critic, in a protest against over-romanticizing the

West, had pointed out historical points and details of inaccurate pioneer description which he thought he noted in the story. The slurs caught Gene's eye and his dander was up. Sick and unable to write a rebuttal, Gene marshaled his friends and friends of Hough to answer. He wrote to Alex asking him to go to bat. Alex wrote me:

'Ford was then Literary Editor of the *Los Angeles Times*; for a starter he gave me a one-thousand-word article on Hough, space in the paper. That was the starter. Next I went to Arthur Sullivant Hoffman, then editor of *Adventure* magazine. Hoffman, like the good soul and square shooter he has always been, consented to devote the "Camp Fire" department in the magazine for several issues to vindicating the memory of Hough. Every worthwhile publication in the country took up the controversy — even the, as Gene would say, "good old *Saturday Evening Post*" came out with a rather lengthy editorial on the matter. If there was a man who would fight for the memory of his friends or for the underdog, that man was Eugene Manlove Rhodes, God bless his memory.'

Professor Walter P. Webb helped carry out the campaign. 'I speak as a Texan who happens to know the facts. My purpose is to show the stuff that this ill-willed review is made of.' And he proceeded to demolish the criticisms by proving: that Texans in 1867 did consider themselves Americans, that the number of cattle going over the Trail was not exaggerated, that the trails mentioned were historical but not easy to place because they were shifting, and by upholding Hough's correctness where the reviewer had misquoted him.

Others took up the refrain, and Gene had the pleasure to see if not actually write for the defense. Information was gathered to prove the size of herds, the correct quality of Hough's descriptions, and all other details. It was a lively fight. Even the charge made by the reviewer that Western women 'were gaunt, homely, hungry, leading a raw one and rawhide existence' was answered and proved mistaken. Were they not too pioneers who had built America?

Gene put as much work on this enterprise as would have completed a fair-sized story. We still have the galleys of the Camp Fire letters.

Mother died the first of April, just as her crocus beds were a mass of bloom. My beautiful mother, fashioned of the stuff from which martyrs are made, to do right, at no matter what cost. Gene was very fond of her, but stood in considerable awe of her. He wrote in her copy of *Good Men and True*,

> *Dear Grandma:*
> Here's the little book we wrote together, up on the good old farm.
>
> Your loving son,
> Gene

Mother was so proud of this book.

There was no tie now binding me in New York. Gene and I could be always together. When Gene used to go away, on his return I would rush to greet him with, 'Where have you been?' Because I was so lonely a person without him, he wrote this poem 'Recognition' for me and said it was my very own poem. It was printed in the Poet's Corner of *The Saturday Evening Post* and treasured in my heart.

RECOGNITION

Oh, once the world was wide to me, and once the years were long
Where dream and day they fled away with laughter and with song;
And once when April walked the world — unguessed, unwarned, unknown,
My love and I met face to face, and walked no more alone.
No words had we of doubt or fear, no thought of loss or wrong,
But 'Oh my dear, and is it you? Where have you been so long?'

. . . .

Last night I climbed a star way high, beyond the outmost sun,
Where friend and foe we lost below, they gather one by one;
I know not if the wall were high, nor marked the way I trod,
Nor if the street might lead my feet before the throne of God;
I only know who met me there and drew me from the throng —
And 'Oh my dear, and is it you? Where have you been so long?'

In August we planned to drive in our new Ford coupé to West Virginia to visit son Fred. I wanted to take the camp kit, but my lord was firm. 'Nothing doing. We will buy our meals.' So we nearly starved to death. The climax came late one afternoon. We were both as cross as bears, snapping and snarling like a couple of mad dogs. As we went through a little town in southern Ohio, a sign caught our eye, 'Home-cooked Meals.' This was an innovation then. We stopped and were served an exceptionally delicious meal. A transformation! Our snappings and snarlings were forgotten. It seems we had just been outrageously hungry.

Huntington, West Virginia, was a beautiful town with wide streets and lovely shade. We had a month-long, enjoyable visit. The way back through the Shenandoah Valley was a day of going ahead and doubling back in hairpin curves. Wonderful scenery and forests, but you didn't seem to get anywhere. It was late when we reached Stanton, where we had had the good meal, and went on. We found a camping place in an oak grove where some sort of picnic or gathering was in progress, with lots of noise.

It hadn't rained for a long, long time and happened to remember about it just then. Our tarp was old, and how it leaked! I prodded Gene in the ribs from time to time to report new leaks, but he just grunted and slept blissfully on. Our quilts were wet through, our pillows were sodden, and worst of all when we rolled this wet mass up next morning, horrible worms from the oak trees had crawled under our pillows for shelter.

As our bedding was wet, we went to a fashionable hotel that night, the only one within reach. Gene wore overalls. In the morning some aristocrat beckoned him imperiously and told him to back out the man's expensive car. With no demur whatever Gene climbed in and backed it out. It's a wonder he didn't wreck it in that jam, his driving was so temperamental. The man gave him a fifty-cent tip, the only tip Gene ever received in his life. He thought it was a wondrous joke.

Gene ordinarily had good results with his driving, but his guardian angel must have had to hump herself. I've many soul-stirring memories of trips.

In early summer that year my brother George had attended a Cornell reunion. I wrote him that I came very near attending a reunion too. Gene and I went to Tioga Center on the Fourth to see two ball games played by the Apalachin team. Coming home Gene picked up a tramp. It began to drizzle shortly after, and the pavement became very greasy. When we got up past the place where Gene had in another accident wrecked his beloved 'As Is,' a car ahead of us pulled out of the nearly solid line of traffic, to pass a slow-moving car ahead. With a view to hurrying home, for it was five-thirty or thereabouts, Gene pulled out after him, so quickly that I didn't have time to stop him. I just gasped, 'There's another car coming!' for I could see ahead and he couldn't. The car we were following swung back and left us facing this swiftly moving big car. Gene swung sharply back, shutting off his gas as he did so. Our car crossed the concrete and poised, shivering, on the grassy strip bordering a ten-foot bank. Then by some means Gene swung the car back on the concrete, where it went over with a crash. I didn't lose consciousness, and I didn't make a sound. Gene being more or less on top of the heap proceeded to climb out. I sat for a breath staring at the tramp, who kept saying, 'Get me out of here, I'm hurt.' Then a thought: 'Heavens, the gas tank will probably blow up next!' I crawled out through the torn top backwards. Somebody stood me on my feet. I don't remember how the tramp got out, but he wasn't hurt, only scared. Gene and a dozen men, with a 'Yo-heave,' set the car on its wheels again.

When we came home, past the long line of Apalachinites and strangers stretched out along the roadside to see us pass, last of all was the tramp. As we came by, he saluted and I knew he had been a soldier. Alan looked at us in amazement when we drove into the home yard. We had started out so gaily in the morning. Now we looked so queer and bedraggled with the top out of the car and felt so incredibly silly.

It was at about this time that a friend of ours in Memphis, Tennessee, when calling on a lady, saw a volume of Gene's on her library table. He smiled and said, 'That man is a friend of mine.' She replied: 'He is a friend of mine, too. He autographed the book for me.' Our friend turned to the page. 'That is not Gene Rhodes's writing! I know it as well as I know my own.' 'Oh, yes, it is,' she stoutly averred.

It seemed that a man was impersonating Gene. He autographed books, he did all sorts of things; he even gave lectures. Gene said if he could send his bills to this impostor and have him pay them, he wouldn't put up much of a kick. In a letter from Memphis, Tennessee:

> *Dear Gene:*
>
> Several days ago Doctor Aikman picked up your book — *Good Men and True* — and remarked that he knew the author very well. I told him he must be mis-

> taken as he lives in the West. He said no, he had been in Natchez off and on for four years and that he called himself Doctor Holmes. Doctor Aikman's description of the man did not tally with yours at all, except in characteristics. He would tell Doctor Aikman of certain articles that were coming out in *The Saturday Evening Post*, and sure enough they would appear. Something queer about it, don't you think? Mr. Griffen, who has a room here, tells me the same thing about the man. Mr. Griffen is the editor of the *Evening News* and has been very much interested in this man ever since he knew him.

The following letter was to our friend from an acquaintance.

> Did sister tell you about the man that claims to be Eugene Rhodes? It is the most amusing thing I ever heard of. It must be some relative, possibly a half brother. Doctor Aikman has been so interested in finding out, for he says this man is rather clever, but he is dark and rather stout, and as I remember Mr. Rhodes he was slender and rather blond.
>
> Now if you have been masquerading around through the South under the cognomen of Doctor Holmes I want to know something about it. If not, there is a mystery here, and I am all the more interested, so let me hear from you about it.

The mystery was never solved. Gene never succeeded in unmasking this man. He died finally, we were told. Whether he was buried under the name of Eugene Manlove Rhodes or Doctor Holmes is something we shall never know.

Late the next summer we packed a few things and

stored them in the granary, scattered the rest of our belongings to the four winds of heaven, loaded our Hupmobile touring car right to the roof, and started for New Mexico. It wrung my heart unutterably to leave my beloved homeland, but I had told Gene that when Mother and Father were gone he could do the deciding on our future home. He had been so fine to let me look after them all those years.

Among the things that went with us in the car was an especially nice copper tea kettle. By some means we lost it. Often, even after we came to California, Gene would look up from his book and say with a sob in his voice, 'I ho-ope our tea kettle is happy.'

CHAPTER XII

Santa Fe and Tesuque

We were at last on our way back to New Mexico. A friend sent us a copy of the *Santa Fe New Mexican*, on the editorial page of which we read, 'Sante Fe is waiting to welcome Eugene Manlove Rhodes.' Instead of the expensive car such a tribute called for, with a second car perhaps for the maid and valet and luggage, it was a very travel-worn and mud-spattered equipage that drove up to the entrance of the De Vargas Hotel on October 12, 1926. And just as I stepped out, my stocking supporter broke. I challenge anybody to enter a fashionable hotel with 'the haughty calm that marks the cast of Vere de Vere,' with a dangling stocking supporter.

Our first guest was N. Howard Thorpe, wearing a ten-gallon hat; a most picturesque figure, tall and graceful. In his collection of old cowboy songs and some poems he had himself written, was

WHAT'S BECOME OF THE PUNCHERS?

What's become of the punchers
  We rode with long ago?
The hundreds and hundreds of cowboys
  We all of us used to know?

Sure, some were killed by lightning
Some when the cattle run,
Others were killed by horses
And some with the old six-gun.

. . . .

Gene Rhodes is among the highbrows
A-writin' up the West,
But I know a lot of doin's
That he never has confessed.

He used to ride 'em keerless
In the good old days
When we both worked together
In the San Andres.

Building big loops we called 'blockers,'
Spinning the rope in the air,
Never a cent in our pockets,
But what did a cow puncher care?

Gene was indifferent in just that way. He said he didn't care for money, and I can readily believe it. We were always up to our necks in debt. But then, I don't believe men worry about debt as women do. Back in Apalachin one of the denizens once said: 'I guess Gene must be broke. I heard him singing when he came down the street this morning.'

N. Howard interested his friend, Kate Chapman, in our case and we were speedily settled in Acequia Madre Street in a quaint little house built of the blinds from a big hotel, with roofing paper covering them — a black house, trimmed with blue shutters. But Gene had never lived in Sante Fe and it hadn't the same pull on his emotions that southern New Mexico had. Furthermore, he was constantly tormented with bronchitis, even in that sunny country, for Sante Fe and later Tesuque were sometimes snowy and slushy. The specialist he consulted gave practically no medicine but prescribed a diet and setting up exercises. In no time at all, the cough was under control.

Alice Corbin Henderson took us out to Tesuque to see her daughter's house, which we rented for the winter. It was the most palatial place I have ever lived in. On the way out Alice chanced to ask Gene if he had ever been in Santa Fe before.

'No, but they once tried to make a permanent resident of me.'

Then he told the story of the night when he, unarmed, had been held up by five or six men, all armed. Gene had jumped from the buckboard out on them, snatched a gun from one, and turned the tables on them. The five men swore out a warrant for him. But the Judge who heard the evidence (although he was Gene's political enemy) rendered judgment: 'These accusations are so palpably false that I have no choice but to let this prisoner go free.' Gene walked out of the courtroom and did not see the Judge again till we met him in Santa Fe. Dear old Judge McFee, of whom Gene said that he prayed as if he knew the Lord intimately.

Old and new friends came to visit us at Tesuque. Mary Austin came, bringing little Christmas cakes made after a recipe kept for generations in her family. She and Gene were speakers at the Old Palace Museum and had both seen their early stories published in *Out West*.

Doctor Lummis, too, came, saw the charming studio in the house, and stayed to work. Tanned and tall, a clever performer on his guitar, a splendid singer of the old Spanish songs, hundreds of them, he might have been a gypsy. The Indians all but worshiped him. His encouraging words when Gene first started writing, 'There is red blood in this,' we had never forgotten.

Gene regarded Doctor Lummis with veneration. Nevertheless, when at one of Doctor Lummis's parties, to which celebrities from all over the world were invited, Gene was asked to write in the guest book, Gene wrote at the bottom of the right-hand page, 'All I have and all I am I owe to . . .,' and looking up impishly into the face of the man who had set his feet on the literary path, turned the page and wrote, 'my creditors.'

In the early days of our correspondence, Gene had written me of his visit to Doctor Lummis's remarkable house in Los Angeles. At Gene's knock, the distinguished man had leaned out of the window of his upstairs study and shouted: 'Who are you? I think I can lick you, whoever you are.'

There could have been no more promising introduction for Gene. He took him to the splendid library, formally presented the books, and left. 'You can read all you want to. I have some work which must be done.'

They sat there for several days, Gene silent among the books, abroad on trips to Arabia and Spain. That was the beginning of a friendship which was to be forever unbroken. There was little difference in their ages, but Gene said Lummis had the older soul, filling a place in Gene's life midway between the experienced uncle and the beloved elder brother. When Gene had brought out his first book, Doctor Lummis wrote to him:

> You have done a very extraordinary thing. Very uneven, in places hazy. Not entirely pulled together in a final Drawstring. A novel made up of episodes. But you have made the Best talking book that ever came out of the mouth of the West. The language they use on occasion is frequent and painful and free.... And to my surprise you have some Desirable ladies.
>
> ...I often think back to the times I rapped your knuckles for doing just what you do now. I never saw any work of yours I didn't admire. I never saw any of it that I didn't want to kick you for not doing it better as you are perfectly competent to do.
>
> ...I have enjoyed this book as few in many years.

When a friend of Gene's from the old days, a former governor's wife, Mrs. McDonald, a widow now, came alone to Sante Fe to attend the inauguration ceremonies for Governor Dillon, we wanted to entertain her. We had a very small party indeed. My table linen, which was nice enough to do honor even to this lady, was back in my trunk in New York. Not being overburdened with money, I bought a cheap coarse tablecloth and paper napkins. The guests were all such thoroughbreds that if they were aghast at my napery, they disguised it beautifully. Gene rather emphasized his attentions to Mrs. McDonald's niece, as he often did to the young and lovely. The aunt smiled and said, 'I notice when they reach Gene's age, they get sort of doddering!'

Gene was extremely susceptible. He had a 'waiting

list' of twenty-five or so to step into my shoes in case of my demise. Whenever he met an extremely attractive woman, he asked her if she didn't want to be put on the waiting list. Of course, she always did. A very dear friend of mine who occupied third place on the list died, and he very promptly moved Betty Russell, a former editor of *Scribner's*, up to third place. I told him it wasn't honorable, but he didn't care. In a grave moment one day he said, 'I have never had a woman listed for second place.' 'Why not?' I inquired. 'Because you occupy that as well as first place. There would never be another.'

After Betty Russell went home, she sent me a package marked POISON! I was at the dinner table when Gene came in with it. I quite trembled. 'Do-o you think I should u-undo this?' I took off the string and found a box of mixed flower seeds for my flower garden.

Gene was irresistible. He was like some cajoling small boy always bidding for attention. If you would say to someone in his presence, 'Poor George!' he would instantly look woeful and say: 'I want to be felt sorry for. I feel bad.' You would have to be more than human not to have patted that coaxing head. Oh, yes, how could they not have loved him?

The Theodore Von Soelens were often guests at El Cuervo, 'The Crow's Nest,' as our Tesuque ranch was called. Mr. Von Soelen came one day alone, saying that his wife was ill. It so happened that an old Mexican woman who lived on the other side of us was sick at about the same time. Gene suggested that I send the poor thing something to eat, a proposition to which I readily agreed. I sent Gene to town for oysters to make stew. It was a snowy day, and almost night when he came back with the oysters. I quickly made the soup, and thinking that the poor soul probably wouldn't have any crackers, I cut a Quaker Oats carton in half and filled it. The soup I put in a lard pail and sent Gene off with it, telling him to hurry home for supper was ready. He asked if he should take the car, to which I answered, 'Good heavens, what for?' I waited and waited and waited, finally concluding he had met someone to talk to. After such a long time he came in wearily.

'They were not home. They had gone in to the Apache Club for dinner.'

'Who?' I gasped.

'The Von Soelens.'

'You don't mean to tell me you took that soup to them! I made it for the old Mexican woman.'

We were stupefied and then began to laugh till the tears ran down our cheeks.

'Don't ever tell them!'

I agreed not to, but it was too good to keep and in the end he told them himself.

We had been in Sante Fe only a short time when Gene decided to go to see his brother Clarence, who had a ranch at Mesquite after practically a lifetime in old Mexico, where he had superintended a silver mine. So eager was Gene to see Clarence that we went down by way of the dreaded La Bajada Hill.

It was mid-afternoon when we reached their home. Gene's sister-in-law, Jessie, came out. He kissed her. Neither she nor Clarence had seen Gene for twenty years or so; he had changed and was wearing a Vandyke beard, which would disguise anyone.

'Don't you know me?' he asked.

'No-o-o —'

He looked at her accusingly. 'Do you let all the strange men you meet kiss you?'

'Gene!' she shouted, and kissed him again.

Clarence had cotton-pickers at work in the field to which Gene's nephew Hinman took him.

'Dad, here is another man wants to hire out.'

Without looking up, Clarence answered, 'All right, I'll take him on.'

After a delightful visit, Gene's restless foot began itching again and we were back on the road, a few days after we had come to Mesquite. Jessie killed two chickens for dinner the day Gene decided to go, but even that couldn't induce him to stay. She then cut out all the white meat and livers and gave it to us, with a big lump of butter to fry it in, and we camped on the desert for dinner. A mesquite fire, coffee, and chicken fried over the mesquite coals, what delight that was! Gene hardly tasted it. Something he had eaten disagreed with him and he had an attack of ptomaine poisoning.

On the way home we circled around to Tularosa. A scene of desolation met us. The magnificent cottonwoods, centuries old, in the shade of whose interlacing branches Gene and I used to ride, had all been cut down. Lombardy poplars had been planted in their stead, but what good would Lombardy poplars do in that sun-baked desert?

Back in our beautiful house in Tesuque, Gene began work on *The Hired Man on Horseback.* On our trip from Mesquite, we had seen Fred Crosby, superintendent of stock at the Mescalero Reservation, riding along the horizon, erect in his saddle. He had been foreman of the Bar Cross, and Gene had worked for him four months getting wild cattle out of the mountain brush, such rough country that the cattle company didn't even gather them all, fearing some of the cowboys would be killed. Gene had the superb Crosby in mind when he wrote his poem.

It was his vindication of the cowboy, flung in the teeth of a world that dared to belittle his beloved cowboy. Gene's romance was there, a great deal of his philosophy. I can see him in almost every line of it. No better description of his romantic years will ever be written than

> Merry eyes and tender eyes, dark head and bright . . .
>
> Doggerel upon his lips and valor in his heart . . .
>
> The hired man on horseback goes laughing to his work . . .
>
> The hired man on horseback has raised the rebel yell . . .

Its publication brought out a storm of cheers and protests. I think it caused more excitement than anything else he ever wrote.

CHAPTER XIII

Champion of the West

When you are near an object, it is easy to be blinded to its outstanding qualities. I am giving you William MacLeod Raine's description of Gene as he wrote it for *The Student Writer*.

> Over the telephone a voice came to me, one with a note of whimsical gaiety in it. (Where had I heard that voice before?)
>
> '... Eugene Manlove Rhodes talking. At the Oxford Hotel ... I'll be in the lobby. You'll know me because I'm wearing a sombrero, and I'll have my hands in my own pockets.'
>
> (I knew now where I had listened to that voice — in *Good Men and True*, in *Bransford in Arcadia*, in *Copper Streak Trail*, in a lot of *Saturday Evening Post* short stories.)
>
> I would have known him even without the identification tag he had given me, for Rhodes is like the stuff he writes. It is an extension of his personality, so to say. He is whimsical, original, full of a certain philosophic but kindly faith in human nature. When you read his books you know him. When you read his letters you know him better....
>
> Slender, gray, a bit of a dreamer, with eyes that warm easily to humor and appreciation: that is the impression

one gets of Rhodes across the table at lunch. He is quite unconventional and therefore full of good copy, none of which he ever uses for press-agenting. That would seem to him cheap and would be wholly out of character....

Rhodes began to write because of indignation. He loved the West, and he resented it that the East was taking seriously Alfred Henry Lewis's burlesques of Wolfville. His corner of New Mexico — between White Oaks and Tularosa — was a poor strip of ground, but it was rich in men. Range foremen, outlaws, sheriffs, legislators, successful merchants, crack ropers, and riders developed here. When New Mexico became a state, the first governor, the first congressman, and one of the first United States senators came from this small section. It bred leaders. He felt the urge to tell the world about it. So he wrote.

You feel in Rhodes's writing that he is wholly a democrat. He looks inside to see what a man is. The things he has added to himself — stocks and bonds and farms and city blocks — are not of the least importance. Social standing is nothing. All he cares for is that essential quality that makes the man.

The only thing of which Rhodes is intolerant is intolerance. He is generous to his fellow writers. In his letters and in talk he is always ready with his hearty 'good stuff.' Nobody reads other Western writers more appreciatively than he does. Owen Wister, Emerson Hough, Kenneth Harris, Stewart Edward White, George Patullo, Peter B. Kyne, William R. Lighton, H. H. Knibbs, and B. M. Bowers — he finds them all true craftsmen in depicting the country they write about. Some novelists of the West he does not care for. He does not say so. He just does not talk much about them.

'All those chaps wrote about the country they knew,' he commented. 'And all of them represented the cowman as extraordinarily efficient because he did his own thinking and lived by no formula.' He added, presently: 'The cowmen were all alike in this, that each was entirely different from others. Each was an individual, a real person.'

Talking with Rhodes one gets the animating spirit back of his work. The West was not only a land of splendid hazard. It was that, plus the spirit of unconquerable youth. Each day was a *new day*. Every sunset was something to marvel at. For this was the most engaging planet in which the range rider had ever been a dweller. In those days when the shining antelope flitted through the sagebrush the man in chaps lived in the Youth of the World.

We came in time to the important question. How do you do it?

'I do it in the worst way in the world,' Rhodes answered. 'If I tell you how it is only that young writers may use me as a dreadful example. I mill over my stories a long time. They take form in my mind — characters, settings, and incidents. The whole story is in my brain, complete, finished, before I begin the first chapter. Every incident of the plot is there. Tell the youngsters not to do as I do. It's a wearing business — like playing chess in your head without a board to look at.'

'You don't mean that you don't make any notes during this period of incubation?'

'Oh, no; I make notes. Lots of 'em. I paste 'em up over the room in more or less orderly sequence. By the way, here's a mechanical detail that might be worth while. I use different colored paper — always in neutral tints that won't be hard on the eyes — to show whether my notes are the first, second, third, or twelfth draft of the story. By that means I don't get them mixed.'

'What do you mean — twelfth draft?'

'I work my stuff over and over. I write it and rewrite it and write it again before it goes to the stenographer.'

'You're not a rapid writer, then?'

'No-o, though I have worked rapidly under pressure,' Rhodes said. 'I suppose it takes me about eight months to do a novel, working nine hours a day. Yes, those are long hours — too long. If the stuff works out right I do about twelve hundred words a day.'

'Your characters — are they tractable? Do they stay where they are put?'

'They do not. A minor character will begin to take the whole show away from the chief ones. Then another will become obtrusive. You see, the star system doesn't obtain on the range. It does not play favorites. A man holds about the place to which his abilities entitle him.'

'You take your characters from life?'

'About fifty per cent of the characters in my stories are real. Some, of course, are compositions. Pringle is an imagined character; that is, I did not have anyone distinctly in mind when I conceived him.'

'Any suggestions for young writers?'

'They ought to know what they are talking about — ought to know intimately and closely. A piece of work can't be authentic unless it has this background of knowledge. Nothing else will take its place.'

'Imagination?' I hazarded.

'Imagination has to have something to work on — practice and definite information.' Rhodes offered one more suggestion. 'It's a good thing for a writer — old or young, it doesn't matter — to read his stuff aloud, both to himself and others. We're both eye-minded and ear-minded. The ear catches repeated words that the eye misses. It detects stilted and still phraseology. You discover that you are overplaying or underplaying a situation. Besides, you get another point of view, one more detached from the product.'

To his friend, Professor Walter Webb of the History Department, University of Texas, Gene expressed his theory of writing. 'The way to write is to do so. When you have something to say and say it your own way, you are getting somewhere. Hints from old hands — or better still, hints from disinterested readers — may give you useful points about what *not* to say and how *not* to say it. But the affirmative part is your own. I am firmly convinced that my life has been shortened, my sunny disposition spoiled, and both stomach and brain made prey to indigestion through reading — and making suggestions upon literally thousands of scripts. Some few of these people arrived — but most didn't. For those few it was a pleasure — and for the others simply undiluted hell....

'The only advice to beginners which seems to bear the acid tests is this. Read your story aloud three times. Once to yourself. You will find errors of omission and commission that way which might otherwise escape you, particularly the stiff, the stilted, and the hifalutin. Next, read aloud, always aloud, to a sympathetic auditor, who will make helpful suggestions. Last, read aloud or have it read aloud to you by someone who is either hostile or indifferent to your point of view. Indifferent is best. That will bring out the faults, if any. Better still, it will show if you have not made your premises and statements clear. In stories with a Western setting, most particularly, there are conditions which are so much a matter of course to you that we forget to state them, whereas the non-Western reader has no idea of anything of the sort.'

Of all Gene's novels, in his own judgment *Stepsons of Light* was the favorite. 'I have a wistful feeling toward that book that I have not for the others, probably because it owes little to fancy, being nearer to history than to fiction or autobiography.' He earned that mild but lasting enmity of Jody Weir, who lived near us in Santa Fe, for the incident in the first chapter of that book happened just as recorded and in exactly the place named.

In spite of the success of his novels, Gene's own preference was for his short stories. That he could not have them published in book form was a source of lasting disappointment to him. In 1926 he wrote to Houghton Mifflin Company, who had been publishing his work for four years: 'I will never deny that it is a bruise to me, learning that a book of short stories (not about degenerates or imbeciles) hasn't a Chinaman's chance in These States. My sorrow is largely for myself, who am no novelist at all, but just a teller of tales ... the longer my stories the poorer they are, for indeed I have a great gift at the omitting' — to cut out 'the gauze and effect,' as he phrased it.

Gene had a remarkably clean mind. I don't remember ever hearing him tell a risqué story. He liked books along these lines, and was proud to have for his publishers a firm that through all this avalanche of literary filth, had put out not even one book that was off-color. His own were straight. 'A good story,' he said of 'Tie Fast Men' which *Cosmopolitan* published, 'but probably not a popular one. Can't help it, but only one seduction in the story.' He used his stories as a means of getting his ethics of honor and loyalty and courage across to the reader. He used one historical character in every story, he wrote a friend, like a tuning-fork — to chord the rest of the story.

I think perhaps he made a sort of lost knight over yonder, straying from one sleeveless adventure to another, looking wistfully upon first one lovely lady in distress and then another. Gene always had a romantic regard for the opposite sex, irrespective of her station in life or her morality. Alex McLaren witnessed the following characteristic episode. It was at the time when the 'Fatty' Arbuckle scandal was the universal topic. Gene was playing pool next to a table where several hard-looking characters were lounging. One of the roughnecks made an exceedingly ugly remark about Virginia Rappe. Dropping his cue to the floor, Gene settled his piercing eyes on the speaker.

'I don't like to hear a man make a remark like that about any woman,' Gene said quietly and evenly. 'The girl is dead. It is the hour of her funeral.'

'What d'yuh aim doin' about it, Dad?' the roughneck snarled.

'My first suggestion is that you take back what you said.'

'I don't take back anything I ever said about any damn floosie. What do you think of that?'

For answer, Gene gathered up a handful of pool balls and turned them loose with devastating accuracy. When Gene thought he was in the right, as he generally was, he was never slow in backing up his convictions.

After all, Gene understood the women. 'Reflections upon womankind always stir up trouble. Lots of the flappers — most of the flappers — are only doing what the sixteen-year-old boy used to do when he tied a plow-handle Colt forty-five low down on his thigh. Imitating and "showing off."'

Privately, he preferred real humor. He delighted in concocting quaint and amusing keynotes to his chapters, quoted from works that were also drawn from his imagination:

> 'Money was so scarce in that country that the babies had to cut their teeth on certified checks.' — *Bluebeard for Happiness*
>
> 'A fine face, marred by an expression of unscrupulous integrity.' — *Credit Lost*

And he disliked having his characters misunderstood. His Jeb Rider of 'The Tie Fast Men' was not a 'bad man' as the editors made him, but a 'lost dog.'

True to his democracy and his sense of fairness he defended the underdog in literature and life. The Mexican, for instance. 'Since the days of the Invincible

Armada, the English have been drilled, from the cradle on, to hate and fear and despise the Spanish. In the English novel, the Spaniard is the villain ex officio. Failing the Spaniard, the villain must be a man with dark complexion and good teeth.

'In this country, the Mexican has fallen heir to this race prejudice. The Mexican in our novels is a man of straw: not only a scoundrel, but a stupid and feckless scoundrel, sure to be outwitted, outfought, and foiled by any blond in the book.... The people who write this tosh know nothing about Mexicans.... The Mexican has his faults, like the people in forty-seven of our own states: but, generally speaking, he is hospitable, courteous, frugal, hardy, proud, uninventive, generous, gay-hearted, unthrifty, unindustrious, liberty-loving, cheerful, patient, and brave.'

On our drives past the State Penitentiary, we always sailed by quickly. Gene did not want to visit it for he was dead sure that he would know some of the men there, and he would have grieved to see them shut up there, away from the life they loved. For all his stern code of law-abiding he had a soft spot in his heart for men who had taken the high trail. Many an outlaw had he sheltered and warmed and fed in the old days. One of my early experiences when I first went to Tularosa was Gene's giving aid and shelter to one of his cowboys who had made a misstep. The youth was 'hiding out' in the White Sands. Gene sent a horse by another cowboy to bring him back to our place. A strong wind was blowing from him to the horseman.

The sand was blowing so he couldn't see if it was friend or foe. He shot and ran from bush to bush for shelter, and shot again. The rescuer nearly lost his voice shouting to him to stop shooting. He finally reached him. The young outlaw stayed out in the orchard below the house where he could watch the road the sheriff would travel.

With the same faithfulness and with more fervor, Gene defended those who carried out their duties as law-enforcers. Such was his defence of Pat Garrett. True, Pat had been on Gene's trail for a minor offense. More significantly, Pat was of the opposite political party in the days when Las Cruces was divided so sharply that Republicans walked on one side of the street and Democrats on the other, while one of the judges insisted that his wife accompany him when he went from district to district as a protection against shooting.

Miss Elizabeth Garrett, blind daughter of the sheriff and singer of note, was as ardent an admirer of Gene, as her father had been his political enemy. For her sake and that of justice, Gene took up the cudgels for Pat in answer to criticism of him resulting from Walter Noble Burns's interpretation of the story in *The Saga of Billy the Kid*. Before the Woman's Club and the Kiwanis Club Gene spoke in justification of Garrett's killing of Billy. Gene's 'In Defense of Pat Garrett' appeared in *Sunset Magazine* for September, 1927.

It was a magnificent defense.

'If you have not read *The Saga of Billy the Kid* by

Walter Noble Burns I hope you do. The book is written with color, fire, and charm: the tragic events it chronicles are of surpassing interest. If it were a novel, it would command my unstinted praise. As history, it is misleading.' Then Gene went on to show, first, that Mr. Burns had evidence from one side more than from the other. He spent much time with the Coes who fought with Billy the Kid; he did not talk to Sheriff Brady's son to ask the circumstances of Brady's murder by the Kid. Gene admitted that he thought Billy the Kid had fought on the right side in the Lincoln County War of 1878, about which the truth will never be known in entirety, but when the amnesty was granted the fighters by Governor Lew Wallace, Billy the Kid deliberately chose a life of outlawry. He murdered unarmed men. Taken into custody and chained to his guards, he filed the irons and killed the officers. His capture by Garrett was part of an earnest program of enforcement to which the new sheriff had pledged himself. When the Kid suddenly appeared on the porch of the house where Maxwell was sheltering him and found Pat Garrett there questioning his host, it was a matter of who should shoot first. Had not Garrett fired, he would have been killed.

True, as Burns had stated, that Garrett and Billy the Kid had been friends. They had, at least, known each other. Gene, himself, admitted knowing many outlaws, for reasons generous or astute. But the decision between the law and the outlaw was as fair as such fight could be. In Gene's opinion, Walter Burns had been carried away by his enthusiasm for the subject of his biography.

While preparing 'In Defense of Pat Garrett,' Gene had reason to think that Burns's date for the capture of O'Folliard and Billy the Kid on Christmas Eve was wrong. After forty-seven years, he remembered it as December 21, without the sentimental appeal of the former. In confirmation came a letter from Jim East who had been with the Texans 'bringing the law to Pecos.'

> I could not find a single man to confirm my memory and there was not a newspaper of December 1880 left in any newspaper office in New Mexico. But I remembered it as December 21 — after 47 years! Now comes this letter from East — the last survivor and he says my memory is right.
>
> From this you [he was writing to his Boston publisher] will get my private problem — which is at once a trial and a satisfaction. Every line I write is written for two audiences — the casual and highly hypothetical reader, and the oldtimers, the eye-witnesses, who instantly detect the slightest divergence from the facts. If my psychology isn't in straight (but it is) I hear from them. If a single strap buckle or byword was not au fait and okey — I'd hear from them. You bet. So I have my private consolation when the New York Critic describes *Stepsons* as a 'typical navy league novel.' Omigosh, I wonder what a navy league novel is....
>
> From East's letter and mine you get a glimpse behind the scenes. The legends of New England, New York, Virginia — you know them. Miles Standish, Ethan Allen, Paul Revere, Sir William Johnson, Walter Butler, Noah and Jonah and Captain John Smith. Well —

we have a carefully graded hierarchy of our own — of which the East knows nothing, not because they were not notable men, but because they were not in the Fourth Reader.

As for Pat Garrett — he was for us what Hector was to Troy. But there are hundreds of others of whom the East has never heard and will never hear. We remember Adobe Wells as you do Ticonderoga or Braddock's Defeat. We have three memories where you have but two; that we remember Quanah Parker as well as King Philip and Tecumseh makes us but so much richer.

CHAPTER XIV

Native's Return

GENE'S longings for his own part of New Mexico increased. When summer was upon us, we yielded to the call, boxed our possessions, and shipped them to Alamogordo. We travelled along in our car.

The first night we stopped at an auto camp in Carrizozo. The rough board door of our primitive cabin fastened outside with a hasp. Our simple supper over, Gene went in search of some of the oldtimers. After a few minutes, I decided to follow him only to find myself a prisoner, locked in from the outside. It was nearly daylight when he returned, deeply chagrined to find out what he had done. I told Mrs. Crosby, the wife of the Hired Man on Horseback, about this episode. She matched it. Gene had come to their ranch once and stayed overnight. She put him up a lunch in the morning. (He told me he sat down and ate it all as soon as he was out of sight of the house. He didn't want to bother with lunches.) Taking her water pail, she was about to start out for the arroyo. Stopped at the door! It was hooked on the outside. She didn't know what in the world to do. The men were gone and might not get back until the next day. But she solved the problem by climbing up on her table and cutting the screen from a window. She probably had a long wait for a new screen.

When we reached Tularosa we were bitterly reproached for not settling there. Gene explained that cutting down the cottonwoods had settled that. We were going on to Alamogordo. Once there, we rented a newly painted and papered, tiny house on the corner opposite the mansion of Gene's friend, Oliver Lee.

Living in a furnished house, I longed for something of my own. In salvation, the ladies of the town arranged a rummage sale to which I was invited as a clerk. Among the items contributed was a small dressing table with a mahogany framed mirror with the frame scorched by a candle flame. It had been brought across the plains in a covered wagon and had been given by the granddaughter of the pioneer woman who had brought it. I bought it. At last I had something of my own. How I loved it. It was stolen from our New Mexican house after we left there.

One of our favorite pastimes was to drive down to see the express from the East come in, playing that our son Alan was on board. We would watch the Pullman crowds anxiously, telling ourselves that it would be dreadful to see him descend from a second-class coach. We were not expecting him and wouldn't have cared what part of the train he had come on, should he arrive. Then, before I had unpacked our trunks and boxes, Alan came — late at night, in his car. He had broken a spring and had it chained together. It was a feat to go through the sand dunes around Oro Grande in the daylight, but he had accomplished it at night. Naturally his father was downtown and saw him first. There was no gauging my happiness. His father helped him to get a job with the Highway Department and we settled down contentedly.

Gene was writing one evening when we heard a small voice at the door. Gene opened it and the most wretched black kitten 'just elbowed his way in.' One eye was dug out, the other was ailing, and his poor little backbone all but stuck through the skin. We fed this unhappy mite and washed his eye with boracic acid. He sat bolt upright on a chair beside Gene the whole night through. That settled that. He was Gene's cat. He was baptized Henry Clay. Henry grew fat, rolypoly, and playful. We fed him fresh steak; nothing else would he eat. When Mrs. Lee gave us a beautiful young white turkey from her ranch for our Christmas dinner, we all looked forward to seeing Henry revel in the bones. Would he? He would not even taste them!

Gene was writing a story, but even with Henry Clay's help he was going very slowly. Thinking to inspire him to quicker work, I suggested that we go camping in the San Andres, Gene's favorite haunt, whenever the story was finished. It was all to no avail. The offer was made in October, but it was December before the story was finished and sent away.

Then, to my intense surprise, Gene announced one morning that we were going to the mountains. We rolled up our camp bed and took the camp kit and departed. After we had driven through Tularosa, the wind came up and the day turned cold and disagreeable. It was a great relief when we entered Gene's cañon out of the stinging blow. We had an old-fashioned open touring car but practically never used the side curtains, for their flapping annoyed Gene exceedingly. We stopped to camp in a clump of trees on the Lenox place, where Gene had once pastured stock but which he had not homesteaded. Mr. Lenox had bored for water and, as a result, had a place ornamented with orchard and flower garden. We drove up to the house to announce ourselves. An attractive young woman was there alone. A loaded six-shooter lay on the library table.

That night after we had let down the driver's seat in the car, stretched a tarp over the entire top to shut out the wind more or less successfully, and had made up our bed, we heard hoofbeats and a man on a beautiful black horse rode into the circle of the firelight, introduced himself as Louis Lenox, and said he had come to take us over to his house. We went with him, just to spend the evening, but the warmth from the huge fireplace, which must have held nearly a cord of wood, and the constant stream of cowboy stories made us drowsy. In the end, we stayed overnight, tucked under a feather bed while outside the wind was howling with even greater fury. In the morning when we went over to our car, even our African water bag was frozen solid. We started back immediately for our home fire and the smile of Henry Clay.

In April, next spring, we drove to Roswell to see Major Fulton of the Military Academy, who wanted

Gene to meet a pioneer woman. The month of March is usually a period of sandstorms, but this year New Mexico waited 'to do herself proud' in April. The wind blew so that I couldn't keep my hat on. I stopped at the Agency store at Mescalero to get some elastic. When they had none, I asked in desperation for a pair of shoestrings and some safety pins. But no pins were to be had, until the storekeeper's wife came to my rescue. I pinned on the shoestrings, tied them securely under my chin, and 'let the hurricane roar.'

As we came down a long mountain road leading to Roswell in the distance, a huge cylinder of dust appeared on the horizon, rolled swiftly toward the city, swept through it, and vanished, only to be followed by another and another in a seemingly endless parade. It was through storms like this that Gene had once gone hunting for cattle and horses, interminable miles.

In Roswell Gene talked over her experiences with the pioneer woman, who took us to see a Mexican who had gone with Chisholm on one of the first cattle drives. He spoke no English, but she acted as interpreter. The poor old man put out his hands, the palms of which were drawn together where the Indians had tortured him. He told about being with his mother in a house near the Rio Grande when the attack had come. She told him he was small and might be able to get away, if he went alone.

'Then she kissed me and made the sign of the cross on me, and blessed me. I never saw her again,' the old man said.

All the misfortunes that could come to a mortal had come to him, but he smiled bravely, held out his shriveled hands, and said that nothing could harm him, for his mother had made the sign of the cross and blessed him.

Weather conditions made it urgent for us to start home at once. We got up at five o'clock in the morning to cross the Staked Plains before the wind came up. When we reached the mountains we met sleet and nearly froze. Then the road dropped down from the White Mountain into the balmy air of Tularosa basin. On our window sills when we arrived home, we found drifts of white sand from the White Sands eighteen miles away.

Alan drove back to New York in June, 1928, with me as passenger for a two weeks' visit. 'Hick' Haynes, who had a ranch out of Alamogordo, invited Gene to stay with him. He had a man cook who would see that Gene as well as I had a vacation. But Gene elected to stay at home. He was lonesome, didn't eat as he should, and cut out smoking, he who had always smoked incessantly. On Sunday morning, when I was still en route to New York, he had a violent attack of enlargement of the heart that all but carried him away. He had been out on the porch at the time and noticed by the iceman who lived down the street. When this friend found him, he rushed for a doctor, only to find none in town. But the superintendent of the hospital came immediately to administer two hypodermics of strychnine. She told me that his heart wasn't even beating, that it was enlarged until it filled the entire cavity and was quivering like jelly.

Mr. and Mrs. Edmond Lewis took care of Gene, even to obeying his instructions that I should not be informed and alarmed. All unknowing, I wrote and asked if it would be all right to stay another week to wait for a friend who was going to Vancouver and could accompany me part way back. When I did come back, Gene was at the station to meet me and the dreadful news was not told until later.

We had planned a trip over the state to collect first-hand material for the 'Old-Timer' book which Gene and Clem Hightower were to write and Houghton Mifflin Company publish. We felt we had to go on the trip, although the doctor warned that Gene would die. My only answer to that was that he would die if he stayed there where it was hot and breathless, and where even Henry Clay was gone. We had found our poor kitty dead under the porch. Only the faint interest in the camping trip kept Gene's spirits flickering.

So began a long journey to visit and interview. We went first to see Judge Fall at Three Rivers, in whose defense Gene later planned the last chapter of his book. Then on to Socorro, once hangout of desperadoes. On the way it began to rain and the newly paved road became slippery as molasses. Seven cars went in the ditch, including ours. When Gene tried to chop some small brush to put under the wheels, his heart protested and I had quickly to put a drop of nitroglycerine on his tongue as the doctor had instructed me. After the rain stopped, we were started on our way with some slight help from another driver. It seems that nowadays it is always everyone for himself in such a crisis, even in New Mexico. But it was never that way in the old times, Gene used to say. Another few miles and misfortune was still dogging us. A rear spring slipped and acted as a brake to stop the car. It was a tired and hungry pair who were finally towed into Socorro.

We started along the dimly lighted streets to find a place to eat. Gene shouted to a group of men sitting on a bench some distance from the sidewalk and a surprised voice answered:

'Gene Rhodes, or I'm a sinner!'

It was N. Howard Thorpe. He piloted us about during our stay, even showing us several desirable pieces of property. I confess I would have liked to have settled there, but Gene said he detested the place. He had seen a man stamped to death in front of the post office and it had spoiled the place for him entirely.

From Socorro we went on a-visiting. Among the people we saw were the Ottamon Stephenses, whose new books, heaped on the floor, Gene eyed wistfully. Mrs. Stephens told me some of her experiences when she came, a cultured young English girl, to the frontier where her husband spent much of his time away, hunting and trapping. She looked out her window one time to see a band of Indians in paint and war bonnets galloping their ponies down over the hill. They came to her door, which she opened. She dared not do otherwise. A big Indian pushed her to one side and strode noiselessly into the room. The Stephenses numbered among their possessions an old-fashioned music box that was played by turning a crank. He motioned to that and she understood that he wanted her to play it. She played all the records and thought, 'Now they will kill me.' Instead they grunted and moved from the room. The last Indian to go handed her a handsome Indian bracelet. They were on their way to some Indian festivities and not on the warpath as she had thought.

After our trip, Gene lost his putty-colored complexion and looked himself again. Just in time, too, for our landlord wanted to rent our house to a school-teacher's family and we had to load our possessions to move — on three days' notice. We went over to the Rock House at Three Rivers which the Falls had offered to us when we last saw them.

The Rock House was known the country over. It had been owned by Mrs. McSween Barber, whose husband, McSween, had been shot in the Lincoln County War. She figured in Emerson Hough's *Outlaws*. The Jim Nabours in Hough's *North of '36* had lived in a house now mostly in ruins below Rock House. In the ravine back of our house stood Mrs. McSween's cookhouse, which I used as a laundry, although the entire wall facing the ravine was gone. Rock House itself was built of hewn stone, had monstrously large rooms — the living-room, for example, thirty feet long — enormous fireplaces, and wide windows that looked out directly over the rocky and rugged majesty of the White Mountain.

The doctor had told Gene he could never ride again, never do another day's work, and many other 'nevers.' Whereupon Gene began to clean the tumbleweeds and dead leaves out of the concrete ditch that brought water to the house. It was a mile long. He rode horseback. He was as good as new.

But that winter we both had the flu in the Rock House, a real adventure. 'The wind was blowing in turret and tree' with such an uproar that we took refuge in the guest room and cooked the little bit we wanted to eat in the fireplace there. Gene was frightfully sick, running a temperature high enough for delirium. 'I all alone in the night, guarded the pass that leads to the Valley of Death.' Before he was safely through the illness, I had a proper case of laryngitis when I could neither lie nor sit in bed with comfort. And the wind! It blew for days and nights on end. The entire plain was blotted out with dust.

The summer of 1929 put us back on our feet. Gene was writing again and the stories sold. We were able to send my brother George payment of a note long overdue and our two-hundred-dollar grocery bill at Mrs. Fall's store was settled. The prosperity all began with Engle Ferry.

Gene had come to bed one night whispering jubilantly, 'I've made fifty dollars.'

'How?' I inquired sleepily.

'I've finished my Engle Ferry poem,' he answered.

Engle and Engle Ferry were living parts of Gene, and when Elephant Butte Dam, built by the United States Reclamation Service in New Mexico, made a lake forty miles long, a hundred feet deep over Engle Ferry near old Fort McCrae, Gene wanted it commemorated.

Engle Ferry is narrow and deep,
The current is strong and the banks are steep;
Teamster and horseman, they praise the Lord
For the stony footing of Engle Ford;
Scoured and cleansed of quivering sand,
The safest ford on the Rio Grande.
The patient oxen may drink their fill,
With thankful eyes on the farther hill;
Drink, and lean to their yokes again,
Toiling over, with heave and strain,
To night, and rest, and the scanty sward
Of the starlit meadows by Engle Ford.

A winding road upon either hand,
Between black lava and yellow sand,
Between red water and close blue sky,
Leads to the ferry when floods are high.
Chain your wheels with a double hitch,
Skid and lurch on the last steep pitch,
Slide on the ferry and close the gates,
Block your wagons — and trust the fates!
Clouds brood low on the sultry air,
Stabbing the gorges with lightning flare;
Angry echoes from hill to hill
Mutter and clamor and threaten still;
The pulleys whine to the cable's strain —
But Engle Ferry is crossed again!

With the same zest, he took up prose again in the

defense of Engle. The postmistress wrote Gene that the spelling of Engle on the railroad station had been changed to Engel, for one of the directors of the road and they were taking steps to have the spelling of the post office changed in the same way. Gene and Will Barnes of Washington, D.C., immediately took the matter in hand. *The Santa Fe Mexican*, too, came to the rescue.

GENE RHODES AGAIN LIFTS LANCE FOR AULD LANG SYNE: ENGLE SHALL REMAIN ENGLE

Story-teller of Other Days Opposes Changing Name of Historical Spot, So Called in Honor of Pioneer Engineer Who Hung the Hanging Bridge, Built Raton Tunnel, and Put Cogs on Pike's Peak; Railroad Company Would Alter Name to Fit Later Official.

Engle, New Mexico, named after R. L. Engle, pioneer railroad construction engineer and one of the first blazers of the steel trail in the southwest, is not going to be changed to 'Engel' to fit the name of a vice president of the Santa Fe Railroad Company — not if Eugene Manlove Rhodes and fellow oldtimers can prevent it.

The protest against this proposed change has reached the ears of the Postmaster General, and other higher-ups, and Mr. Rhodes, the well-known story-writer, now resident at Three Rivers, New Mexico, has just addressed a letter to U.S. Senator Bronson Cutting of New Mexico, asking his good offices to prevent this iconoclasm.

It seems that Gene and his friends have the goods in this case, and that Engle was indubitably so called in

> honor of said R. L. Engle, who was one of those hardy men of yore who bore the burden and the heat of the day and the chilly snows of the Rockies in order that we and our children's children might pay the Pullman surcharge. The son of R. L. Engle has furnished convincing proof that the station was named for his father at the time the senior Engle was doing the survey work and construction work for the Santa Fe in that part of the territory, in the seventies. But the fact had been written on the scrolls of fame by Rhodes before this data was added.
>
> IMMORTALIZED BY RHODES
>
> Engle was immortalized by Eugene Manlove Rhodes some years ago in his installment story, 'No Mean City,' published in *The Saturday Evening Post* and one of the finest things Rhodes has written; a romance with Old Ben Teagardner as its chief character, an epic drama beginning with the Spaniards who thirsted on the Jornada del Muerto, and ending in the deep waters of Elephant Butte Lake, crystal-blue sepulcher of adobe haciendas of yore....

'Pegasus at the Plow,' second poem in the line, was published July, 1929, in *The Saturday Evening Post* and 'My Banker,' also that summer. A season of poetry and sentiment, indeed. I told Gene with great glee that, devoted as he was to New Mexico and all her works, it was a New York pasture into which he turned his team at night. And 'My Banker' has a story.

After we had been away from Alamogordo nearly a year, we went back for a day. In the café where we were lunching, a woman came up to me and pleasantly said it was nice to see us back in Alamo again. Although

I expressed my pleasure at being there and made a few remarks about the changes in the town since we left, I was more piqued to know who she was. Then she dropped a bomb at my feet.

'You know, Mrs. Rhodes, I have never met your husband.'

I had to admit that I didn't know her. She was the banker's wife, the banker from whom Gene borrowed money, because he said that was what bankers were for. It had been to Mr. Hollaman, the banker at Alamogordo, and to Jack Spencc, at Tularosa, with no partiality shown, that Gene had written his verses.

MY BANKER

Who is it, when I'm feeling blue,
Sends me a cheerful line or two
To say my note is overdue?
        My banker.

And who sends back my check again
Stamped 'No Funds' in his ghoulish den —
The saddest words of tongue or pen?
        My banker.

Who is it, when my notes fall due,
When coin is scarce and friends are few,
Who says, 'Oh, yes, you can renew'?
        My banker.

Of all my friends beneath the sun
Who, think you, is the only one
Who never says, 'It can't be done'?
        My banker.

When times are hard and days are black,
When care sits heavy on my back,
Who is it furnishes the jack?
        My banker.

Now I've been wicked and I've been weak,
And I've been dumb in the hour to speak,
And I've spoke high when I should ha' been dumb
And missed my chances for martyrdom.
And I've been foolish and I've been fond,
But when I come to the Great Beyond,
When Peter grumbles, 'Now, who are you?
And why do you think I should let you through?'
I'll cock my hat and I'll blink my eyes,
And I'll say, 'I never was good or wise,
And I can't think up any likely lies,
But brace yourself for a great surprise;
Under the sun here is something new,
So open your gates and let me through —
The first who ever was grateful to
        A banker.'

As if this encounter wasn't bad enough, just before we left for California Gene wanted some books he had loaned Mr. Hollaman. I was going to Alamogordo with Mrs. Norton, so he asked me to get them for him. 'Where does the banker live?' He replied: 'Two or three doors from the post office. Inquire when you get down there.' I inquired, but it was a bit confusing, for people lived in one end of the post office block, and I didn't know whether that would count for a house or not. I counted what I thought was three and went to the door to ask if Mrs. Hollaman lived there. The lady I was addressing said pleasantly, 'I am Mrs. Hollaman.' Of course, it was the banker's wife again. I told Gene if I ever asked that woman a third time who she was, I'd go out and hang myself to the nearest tree.

That summer our boy Alan was married in Binghamton, New York, to a Boston girl and took her West with him for a wedding trip. One evening in December when I had gone early to bed Gene rushed in.

'You better get up! Mrs. Norton (the electrician's wife at the Fall ranch) just phoned that Alan stopped there to inquire the way.'

I climbed into my clothes in a hurry. We lit all the electric lights in that big house until it looked like a Christmas card in the darkness. Gene had saved some dry cedar brush for the occasion. As they came in, he heaped it on the fire to crackle and snap in the huge fireplace. I shall remember that fire always, and my tall son, and the big blue eyes of my new daughter. Alan and Betty remained in the West for the next year. While they were in Alamogordo, we took many camping trips together to show Betty the wonders. One notable trip was to the Ruidosa, where we camped under the pines beside the noisy river where the trout hide. This beauty spot is described in the first story Gene wrote: 'The Hour and the Man.'

In the spring, in March sometime, Alan rigged up a four-wheeled trailer to carry all his household plunder, fastened it to his little Ford sedan, and he and Betty were off for New York. We went with them as far as Three Rivers post office, presumably to get the mail, really to have that much more time with him before we were left alone. I watched that small car go down the long road between the ominous mountain ranges with the trailer bobbing along behind them like some enormous tumblebug. I wondered if they would arrive safely. Narrowly, they did. A tornado followed them across Arkansas, but only overtook them in a deluge of rain in Memphis, Tennessee.

Betty left her cats with us. The kitten Gene named Mussolini, but he said he didn't know whether it was Mussolini or Messaloni, so we could call it Mess or Muss as the occasion seemed to warrant.

The Dohenys foreclosed the mortgage on Judge Fall's ranch and took it over. We remained in the Rock House, sharing it with the new manager for some time before moving to Half-Way House (halfway between Three Rivers and the Rock House). The manager was a business man to his finger-tips, expert in making reports and saving at every possible turn. But he was also generous and thoughtful. We were proud to have his friendship.

Mrs. Norton, the electrician's wife, had taken over the work of running the power plant. The wells down the cañon were operated by electricity. She climbed down the ladder into those wells in her high-heeled slippers to turn the switch which sent the water gushing out. Or she would climb up to the top of the massive engine in the power plant to start that. She made a good job of it too, waved hair, lacquered nails, and all.

One of Gene's favorite stories was of our call to the power plant. Mrs. Norton was in another room primping. Her small daughter, aged four, sat in an overstuffed chair, small finger-tips together like an Episcopal clergyman, as she entertained us. The child Fay had no children to play with and had rather an adult manner from always associating with her elders. Her mother was very careful of her language.

The subject of goldfish came up — it seems the druggist in Tularosa had some for sale. Regarding her finger-tips reflectively, Fay said in a benevolent manner like her mother's, 'We had some goldfish once,' adding in a deep bass voice like her father's, 'but the G—d damn things died!'

Fay had a lively press agent in Gene from that time on. Another young friend who was a happy target of his wit as a result of a visit to Rock House, was pretty Kitty Crosby. For her he wrote 'Relativity for Ladies.'

Oh, cunning Kitty Crosby, who kept all joy astir,
  Who made me promise faithfully to wait a while for her!
The dainty Kitty Crosby who was my valentine,
  When I was only twenty-three and she was only nine.

Ah, coy was Kitty Crosby when she was older grown;
  A maid demure and winsome but cold as any stone.
I could have boxed the minx's ears who called me Uncle Gene,
  When I was turning thirty-five and she was seventeen.

The busy years, the crowded years — how winged and swift they ran!
  The girl became a woman and the boy became a man.

But when I named the promise true, she only laughed at me —
The day when I was forty-six and she was twenty-three.

Oh, cruel Kitty Crosby, how could you use me so,
Deride your loyal lover and bring his heart to woe?
Oh, canny Kitty Crosby, you never can be mine —
For now that I am sixty-two, you're only twenty-nine!

CHAPTER XV

Oldtimers

BACK in 1927 when we had first returned to New Mexico, it was suggested to Gene by Harrison Leussler that he write his autobiography. This seemed to Gene to smack of 'Windy Bill,' for he wrote: 'I have done nothing to autobiograph about. This is a poor place for delusions of grandeur. Ulysses lives next door, Du Guesclin across the street, Marco Polo in the next block. Every third man (over fifty) has been a Texas Ranger, a frontier sheriff, or a cowman whose ventures have ranged from Canada to the Concho. Alex McClaren ranges casually from Scotland and Spain to Peru and the Brazilian highlands. My own Uncle Ben Teagardner — concerning whom I have a novel half done — was wont to pass lightly from Hong Kong to Australia, Chile, and Alaska — although, of course, New Mexico was always the earth's center to him. It is always that, once you have lived here. Of men over fifty, hereabouts, I am the most parochial. A parish to be proud of — yes. But that reflection does not make for biography. Also, it is a task for which I am unfitted by training and inclination. Do your work and keep your mouth shut; it was so my father taught me, and the lesson is in my blood and my bones.'

But the remorseless and implacable Leussler, as Gene called him, had his way. Gene talked with Clem Hightower and the two, oldtimers of the same period, agreed to collaborate. What Gene didn't know about it, Clem did. Their knowledge dovetailed in the most surprising way. Clem had come to New Mexico in 1877, had lived in every corner in southern New Mexico and several of the northern counties. He was government teamster and packer for years — including most of the Apache campaigns, cowboy and rancher, freighter and member of the House of 'Reprobates' from Lincoln County, and stood high in the annals of the state as a politician. (He also stood high in his own right. He must have been more than six feet tall.)

Together they discussed collecting material for a story in which they had had their fingers — elbow deep. They met in a hotel dining-room and sat there talking for hours. Mr. Miller, a bookstore man from Albuquerque, was present. Gene said he seemed vastly interested, 'but possibly he was only stunned.' Anyway he didn't go back to his store till they left. They built maps of knives, forks, and spoons, augmented by drinking glasses and salt dishes. 'Them was the days.' Gene summed it up, 'I have lived in exactly that place and time I would have chosen from all recorded history.'

It was to be an enormous task to hunt up the oldtimers to verify stories — all the way from Jim East in Tucson, Arizona, to Charlie Goodnight at Goodnight, Texas. Gene well knew that the boys would catch the slightest discrepancy. The boys! Goodnight was eighty-eight, Jim East eighty, Blackwell eighty-five, Cole Railston sixty-seven. But they would all talk to Gene and Clem, oldtimers with their own ethics, telling as never before the stories of the killing of Apache Kid by Charley Anderson, Walter Hearn, Bert Slinckard, and others. And as he worked, Gene recalled incidents he had half forgotten. 'Harvey Moreland and Sam Adams and myself were exactly of an age. We had worked together for a week, building a stone house for Pres Lewis. The house stands yet. But when we finished it, Harvey and Sam rode west and I rode east. They were killed next day, building fence with Charlie Stevenson. Charlie and Sam had guns, so the Apaches shot them. But Harvey was unarmed. They staked him out — crucified — and drove a crowbar through his head.'

To his publishers, Gene wrote: 'We knew all about each other. Every man was weighed and placed. You are safe in saying that Clem and I know what we are talking about and that we can tell you the inside story of our little parish. As it has fallen to my lot to defend Pat Garrett's memory, it may interest you to know why he did not take my tip (in regard to the Barbee murder of a deputy sheriff on my ranch). It is because we were bitter enemies. One of Pat's deputies, Walter Danburg, rode after me nearly four hundred miles, just behind me but never quite catching up, from Alma to Roswell. I know that I made that ride pretty briskly, but I didn't know that anyone was chasing me. I was in a hurry. And I can't even guess what he wanted me for. There were so many things. Innocent, says you? Possibly, but probably not. Probably guilty as all get-out. Desprit Ambrose....

'Clem and I were not gunmen. But we lived among gunmen all our lives and held our own with them, just as hundreds of others did, quiet people who let whiskey alone and were lettered like a football player: large, invisible letters which said for all to see "Use No Hooks." Killing went mostly with whiskey anyway. Life is not so tame here, even now. Gentleman at next ranch shot another gentleman last Saturday — shot him in the leg and neck — and was arrested here, in this very house last Sunday by Pete Johnson — son of that same Pete Johnson of whom I wrote in *Copper Streak Trail*. (It seems that the first gentleman was caught stealing the second gentleman's beef. At least they found the beef in the barn from which the first gentleman shot the second gentleman.)'

There was that little matter of a beef in Gene's history, too, of which his friends made much. To encourage the writing of *Old Timers*, Governor Dillon had issued the following amusing pardon for Gene's old, old mistake of serving a guest beef 'not bearing his own brand' in the years before Gene had gone east to live in Apalachin.

STATE OF NEW MEXICO
Executive Office
Santa Fe

March 1, 1928

To Eugene Manlove Rhodes, Greetings:

The Governor of New Mexico is reliably informed that you have been urged to set down in writing a true and reliable account of yourself and your meanderings in and about the great open spaces of New Mexico; that you have seen life as she is actually lived on our plains and mesas, on the *malpaìs* and in our cañons, in our sandstorms and cloudbursts, in *arroyos* dry and in *arroyos* on the rampage, in alfalfa fields as well amidst stones and cactus; that you have led the grand march at many a *baile* and had flowers hurled at you at many a fiesta; that you have sat down to chile-con-carne and frijoles with sheep men and cow men in the good old campfire days, all of which represents a living and turbulently attractive chapter in New Mexico's history of a period now slipping into the past, and which by means of your pen can be perpetuated for the enjoyment of present and future generations, especially for all those who appreciate a drama set in an heroic landscape peopled by men and women of rare courage and rugged endurance — all of which would add to the glory and fame of New Mexico at home and abroad now and in time to come!

It has also come to my knowledge that you are dilly-dallying about rendering this service to the State of New Mexico, that for some mysterious reason you are hesitating to take your pen in hand and sketch into the canvas of the 'Sunshine State' the thrilling detail of your various experiences within her borders.

You are doubtless aware that as Governor of New

Mexico I am vested with the supreme executive power of the state, which includes the pardoning power. Therefore, in case you are bashful about writing a complete and accurate story of your life in New Mexico on account, perhaps, of having got mixed up with cattle rustlers and on certain occasions having found yourself desperately hungry and without means of subsistence you helped yourself to a nice fat lamb or a young heifer on the range — well, in that event, I hereby freely absolve and pardon you. So don't let that stand in your way. Being a man of the plains and a sheep man myself, I know how such little incidents make a fellow take to cover. When I was a boy I often had to travel on foot, so I caught burros along the way to give me a lift; and many times when I was hungry I did not hesitate to raid cow camps. I can assure you on the part of the livestock men of the state that such trifling indiscretions on your part, if any, will be forgotten and we will call it square. Just put down everything and make a clean breast of it.

Now, therefore, I, R. C. Dillon, Governor of the State of New Mexico, by virtue of the authority in me vested, and for the purpose of substantially and permanently advancing the literary, romantic, historical, and artistic interests of the state, do hereby command *Eugene Manlove Rhodes*, a citizen of this state, immediately to proceed to write down a true and accurate account of his career in the said state and have same published broadcast as expeditiously and as promptly as possible for the benefit of the people of this commonwealth and for the enlightenment of the people of this commonwealth and for the enlightenment of the nation at large; and in event said *Eugene Manlove Rhodes* fails or refuses to carry out this mandate, then and in that event the above proposed pardon will be revoked, and the investigations will be instituted looking into the real cause for any failure or refusal on the part of the said *Eugene Manlove Rhodes* to carry out the aims and purposes of this document.

Done at Santa Fe, this first day of March, A.D. 1928.

R. C. DILLON, *Governor*

I don't remember what Gene said when he got the pardon. He was quite furious and if he didn't swear, he undoubtedly wanted to!

The story goes that Gene met Governor Dillon at some gathering and a friend wanted to introduce them.

'Dillon's an old acquaintance,' said Gene.

'Yes, indeed,' answered the Governor, seeing again the poker hands of old days, 'but it was mostly a "passing" acquaintance.'

Anyway, in reply to the Governor's pardon Gene wrote a note. 'A man with your sense of humor deserves a raise.' The letterhead was decorated with a picture of a man being hanged.

Then he decided it wouldn't do to enter the lawless sections into which he would have to go in search of more material about the oldtimers without a gun. And he wrote to the Governor.

Alamogordo, New Mexico,
March 4, 1928

Hon. R. C. Dillon,
Governor's Mansion,
Santa Fe, N. M.
My dear Governor:

(Is that the way to address a governor?)

Your executive order dated March 1 was duly received, and your instructions shall be obeyed at once.

Your promise of clemency shows unusual thoughtfulness and a fine fellow feeling. I thank you — and today I file that signed promise in a sure place.

Time was when I needed a clement friend in the Governor's chair, very badly. There were several such occasions; but one stands out with unusual distinctness, because I was then newly married and my wife was not entirely acclimated.

It was about 1898. I ran across a young fellow — one of the Hargis family of Kentucky feudists. He was broke, hungry, ragged, and lousy. I bought him boots and clothes and a saddle, also deloused him, and killed the fatted calf for him. Unfortunately, that calf — not to go into unnecessary details, there was a clerical error connected with that calf. Now, one of my neighbors was a purist, and he had a steady offer of $500 reward for correction of such errors. So what does Hargis do but wander over to White Oaks and confide my goodness to John Owens, then sheriff of Lincoln County?

These oldtimers are clannish. A man who had never liked me — and whom I had never liked — rode some hundred and fifty miles to Las Cruces, just to bring the good news.

So I went to White Oaks unostentatiously, no man seeing me — and persuaded this willing witness to leave the territory. I did not have to use my persuader, but I escorted him to the Texas line, and spoke to him severely at parting.

Now, in the matter of writing this book about How the Map Was Made, I shall have to visit every county in the state to verify and to make queries; and I would feel all the better if I might keep a gun in my car, for protection, just in case. I therefore respectfully make application to you, asking that you appoint me special ranger, without pay, and all in order that I may have the right to carry a gun, not concealed, in any New Mexico county. A deputy sheriff's privilege ends at the county line — or so I am told. Such an appointment would be gratefully accepted by

Yours truly,

GENE RHODES

Whereupon Governor Dillon sent the following:

March 7, 1928

Col. Eugene Manlove Rhodes,
Alamagordo, N. M.
My dear Colonel Rhodes:

I am delighted to have your letter of the 4th, in which you signify willingness to obey the mandate issued from this office a few days ago, provided you be allowed the slight privilege of carrying an exposed gun. This right is gladly given you, and you may at any time avail yourself of the liberty of carrying an exposed gun. This right is gladly given you, and you may at any time avail yourself of the liberty of carrying an unconcealed and unloaded gun into any county in this state; and to make your personal safety doubly secure, I am today appointing you colonel on the Governor's staff, which will enable you to throw a mantle of authority over your person and conceal hip pockets in a dignified way, making many a trip pleasant that might otherwise be tiresome and vexing.

Now that we have arrived at an amicable and clear understanding you may proceed with the first chapter of the revelations.

With regards, I am, my dear Colonel,

Cordially yours,

R. C. DILLON

Gene remembered how heroically his father had fought and the hardships which he had endured. When he himself was promoted to the rank of colonel, he viewed the 'Staff Officer' on our special license plates with disgust. (They asked me at a gas station in California what a staff officer on the Governor's staff did. In mock surprise I answered, 'He carries the Governor's staff!') When, on one of our trips, we came to the lodge at the entrance of the Grand Cañon, an officer came out and looked at our license plates and said, 'What position do you occupy on the Governor's staff?'

Gene scowled and said in great exasperation, between gnashing teeth, 'A G—— damned *paper* colonel.' The officer laughed so he could hardly paste the complimentary ticket to our windshield.

Gene's oldtimers book was to be his crowning achievement. He studied and planned for it for years. After trying a number of titles and discarding them as inadequate, he selected *The Silent Past.* It was to be a half-history of half a century in his homeland.

> ...He looked down into the fairest valley of all Heaven. Saint Peter sighed, and pointed.
>
> 'We hold the New Mexicans here,' he said. 'We have to keep them hobbled, or they'll go back.'
>
> — *The Strange Vacation of Ormsby McHarg*

He was in high spirits working on it, 'not reminiscences, although some of that, not autobiography by ten thousand miles, but just New Mexico.' Plans for chapters came swiftly: Charlie Goodnight on the dry trail from the head of the Concho to the Pecos, ninety miles without water; the trail herd where Oliver Loving died; the digging of the first well on the Jorñada del Muerto; the West as something other than a place of gun fighting and hate.

We traveled to Deming and goodness knows where. We drove over a thousand miles, looking up oldtimers, getting first-hand information and history. At the end of the year Gene made plans to go to Kingston and to Seven Rivers to verify the story of the Apache Kid and the story of Seven Rivers and to his father's old ranch to see Joel Jones, only survivor of the Seven River Warriors. These trips had to be made before the spring winds when the bronchitis always began. Clem Hightower was to come to visit and work, bringing his chapter on the Greathouse-Joe Fowler story and information he had collected.

The last paragraph of the Foreword as planned describes their feelings. 'We had much heartbreak to name our story. *The West That Was?* But this was one small parish of the West, and each parish had legends like our own. *Masterless Men?* But there is no place nor time where the Masterless Men have not held their own. For exactness, we have called it *Old Timers in New Mexico.* But that is only what the name of the book is called. The book really is *We Point With Pride:* but the tune is not my own invention. Wild Esau sang it first, I think, the generous, the high-hearted, "the man of the field," and it has been sung since by the

CLEMENT HIGHTOWER

luckless and generous and true, in all lands and in all times.' And the book was to end with: 'Such is our half-history; with much omitted, condoned, extenuated: nothing set down in malice. We have seen much shame and evil and storm; but these things are remembered only with effort. The memories that throng unbidden are of pleasant campfires and the kindly sun, the goodly fellowship of the House of Lacking — gay, kind, and fearless. To them, the living and the gallant ghosts — farewell!'

If somebody had only been inspired to grubstake Gene while he wrote this book, a priceless work of Southwestern history would have been placed on record. Gene had to write stories to pay our current expenses and never got enough ahead so that he dared stop. Clem, with all his high hopes, was unable to come, and in the fall of the year was laid to sleep in the hills he loved so well. For Gene, illness stopped his writing, flu in the spring and in the summer bronchitis so badly that he could not speak above a whisper for six weeks.

'The Silent Past!' It will be silent forevermore. Only the few manuscript chapters that were finished give the record. Before he died Gene had the whole book written in his mind, such was his method of working, but it is now irretrievably lost.

From chapters completed:

THE OLDEST ROAD

Cloudless, sun-lined, and silent, the Chihuahuan Desert is little known, even today; a land of *bolsines*, and lost rivers that never find the sea. It is boot-shaped, a larger boot than Italy. The leg is in Old Mexico; the toe is in Arizona, with the Gila outlining the boot-sole; furious and desperate, the Rio Grande broke jail and cut across the instep, chiseling through four mountain ranges to seek the sea; and the heel is in New Mexico. We are to consider the People of the Boot-Heel.

The Kingdom of New Mexico was the first European foothold within the present boundaries of the United States — peace to St. Augustine: It is true that St. Augustine was built at the tide mark in 1665, long years before San Gabriel de los Españolas (1598) or Santa Fe (1605). Even so, a bivouac is not a civilization. Saint Augustine did not leave Florida Spanish; but Oñate made New Mexico Spain. Nor is that all. Two generations before Santa Fe, Spanish explorers had pierced the grimmest recesses of New Mexico and Arizona and made them named and known.

Starting in 1636, Cabesa de Vaca meandered from the Gulf through Texas, possibly along the southern border of New Mexico when Henry VIII was, you might say, scarcely married at all....

Frey Marcos de Niza scouted from Soñora through Arizona to Zuni in 1539. Cardeñas looked down into the Grand Cañon in 1540. Coroñado strolled from Acoma to the Missouri and back, 1540–1542. What did they think, what could they dream of what lay still beyond their outmost voyaging? 'Travelers' Tales' are often tall; but these doubtless told the truth.

Why, then, 'Old Timers,' for men still living? Because it is a true telling. Because while New Mexico is our oldest European civilization, the south of it is our last-won land. Bold and hardy as they were, the Spanish Pioneers found little to their liking in the boot-heel. It was a true desert, waterless, treeless, and grim. They pushed on to the watered high country of the north, where they might find souls to save and gold to gather; and in their going they made our Oldest Road. You may read of it in our first book.

After Don Juan de Oñate had crossed the Rio Grande, where El Paso now stands, he sent out a party of seventeen men to find a wagon road to the north. They made the first wagon road within the present limits of the United States. Even then they followed a trail already timeless; a trail which stretched from Yucatan to the Michigan peninsula; the same trail had led them north through all the eighty years since Cortez burned his ships; the Turquoise Trail. Just such a trail brought ivory apes and peacocks to Solomon — and it is thought the Turquoise Trail was old when Solomon was king.

Here passed the first wagon road, but not the first wagons. The same account[1] says 'the tracks left by Castano's wagon when he was led captive from New Mexico in 1591 were found on May 4th.'

Castano seems to have been an enterprising teamster. There may have been others even before him, but this is the first wheel track in the United States of which we have record. Villagra, in his epic poem describing

[1] Don Juan de Oñate and the Founding of New Mexico.

the Entrada, tells us of the wagon and oxen taken by Oñate into New Mexico. This was in 1598; Shakespeare had just written *The Merchant of Venice*, and was turning a shrewd eye upon *Julius Caesar* as a commercial possibility.

The Oldest Road followed the river to Robledo, near Fort Selden of a later day. Here it climbed the mesa and struck across the desert to Paraje. Of all the long roads to Mexico and Vera Cruz here was the spot most famed and feared, the journey of death, the Jorñada del Muerto. And from rim to rim was eighty miles, if there was water in Laguna del Muerto, thirty miles south of Paraje; ninety miles if the lake was dry and you took the long detour to Ojodel Muerto, five miles west of the Laguna. A fine spring, this Spring of the Dead Man; abundant water and that of the best quality, but it was ten miles farther.

You must climb a ridge and drop down into a deep cañon, with a steeper hill to climb back. North of the spring, the road wound through a narrow and gloomy defile with conveniences for ambush; and the spring was a popular resort for the Apaches. People traveled in caravans for safety when the lake was dry, and if the caravan was strong enough to split — here is what happened. They outspanned at the dry lake; half of their forces stayed to protect the wagons while the other half rode the stock down to the spring and frequently returned. If the caravan was too weak for dividing it prayed and cursed and went on dry.

Fourteen miles south of Dead Man's Spring, shallow

pools in the Cañada de Aleman held water for a little while after a rain, and another march to southward, Las Tinajitas — potholes in an outcropping of rock — held less water for a shorter time; only enough for camp use at best. From Las Tinajitas to Robledo, thirty miles, the road paralleled the river, with hills between; you might drive your oxen ten or twelve sandy miles down to the river. By the time you got back, they would be as thirsty as ever. Except in the last extremity of thirst, men held the beaten road.

The Jorñada was named in fear and shuddering. Why then the desert route? Why did they not follow the Rio Grande? They had the best of reasons. For fifteen miles above Robledo the river had elected to run lengthwise through San Diego Hills. Above this bleak defile the fords were quicksands until you came to the rocky crossing just west of Del Muerto Springs. Moreover the river made a great bend to westward, taking full fifty miles longer to reach Paraje; and the terrain was impassable, spring ridges and deep barrancas, jungles of cottonwood, willow, mesquite, and tornillo, deepest sand. For a wagon to climb even one of these desperate ridges will be dreaded five hundred miles away. There were fifty such ridges. The Rio Grande foamed against them, undermined them, carved their bases to high bluffs. Terrible roads steeple-jacked across this broken country after the American occupation; but not until the last decade was a good road built down the river; and no road mastered the gorge above Robledo until 1928.

For another reason look at the map. For over six hundred miles above the mouth of the Pecos, no stream flows into the Rio Grande from the east; even as every tributary of the Pecos comes from the west. But exactly opposite the Jorñada, no less than eight little rivers fall from the Continental Divide into the Rio Grande. Game and fish and corn, land, wood, and shelter — yes, and four notable hot springs for healing; here was the chosen home of the fierce Apaches. (Other Apache tribes lived on the Gila, and the Mescalero branch held the Pecos country.)

So the Oldest Road did well to cross the desert. On the clean plain there was no chance for ambush; the sand (though the oxen would not believe it) was comparatively light and shallow: and most of the Jorñada was good hard adobe. For two hundred and fifty years the Jorñada route was the main artery of New Mexican travel, and heavy ox-drawn *curretos* groaned along the sandy waste. Kit Carson rode there; Doniphan passed this way; the Texans went north here in '62. When the surviving Texans of the ill-starred Santa Fe expedition of 1841 were led captive into Mexico, they were forced to walk across the Jorñada in two nights and one day, forty hours — and two men, Golpin and Griffith, were wantonly murdered by the Mexican guards, because they were unable to travel. It is pleasant to remember that Demasio Salazer, commanding the guards, was publicly disgraced for his brutality by the Mexican general, Elias, when the prisoners reached Paso del Norte.

Let me here make a confession and outcry. Until the year 1925, I did not know that this First Road had ever been known as other than the Santa Fe Trail, and I supposed that the later road, from Santa Fe to the Missouri, was only an extension of the original road. I had never heard the Southern Road called anything else, and I had never dreamed of calling it anything else. No surprising blunder, since that Old Road led to Sante Fe and ended there when Santa Fe was the outpost of empire. Well! It seems that we were all mistaken. Santa Fe says — and who should know better? — that the Santa Fe Trail started in Missouri and ended in the Santa Fe Plaza. I stand corrected — but I am still surprised and resentful. The modern Santa Fe Trail is assured of immortality; even the brief Butterfield Trail is famous; but this Oldest Road, for all its high and tragic story, seems doomed to be forgotten — only because it lacked a resounding name to trap the eye and fill the ear. El Camino Real, the King's Highway? Why, that is to be merely nameless. It was sometimes called the Chihuahua — Santa Fe Road or the Mexico-Santa Fe Road. Who can make music with such names as that? This road deserved a great name, a name to sing in our memory. It should have been the Santa Fe Trail — it should have been the Great North Road. . . .

OLIVER LOVING AND HIS FRIENDS

Oliver Loving was undoubtedly the first man to trail cattle from Texas. So says Colonel Charles Goodnight, who is still living at the age of ninety-three. In 1858, Loving took a herd through the Indian Nation, eastern Kansas, and northwestern Missouri to Illinois. In 1859 he drove a herd from the headwaters of the Brazos northwest to the Arkansas and up the Arkansas to near where Pueblo now stands, where he wintered. In the spring he sold his herds in Denver. 'He remained there until the Civil War broke out and had much difficulty in getting back home, but through the assistance of Maxwell, Kit Carson, and Dick Wooten, he was given a passport and afterwards delivered beef to the Confederacy during the war, which completely broke him up.'[1]

The first cattle furnished to the Navajo at Fort Sumner were from Albuquerque, Anton Chico, Manzano, and other New Mexico settlements. In 1866, Goodnight and Loving threw in together and drove twelve hundred steers to Fort Sumner. The trail they made was afterwards called the Goodnight and Loving Trail, circling southward around the Staked Plains, across the Colorado, up the Concho, ninety miles across a waterless plain to Horsehead Crossing on the Pecos, and hence up the Pecos to Bosque Grande. John Chisum was close behind with six hundred Jingle Bob steers; he wintered eight miles below the first comers. It is better to let Colonel Goodnight tell his own story. Here is a letter which he kindly sent me in response to my inquiries.

> ... Mr. Oliver Loving and I formed a partnership to handle trail cattle from Texas to the northwest in

[1] Charles Goodnight in *Trail Drivers of Texas*.

1867, commencing in about January of that year. In the spring of '67 we returned to the frontier of Texas from Fort Sumner, New Mexico, or rather the Loving Bend at Bosque Grande, New Mexico, where we had wintered twelve hundred steers and put them in to the Navajo Indian contractors at Fort Sumner during the winter of '66 and the spring of '67.

On our return to the vicinity of Fort Belknap, Young County, we bought and put together five thousand head of cattle, consisting of two herds. Oliver Loving and I took the first one, about twenty-five hundred head. Joe Loving, his son, followed us up with the second herd; both herds were mixed cattle but largely steers.

When Loving and I had reached a point about halfway up the Pecos from the Horsehead Crossing to Bosque Grande, it being late (the latter part of June) and the contracts to furnish the Indians and troops of New Mexico would be let early in July, it became necessary for Mr. Loving to leave the herd and go on ahead in order to make a bid on same. He left us at what was then known as Texas Bend, probably a hundred miles below the mouth of Blue River,[1] or Carlsbad.

Knowing the danger from Indians, I begged him to travel entirely at night and hide during the daytime as I had done on two different occasions, in the same country. I gave Mr. Loving, as an escort, Mr. Wilson, a one-armed cowboy, who was the bravest and coolest man I had, remarkably so. They traveled two nights, which brought them to the Blue River. Mr. Loving then told Wilson that he very much disliked night riding, and having seen no Indian sign whatever, felt

[1] Now Black River.

perhaps I was overcautious, hence decided to ride in daytime.

All went well that day until about two P.M., when Wilson looked out toward the southwest, observed a large body of Comanches coming out of the Guadalupe Mountains, which spurs or foothills lay in that neighborhood. The Indians were making a charge on them (Wilson and Loving were on the plain between the Pecos and Blue River). Wilson and Loving struck due north to the Pecos River, where there were some small sand dunes and brush. There they made a stand, kept the Indians off until night. But during the evening the Indians made a shot which hit Mr. Loving through the wrist and in the side.

He got under the bank of the river and toward morning, thinking he would die from the wounds, asked Mr. Wilson to get away and get to me if possible, as the Indians were all around them on both sides of the water. Wilson swam right down the river through the Indian guard and got away.

I had laid the herd over one day to rest, which made the distance between us greater than he expected. He escaped with nothing but his underwear and hat and traversed that terrible thorny country barefoot.

In the evening of the third day I picked him up exhausted and with his feet in a terrible condition. Mr. Loving had stood the Indians off until they quit him. He then went up the river to where he knew the cattle would later water if the herd was not taken by the Indians.

It happened that there were some Mexicans with their wagons trying to get through to Texas and picked Mr. Loving up, right where Eddy now stands. Loving had been without food for three days and nights, his wounds undressed, and worms in his wrist. He hired them to take him back to Fort Sumner, about two hundred miles. The government ambulance met him fifty miles down the river and took him to the doctor at Fort Sumner. Blood poison set up in the wounded arm, which had to be amputated. The second day the arteries came loose and he had to be reoperated upon, bringing on a relapse from which he never recovered. . . .

Here is another account, from a letter from M. D. Reynolds, who died on January 5, 1829. His brother, Glenn Reynolds, was sheriff of Gila County, Arizona, and was afterwards murdered by the Apache Kid. This country has been paid for.

. . . In answer to your question relative to an account of Oliver Loving's death, I will give you the facts as I know them. I went up the trail in 1867 with a herd belonging to Goodnight and Loving. They took two herds up that year. Goodnight and Loving were with the first herd. I was with the second, which was in charge of Joe Loving, a son of Oliver Loving. Our herd arrived at Fort Sumner about a month after the first herd arrived there, and it was then that I learned the facts concerning the death of Loving, as I give them here. When the first herd got some distance up the Pecos, Mr. Loving decided to go on ahead and find buyers for his cattle. He took Billy Wilson, a one-armed man, with him. Going on ahead they came to a little stream called the Black River, that flows in to the Pecos from the west near Carlsbad, N.M. Here they were attacked by a bunch of Indians. The Indians ran them down to the Pecos River just a short distance to the east, and Mr. Loving was wounded in the arm. Loving and Wilson jumped from their horses and hid in some undergrowth that looked like cane. Their horses and supplies were left for the Indians and they stayed in this hiding place nearly all night. Loving was so weak from the loss of blood that he persuaded Wilson to leave him and go back and meet the herd. Wilson slid into the stream and swam and floated down some distance to get out of reach of the Indians. Then he got out on the same side that he went in and made his way back to the road and followed it two or three days, when he met their herd. During this time he was without food.

Before daylight, the next day after the Indian attack, Loving came out from the river and to the road and started north toward Fort Sumner. He went about fourteen miles and found some Mexicans with oxcarts, and he got them to haul him to Fort Sumner, which they were many days in reaching. Before Mr. Loving found these Mexicans, he was so weak from loss of blood and lack of food that he built up a little fire and roasted his buckskin gloves into a crisp and ate them. When they reached Fort Sumner his arm was in such bad condition that the army surgeon had to amputate it and he soon died from blood poisoning.

That winter after Mr. Goodnight had disposed of his cattle, he sent his outfit back, he bought an extra wagon and a pair of mules to carry the body of his partner back to Weatherford, Texas, where it was buried. When the party reached Fort Griffin, I left them and went to my home, which was near-by. I remember that it was the 29th day of February, 1868.

We give two accounts purposely. What they do not say is that they started from the outpost settlements of Texas and drove about as far as from New York to Chicago, through a country swarming with hostile

Comanches. Fort Belknap, two days west of Fort Worth, was over four hundred miles from Fort Sumner as the crow flies — the length of Kansas. But their trail looped two hundred miles southwards to avoid the waterless plains. Do you get the picture?

'In that enormous silence, tiny and unafraid.'

They do not mention that there were several hundred Indians in the band that Loving and Wilson met. They do not mention that the herd stampeded at Horsehead Crossing, that they worked several days to gather them, that an overwhelming force of Comanches drove off three hundred head of steers; they do not say that these cattle were wild longhorns and that the dullest day of that drive had enough hazard and danger to last an average man a lifetime. These people did not blurb. In fact, if Loving had not been killed on that trip, their reports today would have been something like this:

'We drove a herd to Fort Sumner in '67.'

Billy Wilson's account of the Goodnight and Loving drive of '66 is a perfect example. He says:

'They had some trouble with the Indians, and we considered it safer to all travel together.'

CHAPTER XVI

Friendly California

In 1930, after Alan had gone East, we decided to try the California climate for a time to see what it could do for Gene's bronchitis. He was having a hard time trying to write. Unselfishly, too, he wanted me to have a stove that needed no wood, could be lighted any time by pushing the pilot light. He wanted me to have a laundryman call for the washing instead of having to do it myself. At the invitation of Clare and Jess Lynn of La Jolla, we went over to look at real estate, seeing so many different properties that we were going in circles. Always we came back to a gray house of hollow tile and stucco in Pacific Beach. A huge eucalyptus tree hung guardingly over it, west of it lay the sea, and in front was Mission Bay, a long line of surf beating on Mission Beach and Ocean Beach. To an inlander it was delightful. But the depression was then unheard of; prices were booming. All we could do was to tell the owner we were going back to Three Rivers until the following spring, but would buy his house if available then.

On the fifth of July we left La Jolla on our trip back to New Mexico by way of the Grand Cañon, which we had never seen. But first to Banning to visit Gene's pal,

Harry Knibbs, otherwise known as Henry Herbert. Knibbs and Turbese were in Los Angeles, but Mrs. Phillips, the kindly lady across the street, gave us the key. We took possession. A guest house was being built, of fresh new pine, on the floor of which we spread our camp bed, well pleased with ourselves. Gene immediately lost himself in Harry Knibb's collection of books. New to him were the Milne 'Pooh' books. He read them with great relish and quoted them frequently thereafter, as when he wrote to William MacLeod Raine, some years after, when he had been marching as recruit in the 'Clean Literature' crusade:

'"As long as we all three say it," said Piglet, "I don't mind; but I shouldn't like to say 'Aha' by myself." And sniffing slightly Piglet said, "It is hard to be brave when you are a very small animal."'

'It is not so hot to say "Aha!" all by yourself. By heck, I have been saying "Aha" alone for twenty-five years. When you write my obituary, kindly mention that fact.'

He memorized 'James, James, Morrison, Morrison' and recited it with great perfection on every available occasion.

After two or three days, Harry and Turbese returned. I greeted them at the door and cordially invited Turbese to enter her own house. I had never met her before.

One evening at dusk a rap sounded at the door and a man with the loose-hanging vest of a cowboy inquired in a Texas drawl if he might speak to Gene Rhodes. He was granted that privilege, and Gene took him out in the kitchen and offered him a drink — of water, to his evident disappointment. He came asking Gene for a job. It was *Harry Knibbs!*

Gene said no one but a cowboy could have appreciated the exquisite artistry of his performance.

Another time a gentleman in a white goatee and long Prince Albert coat, accompanied by a lady in clothing of a bygone day, came to call. They were Knibbs and Turbese.

The weather was terrifically hot. Nobody is ever half-baked around Banning. The day we left, our radiator was boiling in no time, going down smooth concrete. I held the door of the sedan open that we might get that much more air.

At four in the afternoon a day later we came to the Cañon, that great jagged bowl filled to the brim with unearthly blue. It makes one wonder what heaven must be like when anything on earth can be so incomparably lovely. We went up to Narajo Point to camp, walking down to the brink of the gorge in the ghostly moonlight. It was breath-taking.

So back home to the Half-Way House and our strange assortment of animals. Shortly after Thanksgiving the autumn before we went to California, Gene had found a hawk with a broken wing on our woodpile trying to eat the turkey head from our feast bird. Gene set a can of water near him. The hawk looked on with sullen, golden eyes. Gene fed him each day. Still the hawk stayed in one corner of the woodpile, shaded with bird of paradise shrubs. Gene said he would be really accomplishing something if he succeeded in restoring that hawk's faith in humanity. Little by little he did accomplish it. The hawk began by taking food from his hand. She would reach out a vindictive claw and grab it. I warned Gene, 'Sometime that hawk will bury her talons in your hand and you will regret it.' Gene then took a small weed and motioned the threatening claw back with it. The hawk took the food in her beak, which was some improvement. Finally she recovered enough to flop one-sidedly into a small mesquite bush. Gene shot rabbits for her, and to prevent the cat from getting at either his pet or the meat, he nailed a circular saw to the top of a post some distance from the house and put the meat on this. Ranger, the cat, would nevertheless manage by some means to get past this barrier. A deadly feud existed between the cat and the hawk.

When Gene couldn't find a rabbit, which was rarely the case, he took a piece of bacon down to the hawk's table. He couldn't bear to disappoint the bird, he said. The hawk flew along to superintend the rabbit-killing excursions. On our return from a few days' absence we saw the hawk up on the electric light pole beside the house, looking intently into the big living-room window to see if we were there. Reassured, she flew away.

Suddenly the hawk disappeared, to be gone for a long time. We cogitated long and loud as to her fate. Gene said finally that there was a possibility that she had gone to attend to her maternal duties. Gene said afterward he hadn't believed this, said it only to console me. Picture our amazement when the hawk returned one day with four small hawks. She stayed around a few days to see that they were properly rabbited and cared for, and then confidingly handed them over to Gene's care. She left and we never saw her again. The pity of it was that after Gene had succeeded in establishing her trust in mankind some unsuspecting person shot her to protect his chickens.

Betty's cat, Bobby, gave birth to quintuplets, all of whom we put in a room behind the garage. One afternoon there was a terrific racket and Bobby and the young hawks came flying out, tumbling over and over each other, all equally furious. The hawks flew up into a cottonwood tree near the door and complained loudly to me that the cat had mistreated them. They had wanted kittens as a side dish to rabbits. I did nothing about it; neither did Gene. Their confidence was destroyed. Their 'twin gods' had deceived them. Was it possible that these gods actually held cats to be more valuable than hawks? They flew away and we never saw them again.

Not so long after the hawks left, on my way down the creek, I heard a funny flopping in a bush. I called Gene, who came down to investigate. There a huge hawk had fallen, caught by one claw in the crotch of a tree. It hung there helpless. Gene brought it to the house, carrying it by the legs at a discreet distance, for it snapped at him viciously with its beak. He put it down in one corner of the yard, in the shelter of the hedge, and gave it food and water.

Mr. Edwards, our neighbor, came by and stopped to

talk a minute. Gene said to him, with solemn face: 'Do you know, Mr. Edwards, that the birds have come to realize that this is a bird sanctuary? A crippled hawk came here today.'

He nodded toward it. Mr. Edwards looked over the hedge. The hawk was nearly under his elbow. Mr. Edwards's jaw dropped in amazement. He didn't know that the hawk flew away shortly after.

It wasn't so comfortable at times, being married to a genius, more like snuggling up to a volcano that unexpectedly poured hot ashes, stones, and lava on your bewildered head, and when this had ceased, you could still hear the rumblings and groanings that retched his soul. Then there were long peaceful times when you forgot all that. And in any state, he was the most fascinating man I ever met.

Gene slept till noon when he was writing. I was 'tongue-tied' by decree at such times, for he wanted to be quiet and study on his story. He wrote *The Trusty Knaves* at Half-Way House. With rare exceptions he went over and over his stories, writing and rewriting, then changing a word here, and polishing a sentence there, never finished until he made the characters so real that he could hear them talk, and see the expressions on their faces, as if they were on a stage. He didn't like to write about girls. His girls, he said, always squeaked when they walked.

When he slept late, as soon as the coffee urn was perking bravely, I took my oranges and coffee and went into the living-room to watch the sun rise on the San

Andres Mountains. That wide sweep of desert and black lava and white sand. Those mighty mountains. The first gleam of sunlight on the facets of the rocks, the rose and the silver and the gold. I sat and looked at this majestic scene morning after morning. What a stage that plain had been for Conquistadores, Indians, prospectors!

I typed on *The Proud Sheriff* industriously, just stopping long enough to cook us something to eat. I didn't even stop to wash the dishes. We finished the story and went down to mail it, not locking the doors. When we came back, I found the spotless white visiting card of Mrs. Anna Simms sticking under the door of that dirty porch. She was my friend and one of the most exquisite housekeepers I ever knew.

We picked up the manuscript scattered over the floor. 'I'll not scrub till tomorrow,' I said to myself. Water was scarce; we had to bring ours six miles in the wooden cask from the power house before this scrubbing could be done. Next day our friends, Mr. William Penhallow Henderson and his wife, Alice Corbin, came to see us. We were so happy to see them that I put my mortification at the dirty house in the background. Thank goodness, the dishes were all washed and put away by then. Gene and William Penhallow talked till dawn, although Gene hadn't slept the night before, after finishing the story. He was so hungry to see his own kind.

So our Santa Fe friends didn't forget us. When Mrs. Fenyes and her daughter and granddaughter came, we laughed again at the 'night message' Gene had sent the youngest:

OH FAR AWAY AND WHERE AWAY
ON SOME FAR MOUNTAIN TOP
OR LOITERING BY THE SUNDOWN SEA
AM THINKING OF YOU STOP

OLD WINTER CAME TO TOWN TONIGHT
WITH SNOW AND SLEET AND SLOP
ALONE I WATCHED THE GLOWING FIRE
AND SAW YOUR FACE THERE STOP

I MADE THE BACKLOG ROAR AGAIN
AND LET THE CURTAIN DROP
OH IT IS SUMMER IN MY HEART
AM DREAMING OF YOU STOP

THE WIRES FORGET THEIR FOOLISH PRATE
OF STOCK AND BOND AND CROP
TO BEAR MY MESSAGE THROUGH THE NIGHT
AM WAITING FOR YOU STOP

TRY YOUR YOUNG WINGS AND SHOULD THEY TIRE
AND SHOULD YOU EVER DROP
HOME TO THE OLD NEST ONCE AGAIN
OH COME BACK TO ME STOP

We had planned to leave for California as soon as *The Proud Sheriff* was finished. I told Gene I would take down the white curtains and wash them to have that much done, but he raised a dramatic hand. 'Not one thing will we change till this story is finished, or you will throw me all off.'

This time we were there before the winds. We arrived

in California the first of March, 1931. Our first task was to make the strange house on Pacific Beach into a home, really ours, where we would be glad when we came back, and sad when we went away.

We had lengthy discussions on what to call this new dwelling. 'Eyore's House' from the *Pooh*? I told Gene he was not muley enough. We almost settled on 'Belle Acres.' Gene said he would have given anything if he, instead of Arthur Train, had invented 'Fallen Arches.' 'Fiddler's Green,' 'The Bimbles.' He leaned most to 'Dun Movin.' We ended by not calling it anything.

My cousin Ralph Boyce invited Gene to attend the Bohemian Hi-Jinks in San Francisco. On the way we stopped at Salinas where Gene had worked during vacations when he had been in college at San Jose. A Portuguese had been in charge of the crew when Gene worked there. On one day Gene had reached the watering trough and unhooked his team before the 'boss' and the latter had to wait until Gene's team had finished drinking. The Portuguese was so infuriated that he picked up an iron bar and struck Gene over the head with it, cutting his scalp so it hung down over his forehead and eyes. His blood streaming over his face, Gene, a slender lad, grabbed the Portuguese by the throat and choked him until his face turned black and his tongue was run out and swollen, before the rest of the crew could pull him off. Then Gene walked five miles in the burning noonday sun to a doctor who sewed his scalp. The manager had been so pleased with this performance that he told Gene he would be put in charge of the crew.

But Gene's 'itching' foot had led him to farther places. But back now in Salinas, Gene found the manager, whom he didn't have to remind of the episode.

After goodly adventures in the Bohemian Grove, we set out for home again. Having supposed that San Francisco would be hot, I had worn my thinnest clothes. Result, a bad case of laryngitis. We made the trip home in eighteen actual driving hours, but during the night we stopped in a Santa Rosa motor camp. Gene visioned himself marooned with my suffering self at that auto camp for a long period. The dust on the trip aggravated Gene's bronchitis. We raced neck and neck to see who could cough most on that interminable drive.

In Pacific Beach, Gene had the satisfaction of having a literary circle of friends about him. He delighted in Max and Margaret Miller. Said he, 'Max has actually read a book I have recommended.' Stuart Lake, who lived up on the hill, Alan Le May, the Holts, one-time minister to Morocco and his wife, and Walt Coburn of Del Mar made up our group. To these should be added the Walter Austins, who wrote not, but were friends.

Busy as he was with his *Old Timers* book, Gene still found time to read about and become incensed by current problems. When it was rumored that the politicians in San Diego were diverting a goodly share of the welfare money to their own uses, Gene wrote a protest to Eddy Orcutt, whose editorials in the *San Diego Union* were a source of pleasure to him. And how deeply gratified he was to read the ringing editorial that appeared as a result of his letter.

WE ARE ALL DISHONORED

'If politicians get one dollar of that money and survive, we are all dishonored.'

The man who wrote that line is important. The money he refers to is that appropriated by the Federal Government for the relief of men and women and children stricken by the economic disaster. But the man who wrote those words is important because he represents the best Americanism that this Western country has produced. When he says 'dishonored,' the word's meaning must be found in this man himself and in what he represents.

We have no right to name him — we have no permission, even, to quote what he says. Our description of him and our reference to his importance will perhaps disturb and exasperate him. His letter to this newspaper was not written about himself — it was written hotly with a full heart, about men who are going hungry while politicians fatten the pork barrel with money voted to relief.

But when this gallant man of the old West says we are all dishonored, his words ought to fan every spark of manhood, every spark of Americanism, into some clear flame. And we, reading the words, ought to know what it means to be dishonored — ought to ask ourselves honestly if we are willing to risk that shame. . . .

Gene read his daily copy of *The Santa Fe New Mexican* with great pleasure. Its editor was among the most brilliant of Gene's friends and dearly loved a joke. I heard Gene chuckling to himself one day and said, 'What's the joke? Let me in on it.' In *The New Mexican* I read the following:

DILLON PARDON MISPLACED, HASTE DANGEROUS

The executive tendency in this as in other states to issue ill-advised pardons and the grave danger of misplaced clemency in the case of offenders has become a matter of public interest again in connection with an instance under the recent administration of Governor R. C. Dillon....

...The Dillon instance, it is alleged, shows how unreliable some of the recipients of executive leniency sometimes prove themselves. It is alleged that in this case the pardoned man counted upon a change of administration to let him out of doing what he promised in the way of going straight and making amends to society.

In the case now being discussed the conscienceless applicant for clemency not only had his request granted, but on the strength of his ready promises he was honored with an appointment by Governor Dillon and given certain privileges not allowed even to ordinary citizens. This fact has increased the indignation on the part of those interested in seeing all men treated equal under the law...

The case in point is that of a man named Eugene Manlove Rhodes concerning whose past certain lurid reports have been in circulation for some years past and who recently left his hangout in the hills near Three Rivers, New Mexico, and made a hasty exodus to California. California authorities report him now residing at Pacific Beach, the description of the man there tallying with that of Rhodes.

This man was granted a blanket pardon by Governor Dillon upon certain representations which Rhodes made to the Governor and it must be confessed that

> *the Santa Fe New Mexican* was inveigled into saying a word in his behalf.
>
> He was then appointed a colonel on the Governor's staff and given the right to carry an unloaded gun here and there about the state, all these being based on his solemn promise to write the true and accurate story of his life and times and have same published by a reputable firm of publishers and made available for public consumption.
>
> A year and more has elapsed, and while it was understood that Rhodes would be allowed all reasonable time to fulfill his promise, the publishers are becoming impatient and a trifle skeptical of the outcome. While the man has not, it is understood, definitely refused to come across, it is reported that he is furnishing various flimsy excuses, alibis, and other things which it is feared partake of the nature of subterfuge.
>
> There is a strong movement under way, it was reported today, to have the Governor make a thorough examination of the case and possibly send Elfego Baca or a detachment of the National Guard to California with requisition papers and return Rhodes here for questioning.

The California sunshine through the windows of our sitting room made big lonesome squares on the floor. I watched them crawl slowly across, day after day. The long pointed fingers which were eucalyptus leaves waved supinely in the never-ceasing wind; the wind, that was lonesomest of all. No hurrying to get supper for a bunch of hungry farm hands, with crusty loaves of fresh bread cooling on the kitchen cabinet. No peas to shell. Goodness! would I ever get the last one shelled? There were no doors slammed, no hurrying footsteps, no eager voice saying: 'Where's Dad? Does he know there is a ball game at Apalachin this afternoon?' or 'Ma, I'm hungry. What is there to eat?' . . . Only silence.

The fledgelings were grown. They were gone. There were only a very lonely man and a very lonely woman, long, weary miles from the special lands we loved.

CHAPTER XVII

The Last L'Envoi

THEN came Beppo! And Damocles!

'He was a kitten, a black kitten with enormous yellow eyes. His mother was poisoned when he was very small and we fed him with a medicine-dropper for many days. It was touch and go to save him. A thin, tottering, pitiful kitten when he first managed to scramble up my stuffed chair to my shoulder, to sing his first little triumph song and to lick my ear as all he could do then for his share of the kindly bargain.

'A plump kitten then, a big-eyed kitten with free choice of two laps to sleep on, a marvelous rubber ball that was all his own, a garden full of flowers expressly for his sniffing tours; proud and happy when he was allowed to walk with two old people who were all the family he knew and all the world he knew. It is charged that cats hold themselves aloof. Beppo never did. He accepted us as equals and was never once unkind.

'A jaunty cat, a swaggering cat, a cat who exacted his rights; a cat who, when he wanted in or out, asked once to have the door opened, and then promptly did his endeavor to tear the wire screen out by main force. When he was six months old, we got another black kitten, just weaning age, for companion and playmate. That was Damocles, who sits beside me as I write these lines.

'Those were the great days! Wild racings and chasings, scampering and climbing — and such a delightful sniffing of every flower, the first thing in the morning! Such wrestlings and fight-teachings! And with this last came problems. Damocles was such a little cat. Before our eyes, Beppo sat him down to consider; before our eyes, even while we watched him, he evolved and perfected a code of ethics. It was, for all intents and purposes, identical with the best codes men have made for themselves, and there was no article of it which could have originated in any heart but a gentleman's. But there was this difference: Beppo did not break his code.

'Damocles was such a little, little cat — sadly tumbled and wooled about by big Beppo, twice his weight. But he must be taught the essential virtues of cat-hood — courage and self-defense and the art to fight. Therefore, small squeakings of dismay went all unheeded. But there was sanctuary — a rattan-bound stool. When Damocles took to the stool, Beppo would put up a tentative paw. If Damocles struck out at it, those gleeful rompings went on. But if the challenge was not accepted, then that was the end of the bout. The little cat was tired, or perhaps the little cat was bruised: Beppo sighed audibly and subsided. Not once was sanctuary violated.

'Again, the little cat was allowed handicap for size.

The top of the great stuffed chair was reserved for him; from that vantage to repel Beppo's furious attacks from the floor. Again, Beppo lay on his back under the rattan stool and the little cat stood on the stool; with this handicap, they waged desperate battle.

'When the little cat was asleep, it was no fair to molest him, not even to arouse him: Beppo stalked stiff-legged, with blazing eyes and bristling mustache, impatient. But it was not allowed to awaken Damocles. Little cats must have their sleep out.

'Milk was for little cats. When milk was in the saucer, Beppo waited complacently until Damocles had his fill. But meat was different. That was primarily for big cats and Beppo sailed in at once.

'They never were angry with each other and never jealous. Damocles pre-empted a tall stool, table-high, and perched upon it to assist at our meals. Beppo watched him admiringly, ungrudgingly, from the floor. Not once did he attempt to poach on the little cat's preserves. We provided a shorter stool for Beppo, after a little. He accepted it gratefully enough, and they sat side by side to assist — but there was never any confusion about the stools. The tall stool was the discoverer's own.

'The great event of the day was when the two cats walked abroad with me; and they were wild with pride and delight the first time the lady of the house made a fourth. Hi, that was a merry time! Such scurryings, such runnings ahead, hidings in a bush, and pouncings out upon a terrified family!

'There was the same ending for each happy day. Every night, at ten o'clock, no more and no less, Beppo eyed Damocles severely, pounced upon him, held him exactly as Punch held his club, and proceeded to make the little cat's toilet. Strugglings, wailings, were of no avail. Eyes ablaze, Beppo turned the little cat over and over and gave him a good washing. And so to bed, a tangle of black legs.

'They had a thousand jolly games of their own devising. Strangest was the irrigation game, in warm weather: to sit side by side with their backs to the rising water, both black tails extended at full length, trying which could longest endure the shiversome touch of climbing water. A twitch or a quiver counted the same as flight itself. It was a weird watching to see them.

'You must know of a sad blemish on Beppo's fame. He was afraid of dogs. Not reasonably afraid, prudently afraid. Dogs filled him with abject terror. It dated back to a luckless hour of his puniest kittenhood. There was a neighbor dog, a hundred miles away. He was a Scotty named Jockson Beetle, a very fine dog, but a terror to all cats to whom he had not been properly introduced. Jockson Beetle came visiting, bringing his family with him, his two kind and loving gods — and neither Jockson Beetle nor his family knew there was any Beppo cat. We rushed out on the lawn to eager greetings — and Jockson Beetle went up on the covered porch where poor Beppo lay asleep. Jockson Beetle saw and charged furiously — and that would have been all, except that the poor frantic kitten performed a miracle of flight along a bare concrete wall. He never got over that fright.

'This was long before Damocles came. And it chanced that when Beppo was almost grown, our next-door neighbor (half a block of vacant lots intervening) had a general cleaning up of a storeroom behind the garage and put out six or eight delightful boxes of souvenirs for the garbage man. Beppo and Damocles promptly went on a tour of inspection. As it happened, I was watching them as they wrestled together in the lee of the boxes.

'Now there lived next door a frolicsome puppy, young Floppit, a black bird dog. His family, I believe, knew him by another name. But his mode of progression was by a series of sidewise leaps and bounds, so I have never been able to remember him other than as Floppit. As I watched, Floppit came bouncing around the boxes. Simultaneously, a long black streak came down the walk. That was Beppo.

'He came to the corner of his own home lot, and turned, every hair a-bristle. The puppy was bounding about, yelping. Damocles had not moved. He had not even fluffed his tail. He regarded young Floppit's antics with puzzled interest, but it had not occurred to him to be scared. Beppo gave one despairing and frantic wail of warning. Damocles did not come. So Beppo went back — this most imperfect gentle knight! True, he did not go back as fast as he came, but he went fast and he did not falter — back to what he dreaded most on earth. Sans Peur is admirable, doubtless — but this was Greatheart. I have no brighter memory from my days.

'Be patient: this joyful story is all too brief. As he grew to maturity, Beppo went in for society. His engagements kept him away for days at a time, sometimes for a week, and he came back all tattered and torn. This caused his family much uneasiness. A rough and uninhabited promontory runs out into the sea just beyond us, and we had heard coyotes there. But Beppo came and went, and our fears subsided. In the fullness of time, Damocles, in turn, made tentative excursions. On his second adventure, Beppo was at home, much the worse from his wars, and very uneasy about Damocles. He sat on the window sill, watching. The lady of the house saw me coming a block away, carrying truant Damocles. Beppo saw us at the same time, she says; pricked up his ears, hopped down, and went to the front door to greet his pardner. This was about four in the afternoon. They had a great visit together for three hours or so. At early twilight Beppo came to me, firmly demanding that I should let him out. I opened the door and he said thank you, as he always did; he strolled down the path with his arrogant tail aflaunt, turned at the sidewalk, flicked his big eyes at me as he turned. I like to remember that it was a friendly look. He sauntered down to the sea: and met there the Terminator of Delights and the Separator of Companions.'

Gene found a map of New Mexico one day on which he noticed that the cañon, where he had staked out his ranch at the age of twenty-one and which had been named Rhodes Cañon in tribute to him, had a new name. Away went a letter to E. Dana Johnson of *The Santa Fe New Mexican* growling Gene's complaints. The day following the paper replied as follows:

GENE RHODES CAN LICK MAN WHO TOOK HIS CAÑON OFF THE MAP OF NEW MEXICO

We started something again.

Mentioned to Eugene Manlove Rhodes the desire to have at least a New Mexico mountain range named after him.

Now it appears this is a sensitive subject. Gene used to have a cañon and somebody took it off the map. He is gunning for that person.

Writing from Pacific Beach, California, on January 20, 'sixty-four years old yesterday and not a lick of sense yet' the most rambunctious of living Westerners deposes and says:

'Now sir — time was when the official map of New Mexico bore the name of "Rhodes Cañon" — for the place where I was the first man. That was my home — the first home ever established in that county. And I had fairly earned that name on that map — not as a literary guy — but as the first man. I will never deny but that I was pleased to have that place bear my name. That was my wages. I was quite satisfied with those wages — but I had earned them. Modesty be damned — I still think that name was entitled to be a fixture on that map.

'Well, some years ago it was taken off — I don't

know who took it off — or why. But I don't like it. I was the only inhabitant in a space as large as the State of Delaware for many years. I laid out the road from Engle to Tularosa — and built it through the mountains with my own hands, my own pick, shovel, hammer, and drill, my own dynamite, fuse caps — and my own brains. I began dreaming that straight road from Engle to Tularosa in 1890 — and if that cañon is ever renamed for some two-by-scantling politician — I'm going to get one map-maker for my collection....

'I had no hand in getting that name on the map. It was given, as a matter of course, by common consent. It was the Rhodes Cañon, just as others were the Lee Cañon, the Nymyer Cañon. I don't know who put it on the map. It had been there for years before I knew it.

'Then someone cut it out? — Why? There must have been a definite motive. It was not lack of space. Between Tularosa and Engle there is nothing else.

'I was 64 yesterday — but I'll bet any man twenty dollars (cash) to twenty (cash) that I can lick the man who took that name off. And I'll give him odds of two to one that I'll try it on the first opportunity. Remember he must have had some motive other than to save the state that much printer's ink. Therefore he must have been hostile to me-wards, and will doubtless welcome my offer. And if anybody thinks I am immodest or shameless — well! I don't give a damn. But the officious ass who made that change — let him beware!!

'— That isn't all, either. I would not like it to have that cañon renamed for La Guardia or Sinclair Lewis or Scott Fitzgerald. But if it should be renamed Mrs. Franklin Delano Roosevelt, I won't stand it.

Yours

Rhodes

'I will have him yet.'

HE'S GOT A PASS

The *New Mexican* yesterday published some explosive remarks from Colonel Gene Rhodes regarding the alleged high-handed action of some vicious person or persons unknown in removing from the map Mr. Rhodes's own private cañon, which he dug in the San Andres Mountains shortly after the arrival of the Spanish conquerors and which for years bore his name without let or hindrance, or interference by all or sundry, while winter's snows and summer's bourgeoning came and went through the long decades, the wild ass of the alkali flat disported himself at will, the Rhodes runners darted through the mesquite with gay abandon, the gray fox dug his hole unscared while the rank thistle nodded in the wind, and generations of tumbleweeds and tumblebugs tumbled over the desert waste unfettered and unsung; Rhodes Cañon's scarred walls stood grim and inscrutable through the years; Gene didn't live there, and probably the less said about where he was or what he was doing the better. Anyhow, he complains bitterly that they took him off the map and offers to lick the scoundrel who did so.

Fair and softly, fair and softly, Colonel. It might be worse. Mike Harrison brought in the latest N.M. road map issued by the Auto Club of Southern California yesterday, and there as large as life, midway between Engle and Tularosa right spang through the mountain range, is 'RHODES PASS.'

Everyone knows that a pass has a cañon beat a mile. There is the annual pass, and They Shall Not Pass, Hagerman Pass, Berthoud Pass, Grant's Pass, Stein's Pass and I pass — what is a cañon among friends when one has a pass? And who wishes to flock along with Horsethief Cañon, Dead Horse Cañon, Cat

Cañon, Burro Gulch, Brewery Gulch, Skull Valley, and their ilk?

We trust the old cowperson will be mollified at finding he has a pass, and we shall use all possible efforts with the U.S. Board of Geographical Misnomers, Bill Barnes, ex-secretary, to get his cañon back on the map. As a matter of fact we insist that he should have more than the modest cañon he claims for old times' sake; and having immortalized the region to millions, we move that all that certain tract and parcel of land lying between the following points, to wit, Tularosa, N.M., and Chloride, N.M., and Magdalena, N.M., and High Lonesome, N.M., be known and designated hereafter officially as Rhodesia and the name of the San Andres Range be likewise changed to Manlove Mountains. Respectfully referred to the state legislature.

Gene's cubicle for writing and meditation was a student house which he bought from the Army and Navy Academy. In the garden behind he planted and patiently trained New Mexican morning glories that grew and climbed and blossomed in great profusion — almost shutting out the dim blue of the Cuyamaca Mountains that fenced him off from his beloved New Mexico. I have seen him looking off there with the eyes of a sleepwalker, and I knew that even then, in spirit, he rode his sorrel Monte horse, his 'red-roan horse of might' up the rocky defiles of his own mountains.

A walk of stepping stones bridged the space from the house to his den. He had an air-tight heater and a single bed with his old cowboy 'breeches quilt' on it.

At the big east window his writing table stood. In a small dresser minus the mirror, he kept his literary stuff. On shelves put up on two sides of the room he kept pasteboard and cigar boxes, all neatly labeled: 'Unanswered Letters,' 'Important Letters,' 'Poetry,' 'Bank Business,' etc.

He had three tin cracker boxes which he kept one on another in the corner on the floor. Clippings which appealed to him, and pictures which amused him, were pasted on the walls. On all the other spaces were maps except where allowance was made for a big blackboard which he had had a carpenter make, placed an easy distance from his writing table. Here he wrote the names of people to whom he must write, funny quips for his stories, and on several occasions I saw, written here:

'Anne Johnston and one sister.'

He wrote in a book to them — to the two of them, although he said it was bad as bigamy to send one book to two girls — 'his latest about Lithpin Tham' which he said must be his prettiest, for 'the wolf's nose pokes through the door.'

> 'Stranger watered his warm horse at Mal Pais spring — halfway across the desert, here. Horse died. Stranger went back afoot, to San Andres as direct. Went to old, long deserted ranch — (once one of mine). No grub. Nothing. He packed a rusty coal-oil can full of water and crossed the desert. Came to Lithpin Tham's camp at sundown, tired and empty and with blistered feet. He says, sezzi, "For God's sake give me something to eat!"'

MAY DAVISON RHODES

> 'Thure,' says Tham. He speaks in a high pitched falsetto. He set his Dutch oven on the fire and then looked up.
>
> 'Mithter, how long thinth you had anything to eat?'
>
> 'Three days.'
>
> 'Three dayth! Why you greedy thon of a gun, do you want to eat all the time?'

When he brought one of the literary lights and said with great ceremony, 'I want you to meet my wife,' or 'My nice Missus,' as the occasion demanded, I always had a little inside squirm of satisfaction. I was tremendously proud of him. He frequently said he would be ashamed to be as proud of anybody as I was of him. But to this day I cannot tell whether I was more proud of his being a top-notch rider — he was a picture on a horse — or of his being in the forefront of the writers. He said I had helped him there, that he never felt he could write unless I was somewhere around.

'... Me, I believe in marriage. Possibly because my own marriage has been so happy. I will say that my wife is the best ever, and I am lucky beyond my deserts. Don't know of anyone else who would put up with my foolish ways.'

To Retta Badger:

'... Behold me sedate and settled. Also about to drink some coffee immejit. My Missus May, she makes me a perker full of coffee every night, she does. And I sit up and write. You'll like my Missus May. I do....'

He even addressed a letter to me in New York, 'Mrs. St. May Rhodes.'

When Gene's new books came out and the author's copies arrived, he always autographed the first copy to me. He would autograph pages full to most people but in mine he wrote simply, 'May from Gene.' I set up a howl. 'You write reams in other people's books.' He took the book from my hands. When he returned it, I read, 'May Rhodes, Her book. From Gene Rhodes, Her man.' I was quite satisfied.

Gene had said he had no fear of the hereafter. 'A Being so great that He can keep the planets in their orbits, without ever colliding, is perfectly capable of dealing with a midge like me.'

Yet he wanted to enjoy the hours he had left. 'I am loath to quit living for a while, being intensely curious. Hard times — but for the first time in my life I see ground for a thinking man to hope for a decent world — in time. I recommend this planet as a good place to spend a lifetime.'

THE LAST *L'ENVOI*

Nothing is left me to dream or do,
  No more forever beneath the sun,
Dangers to dare or strive renew,
  My songs are written, my tasks are done
  And all my battles are lost and won.
Toil cannot tire me nor cares annoy.
  For good or evil my race is run
And smiling, I fashion my last *L'Envoi*.

Stars, that gemming night's radiant blue
  Smile at the follies your light shines on;

The Last L'Envoi

A fairer world than the one I knew
  May well be of you — but dearer none!
  Kind old world, spin round in the sun!
Bright I found you and full of joy,
  All of my paths were with roses strewn,
And lightly I fashion my last *L'Envoi.*

Gentle maidens, if haply you
  Should read this rhyming of one that's gone —
One as lovely, as pure and true
  Loved me, living, and me alone,
  Dying, her eyes through the darkness shone,
Death that dreaming may not destroy;
  Here in the silence I lie alone
  Yet love lives after the last *L'Envoi!*

L'Envoi

Princess, pause of your courtesy;
  Spare but a moment from love and joy.
Muse on the dust that was once my heart
  And the ashes that fashioned this last *L'Envoi!*

CHAPTER XVIII

Pasó por Aquí

Not all the California sunshine could brighten the knowledge that we were old and broken and practically penniless. Could we have had the money Gene so generously loaned to his friends, and which they didn't pay back, we would have been in comparatively comfortable circumstances. No, not comfortable, with him coughing morning after morning till his muscles and ribs were so sore that he felt he could never give another cough — yet he had to, sometimes for two hours. It wrung the very heart out of me. Even Damocles, sitting on his high stool waiting for the torment to be over and he could be told, with loving strokings, that he was 'the old bold mate of Henry Morgan,' even Damocles looked on with sorrowful eyes.

It had reached the point where the question was no longer how many more stories could he write, but could he write *any*? He was too sick to concentrate, to study out the elaborate plots that always made his stories.

Was it only a matter of time, how soon we would be dependents, objects of charity? Our sons would gladly take us, yes, but it would be the same thing. They had all they could do to breast the tide, as it was. This was a bleak shore to which we were drifting.

Then a rainbow of hope shone in our sky. A new friend, James O'Neil, planned to bring out a complete, uniform, and strictly first-class edition of all Gene's books, to be called The Bar Cross Edition, published on a fifty-fifty basis, sold by subscription, a project which would have placed us beyond want for the remainder of our days. Gene was deeply touched. He would dearly have loved to see his books brought out in a brave dress and uniform excellence, like the set of Stevenson, for which he paid eighty-four dollars. Ed Borein, master-etcher of the cowpuncher and the Indian, and Maynard Dixon, Gene's favorite painter, were to do the illustrations.

The hideous monster Want had the country by the throat. It was more vital to have food and clothing than books. James O'Neil, 'commonly known as Jim' to Gene, made Herculean efforts. But the rainbow faded and went out.

John Morgan and his wife, friends, had gone up in the Pine Hills and urged us to come and visit them. We might never have gone but an avalanche of company overtook us, like the waves of the sea. Company exhausted Gene until he was willing. I eagerly assembled our camping kit.

It was a clear, sunny April morning when we left Damocles, sitting disconsolately on the top step of the porch. We waved our hands to him and drove away, as excited as a pair of children out for a holiday.

Visiting away for dear life and settling all the important issues of the day, we drove past a stop light. It was an isolated stop light way out on Thirtieth Street or thereabouts. There was not a vehicle in sight on the street we were crossing, and neither one of us noticed the warning red light.

A burly motorcycle cop descended on us as we were trundling happily along on our way. He swerved up to our car, with an uplifted gauntleted hand, and a face of fury.

'What's the matter with you?' he snarled.

Gene stopped and eyed him in surprise. 'What have I done?' he inquired blandly.

'*Done!* You——ed fool! You drove past the stop light.'

'I'm very sorry . . .' Gene began.

'Sorry, hell! You do your apologizing to the Judge.'

Then we were not going camping after all. It *wasn't* such a nice sunny morning as I had thought.

'Where's your driver's license and other papers?'

Gene fished out the red pocketbook that held them, and said mildly: 'It's my mistake, brother. I was visiting with my wife and never noticed the stop light.'

'You old fool! You have no business driving a car, you should be driving a horse and buggy. Imperiling people's lives this way. Life is sweet to me. You might have killed me!' The burly cop seemed almost on the verge of tears. 'It's lucky for you, you are old, or I'd drag you out of there and punch your face for you.'

Gene was getting fed up with the whole proceeding.

He said wearily: 'That's all right, brother. Tell me what my fine is and I'll pay it and be on my way.'

The cop was evidently surprised. The car was old and shabby like its occupants. He probably thought we couldn't pay a fine.

He said in an aggressive voice: '*I* don't want to fine you. *I* don't want to make you any trouble. But for G—d's sake *look where you're going!*' He whirled his motorcycle and was gone.

Our spirits were considerably dampened. We let the nation's issues rest. When we passed a market where fresh eggs were displayed for five cents less on the dozen than we paid in Pacific Beach, it only aroused lukewarm enthusiasm, for we were not to return by that route.

When we reached the Morgan camp they already had company, so we took a cabin by ourselves, a delightful little cabin with big live-oaks shading it, a good heating stove and lots of wood. I made our coffee with an egg, which beats all the coffee urns in the world. Our friend Mrs. Morgan brought us over some hot cakes and sausage as we were eating breakfast.

Gene announced that we would go to Palomar Mountain to see Louis Salmon, with whom he used to punch cattle in New Mexico. I would have liked to stay another day in that lovely woodsy retreat. Furthermore, the car didn't act too well as we continued our pilgrimage. There was practically no traffic. I was apprehensive that the car might die out on us. We started up Mount Palomar and encountered a sign which read 'No Smoking Allowed.' Gene regretfully knocked the tobacco from his pipe and put it in his pocket. We wound up and up and up the mountain, looking out over mountain ranges shrouded in heliotrope haze.

'This is magnificent,' Gene said. 'New Mexico can offer nothing grander than this.'

We continued to climb higher and ever higher until at last I said, 'Are we going up this mountain forever?'

'Forever,' Gene answered. 'Till we get right up to Saint Peter.'

'What are you going to tell Peter?' I inquired curiously.

'I am going to tell him,' he chuckled, 'that I didn't notice the traffic signs.'

We reached the Salmon home, high terraced, with roses and lippia grass lawn, and two dogs tied back out of sight, which from their remarks were yearning to tear us limb from limb.

The meeting between those two cowboys was well worth the trip. The Salmons have a charming and modern home near the mountain top. A good-sized, well-stocked bookcase stood inside the door.

'Who reads?' Gene asked our delightful hostess.

'Oh, Louis does,' she said smiling.

Gene looked at me and said bitterly, 'And they claim my cowboys don't read.'

They urged us to stay all night and see the sun set in the Pacific Ocean, so many miles away. But Gene said we couldn't stay, he was working on a story, and would have to get home and get to work. I had a sneaking idea that it was the memory of that lonesome black cat on the top step of our porch which was a deciding factor.

'Damocles is sure enough going to be pleased to see us back.'

It was about nine o'clock when we reached home, a warm April night, and the damp, sprinkled lawn smelled in the darkness like the fresh spring pastures back home.

'Kitty, kitty,' I called. 'Cat! Cat!' Gene's usual call.

A slight interval and a black form emerged from the gloom. Not an eagerly welcoming kitty. Quite the reverse. He stalked stiff-legged and sulky at having been left alone in the first place, ate the freshly opened can of cat food that we offered, and stalked out again.

Gene and I looked at each other and burst into hilarious laughter. 'This,' I said, 'is what you get for not staying and visiting with your cowboy as you wanted to. *This* is your reward of merit.'

Gene was so very weak and ill by now, and would often work all night on eight or ten pages, only to destroy them in the morning. *Beyond the Desert* progressed but slowly. He was working with all his might to get the story done, which would pay off our debts and give us a slight balance. At last it was finished. He sent it off without return postage, because he didn't have it. We had exactly forty-eight cents in the world. I didn't even go into a grocery store for three weeks, lest I might be tempted to spend that precious forty-eight cents. My cupboards were fairly well stocked, a New Mexican habit never outgrown.

We put ourselves on fairly strict rations, hoping to tide over till we could hear from the *Post*. We didn't hear and the days crawled by, and despair gnawed at my heart. When we were at the lowest ebb, mentally and physically, Walt Coburn's wife, Pat (God bless her), invited us up to Del Mar to lunch with them. It saved the day. Such a royal meal as she served. It put new courage in us. We came away thinking things were not so bad as we had been forced to believe.

Then the *Post* wrote on that they didn't think they wanted the story. It was too leisurely. They deeply regretted, etc. and were sending it back under separate cover.

Gene promptly wrote them that they could have the story revamped in any way they liked, or a brand-fire-new story, but he had to have some money and right away. They saved our craft. They sent us a hundred dollars by wire. Oh, happy day! They took the story and cut a fourth from it themselves, which saved Gene that work he was entirely unable to do. This cut the price one-fourth as well, to a sum but little more than enough to pay our debts.

He would be scandalized if he knew I was writing this.

He would say, 'Woman! have you no sense of decency to flaunt our poverty in the face of an unfeeling world?' But he wouldn't be *horribly* scandalized, I'm sure, else I wouldn't do it. Our poverty worried us not at all. It was not a grinding poverty and there were delightful oases.

He steadily grew weaker and often had to sit up all night to ease the pain in his heart. After one such night, when the mail came he held out *The Santa Fe New Mexican* and pointed with a waxlike finger to the following open letter. I denounced the writer in no uncertain words. I implored Gene not to notice it. I told him that there was nothing so crushing as silence. Gene made no reply to me.

Monday, April 23, 1934

IS BOOZE CRIME LIKE MURDER? HERE'S ONE FOR GENE RHODES

Some time ago Gene Rhodes wrote a communication to *The New Mexican* which recommended kidnapping be made legal under state supervision, so as to end lawbreaking, bring in a revenue, and control the industry. He based this on alleged increase in kidnappings every time a state issued a law against it.

If this isn't sly prohibition satire, we pass. It was so treated by this paper, and Gene comes back with a look of injured innocence and said he meant nothing like that. Now a Californian takes a real fall out of him:

Gene wrote a card which read:

'The undersigned has no objections to his friends using liquor. But as it is a law of the United States that no person shall have liquor upon his premises, I am observing this rule.'

E. M. RHODES

He tacked this up beside his front door.

Los Angeles, Calif.
April 17, 1934

Editor *Santa Fe New Mexican*,
Santa Fe, N. M.

Dear Sir:

Here is a letter to Gene Rhodes. Kindly see that he gets it.

'*Dear Gene:* A friend left the enclosed clipping on my desk taken from the *L. A. Times.*

'Poor puzzled little man. Well, climb up in papa's lap and rest the little noggin on papa's cigars, and papa will try and clear up something which evidently has the tired little brain pretty puzzled.

'In contemplating crime and its prevention and punishment, Gene lad, always remember that unless the sharp line of demarcation between major crimes, crimes against not only the individual but against society itself, and offenses against minor rules and regulations is kept constantly in mind, resultant conclusions inevitably will be (as we say in Hollywood) haywire. Now, here is the way you can tell whether any given offense is a major crime: if both you and I think it is a major crime, it is. If either you or I honestly and sincerely believes it is not, you can confidently enter it as a minor offense.

'Major crimes such as murder, kidnapping, arson, rape, etc. are conceded to be such by every person of normal intelligence, even those of very rudimentary intelligence. Yes, I'll go further than that. I believe that Ella Boole agrees that such crimes are second in degree only to the consumption of a glass of beer with a swiss cheese on rye, with a slice of Coachella Valley onion and a touch of English mustard. (Excuse me,

Sonny Boy. I hate anyone who drools. There — papa's all right again.)

'It is obvious that if society is to survive it must incarcerate those who would commit crimes of this class, and destroy them if necessary.

'But to anyone willing to reason dispassionately, it is evident that enforcement measures which not only are proper but absolutely necessary in dealing with outlaws committing major crimes, may be wholly unsuited to violators of our minor regulations. To fill a murderer or kidnapper full of buckshot, if necessary to terminate his activities, is society's duty to itself. But to fill a neighbor full of buckshot for driving through a traffic signal, or refusing to stop and surrender to the law a pint of gin, is itself a peculiarly hideous major crime. A surgeon would and should amputate a foot or leg where there was a cancer of the toe, but what would you think of a surgeon who did the same to cure a hang-nail?

'You know, Gene, regardless of what anyone may tell you, man-made laws are not sacred....

'One last thing, Gene. To me, looking back over fifty-five years, the most puzzling thing in all life is the number of people you encounter who are not only willing to point out just how you should behave, but who will, if permitted, do their pointing with a club or a gun. Their way and their method may be right, Gene, but if you try your darnedest to lead that kind of a life you in your heart know you should lead, you will find that Saint Peter is not going to be too harsh with you because you did not insist that I too lead your kind of life.

'There, Little Feller — does that straighten things up a bit? If it makes just one militant prohibitionist the slightest bit more tolerant of the honest convictions of those who disagree with him, my three cents will have been well invested.'

Adios, Gene,

HARTFORD L. BILLSON

215 So. Orange Drive.

Some two weeks later Gene passed a reply to me to type. For the last time he had buckled on his armor in defense of his faith.

EUGENE MANLOVE RHODES ELABORATES VIEWS ON ALLEGED WET HOOEY

(In reply to an open letter to Mr. Rhodes by one Billson, published in *The New Mexican*, kidding Gene on prohibition matters.)

Dear Mr. Billson:

The squib which grieves you had no thought to make wiser or better men of its fortunate readers, much less to tell them anything they did not know. There was a higher hope of a wild, joyful magic which might bring forth a chuckle; a reluctant grin at the worst of it. Kidding, Mr. Billson. The loser kidding the winner, if you will.... What's the matter? Can't you take it?

In some vague and left-handed way you remind me of Frank King's story.

'No, my husband is not at home, Mr. Johnson. But I'm sure he'll vote for you because you got him off for stealing a ham.'

'No, no, madam. For the alleged stealing of a ham.'

'Alleged, hell! Get down and have a sandwich.'

However, if you must be tragic and tolerant about this matter, I will admit that the arguments I summarized were very silly. Let me be clear. I do not mean that all arguments against prohibition were silly...

'You cannot change human nature?' It would be as sensible to say that you cannot change a tree; that you cannot change grass into grain. All history is the story of how human nature is changed.

'Infringement of personal liberty.' Every law is an infringement on personal liberty. I may not kill a deer when I am hungry, drive through a stop sign, or deal justly with an umpire.... States' rights.

On April 25, the day your letter reached me, Hatton Summers, as good a man as ever wore shoe leather, rose up in Congress and denounced the federal 'Crime Bill,' because the Federal Government was encroaching upon the rights of the states. Silly, wasn't it? Silly at a time when the attorney general of these states tells us that the armed and organized service of crime employs more outlaws than the combined force of our army and navy. — Perhaps those are not the exact words which the attorney general used. I am practically living in the lap of the navy, and I am perhaps a little confused on this matter. It is intricate indeed, any time after eight P.M.

As for bootleggers, rum-runners and company. Is their offending to be condoned because, as the girl said, 'It is such a little one'? Liquor dealers and their customers would not obey dry laws. Liquor dealers and their customers will not obey laws made by the wets. They never have obeyed any liquor laws and they never will. In view of the fact that in your own state of California deaths by drunken driving have increased forty per cent in two months, a member of the California Liquor Control Board proposed only last week that the thirsty should be equipped with a license to drink. His idea was that a drunken driver could be punished by having his license to buy liquor taken away from him. You be the judge, Mr. Billson.

Would that program stop one man from drinking if he wanted to drink?

... Lo, the poor bootlegger! Cheered by the applause and laughter of the wets, financed by those who bought their wares — not otherwise — the big shots, with their mobs and machine guns, set up an invisible government in our larger cities and uphold it by force of arms ... I shall be weeping presently....

It was thoughtful of you to readjust my mind for me, and I have only one criticism to offer. Take people on your knee and lesson them, if you will. But when you yearn to make other people 'Tolerant' it gives you an odd look — like a nudist in an overcoat! Again, why should we annoy the subscribers of *The New Mexican*? Myself, I can talk much better than I write, because I can wave my hands around to show what I mean. An old Spanish custom.... The next time you want to take me on your knee for instruction, don't write. I live almost next door to you — 914 Loring Avenue, Pacific Beach, California. Why don't you ... come down and see me sometime?

GENE RHODES

There was never any answer.

A road-runner came to our yard almost daily. We remembered how these long-tailed birds sped before our trotting team for miles back in New Mexico. Gene said, 'That road-runner is from New Mexico. It knows I am homesick for New Mexico and has come to comfort me.' Perhaps he was right. It never came after Gene was gone.

When we were coming home from La Jolla one afternoon in June, I spoke of *The Hour and the Man*, his first story. Gene said reflectively, 'If I hadn't met you I should probably never have written any stories. I was about to engage in a life of outlawry. . . . It looked very attractive,' he mused. An unhappy love affair had put him at the parting of the ways.

June 26, 1934. It was almost noon and Gene had shown no intention of getting up. I said, 'I'll go over to the Motor Court and get a bottle of milk and make you some milk toast.' He was always especially fond of it. He made no answer. I could hardly keep from crying when I bought the milk, thinking how desperately ill he looked.

I made the milk toast and brought it, piping hot, to his bed. He ate it languidly. But the warmth evidently revived him, for he got up, shaved, and put on his good clothes, saying, 'We'll drive up to La Jolla.' He went into the bank and to Reddings' book store, where he bought two copies of *The Trusty Knaves* to autograph. Then to his dentist, where he made an appointment to come on Friday to have his teeth extracted. He thought that might help his heart. I protested to the dentist, 'You couldn't *possibly* take them all out at once.' Gene said firmly, 'Every one.' The dentist compromised: 'I'll see how he stands it.'

As we came from La Jolla that afternoon, he looked over to the home of our friends, Doctor and Mrs. S. Welles Thompson, and said: 'We'd go and see them but they are not at home. I feel like going somewhere.'

I was reassured. He was not going yet. He would live for a long time. Was he not up and about once more?

When we reached home the first galley proofs of *Beyond the Desert* were at the post office. 'Aren't you too tired to do them?' 'No, I'll sleep better if I have this off my chest.' So I read it aloud, he corrected the first galley, and I corrected the second copy from that.

He intended to send one copy of *The Trusty Knaves* to Norton S. Parker for the motion picture possibilities. He had always abhorred the wrapping and tying of books; that was left to me. He said he would wait to autograph the one to Maurice Walsh till morning, when he felt better.

As I was combing my hair that night preparatory to going to bed, he came in laughing. 'This is a good one,' he said. (I presume he had heard it over the radio.) 'Can you make a figure 8 with your right foot and make an O with your left hand simultaneously?' He performed, making an imaginary O on my dresser. I laughed. 'That might pass for an O, but it looks mighty scraggly to me.' We both laughed.

After I was in bed he came in and said, 'What do you think you did?' I said, 'What did I do?' He said, 'You wrapped the book I was going to autograph for Maurice Walsh in the morning and addressed it to the motion picture man.' I said: 'Never mind. I'll fix it in the morning.' He said, 'No, I want it fixed now.' He untied the knots, changed the book, rewrapped, and addressed it.

It lay on the table in the morning, and he so utterly dead. He came to bed at one o'clock and had a succession of heart spasms until morning. Nothing could ease him. He died in my arms at half-past six in the morning of June 27.

For years he had held my promise that he should take his last sleep on the summit of his beloved San Andres Mountains. His home, for home is where the heart is.

I sat in the train waiting to start on my sad journey. I looked up. A slight and lovely lady stood by my seat.

'Are you going all alone?'

'All alone,' I answered.

'You are not,' she said decidedly. 'I am going with you.'

Doctor May Riach, a famous eye specialist, had left an office crowded with patients to be my companion.

So we took him out to his mountains where brave men were quite unashamed of the tears that rolled down their bronzed cheeks. There we left him in his grave dug in the white gypsum. 'Behind the grave there was a perfectly formed piñon tree, and beside it two shapely junipers. They were the tapers that burned at Gene Rhodes's burial.' The simple marker had only the words, 'Pasó por Aquí,' 'He passed by here.' This phrase, used by the Conquistadores when they passed by and wrote their names on Inscription Rock, had struck his fancy. We left him to sleep peacefully in his warm New Mexico sunshine.

Late that night, as we waited for our train at Tularosa, I saw the lightning flashes over the San Andres and knew a thunderstorm was in progress. I remembered having overheard his saying: 'I am going East this summer. I want to hear the rain on the roof.'

Did he hear the rain on the roof, I wonder?

I couldn't end this story of a gay and gallant gentleman on so sad a note, for he was one who loved mirth and all things joyous. The epitaph he wrote for himself is the quintessence of his spirit.

> Now hushed at last the murmur of his mirth,
> Here he lies quiet in the quiet earth.
> —When the last trumpet sounds on land and sea
> He will arise then, chatting cheerfully,
> And, blandly interrupting Gabriel,
> He will go sauntering down the road to hell.
> He will pause loitering at the infernal gate,
> Advising Satan on affairs of state,
> Complaining loudly that the roads are bad
> And bragging what a jolly grave he had!
>
> EUGENE MANLOVE RHODES

THE END

THE PUBLISHED WRITINGS OF EUGENE MANLOVE RHODES

COMPILED BY VINCENT STARRET

Books

1910 Good Men and True. New York: Henry Holt and Company. This title was taken over, in 1917, by the H.K. Fly Company, and a second novelette, not until then published between covers, was added to the reprint volume to give it bulk. Later, this edition was taken over by Grosset & Dunlap, Inc.

1914 Bransford in Arcadia. New York: Henry Holt and Company. Taken over, in 1917, by the H. K. Fly Company, and reissued as Bransford of Rainbow Range. Later reprints, using this second title, carry the imprint of Grosset & Dunlap, Inc.

1916 The Desire of the Moth. New York: Henry Holt and Company. Title taken over, in 1917, by the H. K. Fly Company, when a second novelette was added to the volume. This second story had not previously appeared in a book. Later reprints carry the imprint of Grosset & Dunlap, Inc.

1917 West is West. New York: The H. K. Fly Company. Fly published only the one edition, and all reprints carry the Grosset & Dunlap imprint.

1921 Stepsons of Light. Boston and New York: Houghton Mifflin Company. This volume was published in England by Hodder & Stoughton; but the American edition preceded the English.

1922 Copper Streak Trail. Boston and New York: Houghton Mifflin Company. A later reprint of this title carries the Grosset & Dunlap imprint. The book was published in England by Hodder & Stoughton; but the American edition is the first.

1927 Once in the Saddle. Boston and New York: Houghton Mifflin Company. Apparently the only edition.

1933 The Trusty Knaves. Boston and New York: Houghton

Mifflin Company. Reissued by Grosset & Dunlap, Inc. A London edition carries the imprint of Hodder & Stoughton; but the American edition is the first.

1934 Beyond the Desert. Boston and New York: Houghton Mifflin Company. There is a reprint to be found with the Grosset & Dunlap imprint.

1935 The Proud Sheriff. Boston and New York: Houghton Mifflin Company. Taken over by Grosset & Dunlap, Inc.

Brochures

1921 Say Now Shibboleth. Chicago: The Bookfellows. Contains three short essays — Say Now Shibboleth, King Charles's Head, and the Gentle Plagiarist, of which only the second (an excerpt from an early novel) had previously appeared between covers. The edition, in boards and cloth, was limited to 400 copies.

1934 Penalosa. Santa Fe, N.M.: Writers' Editions. A separate printing of the fourth chapter of West is West, with a Foreword by Alice Corbin Henderson. The edition, in wrappers only, was limited to 500 copies, of which each copy was signed by the author.

Note — About the year 1932 a collected edition of the writings of Eugene Manlove Rhodes was projected by Mr. James B. O'Neil, as a private enterprise, and a prospectus of four pages was circulated asking subscriptions to the set, which was to have contained ten volumes. Unfortunately, support was lacking and the plan fell through. The intention was to call the collection the Bar Cross Edition, and it was to have been limited to 3500 sets at $50 a set. The announcement called for delivery of the books on or before December 1, 1932. It is regrettable that nothing came of this enterprise, which would have brought together all of Rhodes's published volumes in an attractive format, as well as twenty-nine stories that had never appeared between covers.

Magazine Appearances

[It is not immediately possible to date all of Rhodes's contributions to the periodical press, and it is quite possible that there are errors of dating in this (as it happens) premature contribution to what may some day be a definitive bibliography. Nevertheless, it has seemed well to list such titles as one may, and in the same breath to invite criticism and correction. The compiler will be grateful for both, and will gladly welcome further contributions.]

Out West

1902

January	The Hour and the Man
February	Lubly Ge-ge and Gruffangrim
March	A Ballade of Wild Bees (poem)
April	The Captain of the Gate
June	The Bar Cross Liar

1903

February	Loved I Not Honor More
June	Slaves of the Ring
November	The Blunderer's Mark

1905

November	Sons of the Soil

1906

July	Sealed Orders
October	Sticky Pierce, Diplomat

1907

January	A Pink Trip Slip
June	Rule-o-Thumb
July	The End of a Story
August	The Line of Least Resistance

1908

July	A Touch of Nature
August	The Torch

The Published Writings of Eugene Manlove Rhodes

?

The Evening Primrose
How the Dream Came True

The Saturday Evening Post

1907

March 2	The Numismatist (in collaboration with Henry Wallace Phillips)
April 20	The Punishment and the Crime (in collaboration with Henry Wallace Phillips)
June 1	Extra Number
November 23–30	The Come On

1908

October 3	Check (in collaboration with Henry Wallace Phillips)

1909

March 6	Neighbor
April 24	Executive Mind
July 3	The Man with a Country
September 4	Star of Empire
November 30	Trouble Man

1910

January 8–15	Good Men and True
August 13–20–27 and September 3	The Line of Least Resistance

1911

April 8	A Number of Things

1912

October 19	Prince of Tonight
November 30 and December 7–14–21–28	The Little Eohippus (Bransford in Arcadia)

The Published Writings of Eugene Manlove Rhodes

1913

May 10	Sealed Orders
June 28	Consider the Lizard
July 26	Ragtime Lady

1915

March 27	Hit the Line Hard
May 1 (March ?)	The Fool's Heart

1916

February 26 and March 4	The Desire of the Moth
June 10–17	The Bells of St Clemens (West is West)

1917

April 21 to May 19	Over, Under, Around or Through (Copper Streak Trail)

1919

May 17–24	No Mean City

1920

September 11–18–25 and October 2	Stepsons of Light

1925

April 11–18–25	Once in the Saddle

1926

February 20–27	Pasó por Aquí
March 27	Recognition (poem)

1929

July 20	Pegasus at the Plow (poem)
August 10	Engle Ferry (poem)
December 14	Little People (poem)

1930

January 4	Night Message (poem)
August 16	Maid Most Dear

1931

April 18	Einstein's Universe (poem)
April 18–25 and May 2	The Trusty Knaves

1932

October 1–8–15	The Proud Sheriff

1934

May 26 and June 2–9	Beyond the Desert

?

Say Now Shibboleth
The Barred Door

McClure's

[No dates available]

His Father's Flag
Beyond the Desert
The Long Shift
A Perfect Day
Ragged Twenty-Eighth

Redbook

[No dates available]

The Miracle
The God from the Machine
The Bird in the Bush
The Brave Adventure
The Enchanted Valley

Pacific Monthly

[No dates available]

Lex Talionis
Bell the Cat

Everybody's

[No dates available]

The Awaited Hour
Of the Lost Legion (in collaboration with Laurence Yates)

All Story

[No dates available]

On Velvet
Neighbors
An Interlude
Wildcat Thompson
The Fool's Heart

Sunset

September 1927

Defence of Pat Garrett

[No dates available]

Reversion to Type
He'll Make a Hand

The Published Writings of Eugene Manlove Rhodes

Harper's Weekly

[No dates available]

When the Bills Come in.

Cosmopolitan

[No dates available]

The Tie Fast Men
Aforesaid Bates
Journey's End
Shoot the Moon

Note — It will be observed that there are several duplications among these titles; but the stories are not of necessity the same. Rhodes sometimes used an old title for a new or expanded tale. It should be said, also, that many of his short stories ultimately became chapters in his novels. In spite of this, some of his best work is contained in the uncollected stories at present lost in old magazine files.